PRAISE FOR THE NOVELS OF *NEW YORK TIMES* BESTSELLING AUTHOR

LINDA HOWARD

SON OF THE MORNING

"This book is by far Linda Howard's best. An amazing and unique time-travel that blends the elements of a gripping thriller and a sensuous romance."

—*Rendezvous*

"Suspenseful and thrilling from beginning to end, Ms. Howard adds a wondrous new dimension to her already impressive accomplishments. Sensational!"

—*Romantic Times*

"Bestselling author Howard offers a romantic time-travel thriller with a fascinating premise . . . gripping passages, and steamy sex."

—*Publishers Weekly*

"A complex tale that's rich with detail, powerful characters and stunning sensuality. This is a story you won't be able to put down until you reach the explosive conclusion."

—Bonnee Pierson, CompuServe Romance Reviews

"*Son of the Morning* is an incredible blending of romantic suspense, supernatural, medieval, and time-travel genres in what will be claimed as one of the top action novels of the year."

—Painted Rock (online review)

"Linda Howard is romantic suspense at its best. This is a MUST-read. Breathtaking!"

—Donita Lawrence, Bell, Book and Candle
Oklahoma City, OK

SHADES OF TWILIGHT

"Wow! This powerful saga about a wealthy dynasty that is torn apart by a vicious murder will chill, thrill, and excite you. . . . [A] tale of lust, greed, and revenge . . . that will leave you staggered and extremely satisfied. Linda Howard never fails to create a story that will shock, amaze, and warm you with its gifted touch. This is a passion-filled masterpiece."

—*Rendezvous*

"Family, loyalty, love, sex and revenge steam up the pages. . . . Howard . . . maintain[s] tension through a twist-filled plot."

—*Publishers Weekly*

AFTER THE NIGHT

"A real southern scorcher, this book continues in the author's tradition of steamy suspense. . . . The mystery in the story is well-drawn, and it has interesting twists and turns. . . . Author Howard is a master of sexual tension. The rich setting and the characters' fully explored histories contribute to build a powerful force of attraction that her characters are helpless to withstand. . . . Readers should be prepared to spend the entire afternoon under a ceiling fan with a pitcher of cool drinks nearby when they pick up this hot number."

—Nina Bruhns, *Gothic Journal*

"Linda Howard is one of the top authors writing romantic intrigue, and *After the Night* will only enhance her reputation."

—Harriet Klausner, *Affaire de Coeur*

"Small towns are the perfect background for mysterious secrets, and Ms. Howard pens a tale loaded with them. Her sensuous style of writing makes the reader aware of the all-consuming desire between the hero and heroine. Add to this the dramatic climax, and you get extraordinary pleasure from this novel."

—*Rendezvous*

The acclaimed *New York Times* bestseller! *DREAM MAN*

"A contemporary thriller/romance. . . . Sexy, very hard to put down."

—*The Newport Daily News* (RI)

"The incomparable Linda Howard brings high-voltage power and hard-edged sensuality to this emotional roller coaster of a novel, which is sure to keep readers riveted until the final nail-biting conclusion. They don't get much better than this."

—Jill M. Smith, *Romantic Times*

"Ms. Howard has wonderful pacing, a good ear for dialogue, and knows how to turn on the steam. *Dream Man's* mix of drama, violence, paranormal ability and sex makes it a perfect candidate for a USA Original Picture."

—Suzanne Kennemer Dent, *Birmingham Post-Herald* (AL)

" . . . Steamy romance. . . . Hollister makes the perfect romantic hero. . . . Howard's writing is compelling, especially the murder scenes."

—*Publishers Weekly*

Books by Linda Howard

Kill and Tell
A Lady of the West
Angel Creek
The Touch of Fire
Heart of Fire
Dream Man
After the Night
Shades of Twilight
Son of the Morning

Published by POCKET BOOKS

LINDA HOWARD

Kill and Tell

POCKET BOOKS

New York   London   Toronto   Sydney   Tokyo   Singapore

This book is a work of fiction. Names, characters, places and incidents are products of the author's imagination or are used fictitiously. Any resemblance to actual events or locales or persons, living or dead, is entirely coincidental.

An *Original* Publication of POCKET BOOKS

POCKET BOOKS, a division of Simon & Schuster Inc.
1230 Avenue of the Americas, New York, NY 10020

Copyright © 1998 by Linda Howington

ISBN: 0-671-56883-3

First Pocket Books printing January 1998

10 9 8 7 6 5 4 3 2 1

POCKET and colophon are registered trademarks of Simon & Schuster Inc.

Cover art by Brian Bailey

Printed in the U.S.A.

This book is dedicated to John Kramer, and to cops everywhere. Thanks, John, for taking me around New Orleans, telling me the interesting stuff and showing me the interesting sights.

Kill and Tell

Chapter 1

February 13, Washington, D.C.

Dexter Whitlaw carefully sealed the box, securing every seam with a roll of masking tape he had stolen from WalMart the day before. While he was at it, he had also stolen a black marker, and he used it now to print an address neatly on the box. Leaving the marker and roll of tape on the ground, he tucked the box under his arm and walked to the nearest post office. It was only a block, and the weather wasn't all that cold for D.C. in February, mid-forties maybe.

If he were a congressman, he thought sourly, he wouldn't have to pay any freaking postage.

Thin winter sunshine washed the sidewalks. Earnest-looking government workers hurried by, black or gray overcoats flapping, certain of their importance. If anyone asked their occupation, they never said, "I'm an accountant," or "I'm an office manager," though they might be exactly that. No, in this town, where status was everything, people said, "I

1

work for State," or "I work for Treasury," or, if they were really full of themselves, they used initials, as in "DOD," and everyone was expected to know that meant Department of Defense. Personally, Dexter thought they should all have IDs stating they worked for the DOB, the Department of Bullshit.

Ah, the nation's capital! Power was in the air here, perfuming it like the bouquet of some rare wine, and all these fools were giddy with it. Dexter studied them with a cold, distant eye. They thought they knew everything, but they didn't know anything.

They didn't know what real power was, distilled down to its purest form. The man in the White House could give orders that would cause a war, he could fiddle with the football, the locked briefcase carried by an aide who was always close by, and cause bombs to be dropped and millions killed, but he would view those deaths with the detachment of distance. Dexter had known real power, back in Nam, had felt it in his finger as he slowly tightened the slack on a trigger. He had tracked his prey for days, lying motionless in mud or stinging weeds, ignoring bugs and snakes and rain and hunger, waiting for that perfect moment when his target loomed huge in his scope and the crosshairs delicately settled just where Dexter wanted them, and all the power was his, the ability to give life or end it, pull the trigger or not, with all the world narrowed down to only two people, himself and his target.

The biggest thrill of his life had been the day his spotter had directed him to a certain patch of leaves in a certain tree. When his scope had settled, he had found himself looking at another sniper, Russian from the looks of him, rifle to his shoulder and scope to his eye as he tried to acquire them. Dexter was ahead of him by about a second, and he got his shot squeezed off first. One second, a heartbeat longer, and the Russian would have gotten off the first shot, and old Dexter Whitlaw wouldn't be here admiring the scenery in Washington, D.C.

He wondered if the Russian had ever seen him, if there had been a split second of knowledge before the bullet blasted out all awareness. No way he could have seen the bullet, despite all the fancy special effects Hollywood put in the movies showing just that. No one ever saw the bullet.

Dexter entered the warm post office and connected to the end of the line waiting for service at the counter. He had chosen lunch hour, the busiest time, to cut down on the chance of any harried postal clerks remembering him. Not that there was anything particularly memorable about him, except for the cold eyes, but he didn't like taking chances. Being careful had kept him alive in Nam and had worked for the twenty-five years since he had returned to the real world and left the green hell behind.

He didn't look prosperous, but neither did he look like a street bum. His coat was reversible. One side, which he now wore on the outside, was a sturdy brown tweed, slightly shabby. The other side, which he wore when he was out on the street, was patched and torn, a typical street bum's coat. The coat was good, simple camouflage. Snipers learned how to blend with their surroundings.

When his turn came, he placed the box on the counter to be weighed and fished some loose bills out of his pocket. The box was addressed to Jeanette Whitlaw, Columbus, Ohio. His wife.

He wondered why she hadn't divorced him. Hell, maybe she had; he hadn't called her in a couple of years now, maybe longer. He tried to think when was the last time—

"Dollar forty-three," the clerk said, not even glancing at him, and Dexter laid two ones on the counter. Pocketing the change, he left the post office as unobtrusively as he had entered it.

When *had* he last talked to Jeanette? Maybe three years. Maybe five. He didn't pay much attention to calendars. He tried to think how old the kid would be now. Twenty? She'd been born the year of the Tet offensive, he thought, but maybe not. 'Sixty-eight or 'sixty-nine, somewhere along through there. That made her . . . damn, she was twenty-nine! His little girl was pushing thirty! She was probably married, with a couple of kids, which made him a grandpa.

He couldn't imagine her grown. He hadn't seen her for at least fifteen years, maybe longer, and in his mind he always pictured her as she had been at seven or eight, skinny and shy, with big brown eyes and a habit of biting her bottom lip. She had spoken to him only in whispers, and then only when he asked her a direct question.

He should've been a better daddy to her, a better husband to Jeanette. He should have done a lot of things in his life, but looking back and seeing them didn't give a man the chance to go back and change any of them. It just let him regret not doing them.

But Jeanette had kept on loving him, even when he came back from Nam so cold and distant, forever changed. In her eyes, he had remained the edgy, sharp-eyed West Virginia boy she had loved and married, never mind that the boy had died in a bug-infested jungle and the man who returned home to her was a stranger in all but face and form.

The only time he felt alive since then was when he had a rifle in his hands, sighting through the scope and feeling that rush of adrenaline, the heightening of all his senses. Funny that the thing that had killed him was the only thing that could make him feel alive. Not the rifle; the rifle, as true and faithful a tool as had ever been fashioned by man, was still just a tool. No, what made him feel alive was the skill, the hunt, the power. He'd been a sniper, a damn good one. He could have come back to Jeanette if it had been only that, he sometimes thought, though he was years past trying to analyze things.

He'd killed a lot of men, and murdered one.

The distinction was clear in his mind. War was war. Murder was something else.

He stopped at a pay phone and fished some change out of his pocket. He had already memorized the number. He fed in the change and listened to the ring. When the call was answered on the other end, he said clearly, "My name is Dexter Whitlaw."

He had wasted his life paying for the crime he had committed. Now it was someone else's turn to pick up the tab.

Chapter 2

February 17, Columbus, Ohio

The package was lying on the small front porch when Karen Whitlaw got home from work that February night. Her headlights flashed briefly on it as she pulled into the driveway, but she was so tired she couldn't work up any curiosity over the contents. Wearily, she lifted her tote bag, crammed full with her purse and papers and the paraphernalia of her job, and endured the usual struggle of climbing out of the car with the heavy bag. It caught on the console, then on the steering wheel; swearing under her breath, Karen jerked the bag free, and it banged painfully against her hip. She slogged through the snow to the porch, gritting her teeth as the icy mush slid down inside her shoes. She should have put on her boots, she knew, but she had been too tired when her shift ended to do anything but drive home.

The box was propped against the raised threshold, between the screen door and the front door. She unlocked the door and reached in to flip on the lights, then leaned down to lift the box. She hadn't ordered anything; the box had probably been delivered to the wrong address.

The house was chilly and silent. She had forgotten to leave a light on again that morning. She didn't like coming home to darkness; it reminded her all over again that her mother was no longer there, that she wouldn't unlock the door and smell the delicious smells of supper cooking or hear Jeanette humming in the kitchen. The television would be on even though no one was watching it, because Jeanette liked the background noise. No matter how late Karen worked or how tired she was when she got home, she had always known her mother would have a hot meal and a quick smile waiting for her.

Until three weeks ago.

It had happened fast. Jeanette had complained one morning of feeling achy and feverish and diagnosed herself as having caught a cold. She sounded a little congested, and when Karen took her temperature it was only ninety-nine degrees, so a cold seemed like a reasonable assumption. At noon, Karen called to check on her, and though Jeanette's cough was worse, she kept saying it was just a cold.

When Karen got home that night, she took one look at her mother, huddled in a blanket on the sofa and shaking with chills, and knew it was influenza instead of just a cold. Her temperature was a hundred and three. The stethoscope relayed alarming sounds to Karen's trained ears: both lungs were severely congested.

Karen had always thought the best benefit of being a nurse was learning how to bully people gently and inexorably into doing what you wanted. While Jeanette argued that she had only a cold and it was silly to

7

go to a hospital with a *cold,* Karen made swift, competent preparations and within fifteen minutes had Jeanette, warmly wrapped, in the car.

It had been snowing heavily. Karen had always enjoyed snow, but now the sight of it brought back that night, when she had driven, white-knuckled, through the swirling, blinding sheets of white and listened to her mother fight an increasingly desperate battle for oxygen. She made it to the hospital where she worked, driving up to the emergency entrance and blowing the horn until help came, but other than the snow, her only clear memory of that night was of Jeanette lying on the white sheets, small and somehow shrunken, rapidly fading into unresponsiveness no matter how much Karen talked to her.

Acute viral pneumonia, the doctors said. It worked fast, shutting down all the internal organs one by one as they starved for oxygen. Jeanette died a mere four hours after arriving at the hospital, though the medical team had worked frantically in their efforts to defeat the virus.

There were so many details to dying. There were forms to fill out, forms to sign, forms to take to other people. Calls and decisions had to be made. She had to choose a funeral home, a service, a coffin, the dress her mother was to be buried in. There were people to be entertained—God!—her mother's friends who called and came over and brought more food than Karen would ever be able to eat, her own colleagues from work, a couple of neighbors. Her throat felt permanently closed, her eyes gritty. She couldn't cry in front of all those people, but at night, when she was alone, she couldn't *stop* crying.

She got through the funeral service, and though she had always thought them barbaric, she now understood the sense of closure ritual brought, a ceremony to mark the passing of a sweet woman who had never asked much from life, who was content with the ordinary. Prayer and song marked the end of that life and paid homage to it.

Since then, Karen had gotten through the days, but that was all. Her grief was still raw and fresh, her interest in work nonexistent. For so long, she and Jeanette had been united, the two of them against the world. First Jeanette had worked, and worked hard at any job she could get, to keep a roof over their heads and give Karen the opportunity for a good education. Then it had been Karen's turn to work and Jeanette's time to rest, to do what she enjoyed most: puttering around their small house, cooking, doing the laundry, creating the nest necessity had always denied her.

But that was gone now, and there was no getting it back. All Karen had left was this empty house, and she knew she couldn't live here much longer. Today she had taken the step of calling a real estate agent and putting the house on the market. Living in an apartment would be better than facing the empty house, and her memories, day after day after day.

The box wasn't heavy. Karen held it tucked under one arm while she closed and locked the door, then let the heavy bag slip off her shoulder onto a chair. She tilted the box toward the light to read the label. There was no return address, but her mother's name hit her. "JEANETTE WHITLAW" was printed on the box in plain block letters. Pain squeezed her chest. Jeanette had seldom ordered anything, but when she did, she had been like a child at Christmas, eagerly awaiting the mail or a delivery service, beaming when the expected package finally arrived.

Karen carried the box into the kitchen and used a knife to slit the sealing tape. She opened the flaps and looked inside. There were some papers and a small book bound together with rubber bands, and on top lay a folded sheet of paper. She took the letter out of the box and unfolded it, glancing automatically at the bottom to see who had sent it. The scrawled name, "Dex," made her drop the letter, unread, back into the box.

Dear old Dad. Jeanette hadn't heard from him in at least four years. Karen hadn't actually spoken to him since she was thirteen and he had called to wish her a happy birthday. He had been drunk, it hadn't even been close to her birthday, and Jeanette had cried softly all night long after talking to her husband. That was the day all Karen's resentment and confusion and bitterness had congealed into hatred, and if she was at home the few times he had called after that, she had refused to speak to him. Jeanette had been distressed, but Karen figured that on the scale of things holding a grudge weighed a lot less than abandoning your wife and daughter, so she hadn't relented.

Leaving the box on the table, she trudged into the bedroom and peeled off her clothes, dropping the crumpled green uniform on the floor. Her feet ached, her head ached, her heart ached. The overtime she was working, in at six A.M. and off at six P.M., kept her mind occupied but added to her depression. She felt as if she hadn't seen sunlight in weeks.

She slipped her cold feet out of her wet shoes and hurriedly pulled on a pair of sweats, then some thick socks. She was cold and tired. She thought longingly of heat and sunshine. Once, when she was only two years old, they had been stationed at a base in Florida. Karen didn't really remember it, but when she closed her eyes, she still had the impression of wonderful heat, of long days under a brilliant sun. Jeanette had often talked of Florida, with longing in her voice, because those days had been relatively

10

happy. Then Dexter had gone to Vietnam and never really came home. Jeanette had moved back to the mountains of West Virginia, where they were originally from, to be close to their families while she waited for her husband's tour of duty to be over and prayed for his safety.

But one tour had turned into another, then another, and the man who finally showed up on their doorstep wasn't the same one who had left. Karen had clear memories of those days, of his sullenness, his long bouts of drinking, tiptoeing around him lest she set off his temper. He had turned mean, and not even Jeanette's unwavering love could hold him. He began disappearing, at first just for a day or two, then the days became weeks and the weeks turned into months, and then one day Jeanette realized he was gone for good. She cried into her pillow a lot of nights; Karen could remember that, too.

They had moved from West Virginia to Ohio so Jeanette could get a better job. There had been those few phone calls, a couple of letters, and once Dexter had actually come to visit. Karen hadn't seen him; he was gone before she got home from her classes. But Jeanette had been glowing, softly excited, and at nineteen Karen was adult enough to realize her parents had spent the visit in Jeanette's bedroom. That was ten years ago, and Jeanette hadn't seen him since. She hadn't stopped loving him, though. Karen couldn't understand it, but she accepted her mother's constancy. Jeanette had been infinitely loving, even with the husband who had abandoned her.

After a lonely meal of cold cereal, Karen made herself pick up the letter again.

"Jeanie—Here are some old papers of mine. Put them in a safe deposit box and keep them for me. They may be worth some money someday—Dex."

11

That was it. No salutation, no "dear," not signed with love. He had just mailed his junk to her mother and expected her to keep it for him.

And she would have. Jeanette would have carefully followed his instructions and even kept that curt note, placing it with the pitifully small stack of letters she had saved from when he was in Vietnam.

Karen's instinct was to toss the box into the trash. Out of respect for her mother, she didn't. Instead, she carried it into Jeanette's empty bedroom and placed it in one of the boxes that held her mother's things. She couldn't bring herself to get rid of anything yet; she had rented storage space and would keep it all there until that day came.

The packing was all but complete. There were only a few items left, sitting on top of the dresser. Karen added them to the box and sealed it with several strips of masking tape across the cardboard.

With luck, the house would sell soon, and spring would come, and she would be able to see sunshine again.

Chapter 3

August 5, New Orleans, Louisiana

Almost midnight. Someone was following him. Again. Dexter Whitlaw turned his head just enough to see the flash of movement with his peripheral vision. Excitement pumped through his veins, and he almost grinned. There was nothing like the hunt, even when he was the prey. They had been after him for almost six months, and he delighted in using his old skills to evade them. He had led them on quite a chase, zigzagging back and forth across the country, surfacing in the larger cities to place another call. He hadn't expected it to be easy, and he hadn't been disappointed, but he knew his man.

After the initial "Go to hell" had sounded in his ear, Dexter had begun his game of cat and mouse. Blackmail could be as brutal as an amputation or as delicate as reeling in a world-record trout on gossamer line. First, he had established his evidence—just a little of it, just a taste of what *could* be released if certain conditions weren't met.

As he had expected, the pigeon had reacted with fury. Far from being intimidated, he had called all his dogs and sicced them on Dexter. Most men would have been dead by now, but Dexter had spent a three-year lifetime crawling on his belly in Nam, learning patience and strategy and the ability to conceal himself so well that the unsuspecting dogs had several times walked right past him, just as Charlie and the North Vietnamese had done in Nam.

Dexter was having a hell of a time. He hadn't felt so blazingly alive since he had looked down his scope into that Russian's scope and known one of them had only a split second to live.

The dog following him now was better than the others. Not as good as ol' Dex, he thought exuberantly, but good enough to give him a thrill. Hell, he even knew this one; unless he missed his guess, he was being dogged this time by no less than Rick Medina, one of the CIA's best wet men back in their old green hunting grounds, twenty-five years ago. Another time, another world, but here they were, the same old players playing the same old game of hide and seek.

Dexter blended into the shadows, hunkering down for a minute while he waited for his follower to make another move. A less cautious man would have shot first and checked his identity afterward, but this guy was smart. Assume Dexter didn't know he was being followed; a hasty killing of the wrong guy would send the real prey so far underground it might be weeks before they could pick him up again. And don't forget to factor in the unwanted attention of the cops. True, for the most part, the cops didn't worry much about the unexpected demise of a street bum, even when said demise was caused by a bullet in the brain. But you could never tell; they might be having a slow day and want some excitement, or a TV news crew might happen on the scene, and the bright lights would prod the cops to reluctant activity—the random occurrence of feces, as one erudite patron of a soup kitchen in Chicago had put it.

Dexter waited. Slowly, his movements ghostly, he smeared dirt on his face and hands to disguise their relative paleness. Then he ducked his head down and remained motionless, comfortable in the knowledge that he was virtually invisible to anyone peering into the deeply shadowed alley.

After several minutes, he listened to the shuffle of footsteps as they moved closer. Maybe it was the hunter; maybe it was just another bum. Dexter didn't move.

The footsteps paused. Dexter pictured what anyone looking down this alley would see: scattered trash, broken bottles, a pile of malodorous refuse too small to conceal a man, except that it did. It had rained earlier; the street lights shimmered on puddles of water. Any empty cardboard boxes that had littered the alley a few hours ago had been taken to provide shelter from the rain. To the average hunting dog, the alley would look empty and unproductive, but Medina wasn't the average dog; he, too, had trained in Vietnam, so he knew how to be patient and wait for the prey to make a mistake.

Well, in this case, Dexter thought happily, he would have a long wait. Dexter Whitlaw didn't make mistakes, not in this. He might have screwed up everything else in his life, but he'd been a first-class hunter. So he waited, long after the shuffling footsteps moved away, long after other sounds of other footsteps took their place. A rat sniffed around his shoes, and he waited, motionless. After a while, he was rewarded when those same shuffling footsteps made a return visit, once again pausing at the alley. The hunter was comparing the way the alley looked now to the way it had looked earlier. Nothing had changed. Satisfied now that his prey wasn't there, the hunter moved on, still using the shuffle because a good hunter never broke his disguise.

The deceptive gait might have worked, if Dexter hadn't once seen Medina use the same drunken shuffle to bait two bully boys in a Saigon dive, drawing them in with the false assurance that the Yankee was too shit-faced to put up much of a fight. The two specialized in drunk American soldiers and had fun beating the helpless boys to bloody pulps after stealing their money. The week before, one of the boys had died of internal injuries, and a certain American faction had begun a ruthless search for the two Vietnamese.

As the man who had found and identified them, Rick Medina had the honor of taking them out. Two clean shots to the head would have done it, but Medina had wanted to play with them first.

Medina was a neat, all-American type guy, good-looking and slim, with his brown hair cut in a short crew and his clothes pressed and creased even in the oppressive heat. He was intelligent and affable—for the most part. When he was pissed, or when he was working, the affability disappeared as if it had never existed, and in his blue eyes was the cold light of a killer.

Medina had lured the two Vietnamese out into a dark alley; they hadn't even tried to conceal the fact that they were following him, so certain were they of his helplessness. They closed on him like hounds on a rabbit, but at the last second, the rabbit had whirled, all signs of drunkenness gone. The knife in his hand had a dull black blade, so it wouldn't reflect light. The two Vietnamese likely never even saw it. All they knew was that suddenly their bodies were licked with fire, Medina's hands darting and leaving behind slashes that never went quite deep enough to kill— not yet, at least. Medina had shredded the two, all the while whispering to them in their own language, so that they would have no doubts about what was happening and why.

They tried to get away but found the alley blocked by several blank-faced Americans, all holding pistols. Trapped, hysterical, they reckoned Medina the least threat and turned to fight him. Big mistake.

Rick Medina was a regular Veg-o-Matic that night. He sliced and diced with mechanical precision. He weaved and darted, and each flick of the knife relieved someone of a body part—an ear, a finger, a nose. The two were hoarsely screaming before he finished them, neatly slicing their throats and letting them drop. Stepping over the bodies, he rejoined the silent group at the head of the alley, his face set and expressionless.

Medina had gone off by himself, shrugging away the offers of company, and when he surfaced the next day, he was his old affable self again, the killings handled and put behind him.

That was it about Medina, Dexter thought. He was a stone killer when the occasion called for it, but not a murderer. As brutal as the executions had been, they were just that: executions. A lesson taught. After that, the young American soldiers had enjoyed a bit more safety when carousing in the Saigon bars and whorehouses. Medina had known he would pay a personal price for doing the two kills and accepted the cost.

Whatever line was drawn in Medina's soul, he had never crossed it. All of his kills had been righteous.

When Dexter considered it, he realized he probably respected Rick Medina more than any other person in the world. Medina had held to his code; Dexter himself had not, and he had spent all these years paying for his lapse.

If anyone could catch him, Medina could.

Knowing that gave extra life to the game.

Dexter finally rose silently to his feet. A glance at the stars told him roughly two hours had passed.

It was time to lose the street bum disguise. It had worked for a long time, but Medina was on the scent now. The alleys and soup kitchens would be the first place he looked, so Dexter would have to make it a point not to be there. Too bad; street bums had an anonymity that almost no other group possessed, because people actively avoided looking at them. The cops didn't waste any time on them, and they in turn weren't likely to talk to cops about anything they saw. But there were other disguises that would serve him almost as well; the trick was to blend in with his background, whatever that background might be.

New Orleans offered a rich variety of possibilities, and Dexter considered several of them as he took a circuitous route to the Quarter, which was always awake no matter the hour or the day. After crisscrossing St. Charles a couple of times, doubling back, always checking, he finally reached Carondelet. All the time, he watched his flank, alert to any sign of a tail, but saw nothing suspicious.

He now went straight down Carondelet and crossed Canal, where Carondelet became Bourbon Street. Tourists still strolled the uneven pavements, newly emerged from the restaurants and bars and strip joints. Some were obviously drunk, holding plastic cups sloshing with beer or Hurricanes. More than a few wore cheap plastic necklaces in a variety of colors, and sequined masks were evident as well, though Mardi Gras was months past.

The bar lights glittered on the wet pavement, and jazz wailed out of the open doors of the bars, colliding with the more discordant, driving beats coming from the strip joints, where bored-looking dancers, both male and female, gyrated their hips and humped poles and pretended to be sexy.

Laughter rippled from one group of tourists, three prosperous-looking young men whose arms were clutched by glittering young women in cocktail dresses. As Dexter watched, a briskly walking man brushed past the group and went on his way, turning at the next street and disappearing from view, with at least one of the young men's wallets inside his shirt. Not one of the tourists realized anything had happened.

It was like watching a movie, as if he didn't inhabit the same world as the tourists. They were oblivious to him, looking past him, through him. Dexter shivered suddenly, despite the thick heat of a New Orleans summer night. He had been disconnected since Nam, but abruptly he felt even more distant, as if the tourists wouldn't be able to hear him even if he shouted.

It was a peculiar feeling, making him shiver again. He walked down Bourbon, glancing in the open doors as he passed, the music and laughter echoing as if from a distance. The foot traffic was heavier here, and cops on horseback clopped by, steel horseshoes ringing on the pavement. Dexter walked faster, looking for a dark alley where he could hunker down for a minute and shake this spooky feeling. This wasn't downtown, though, this was the Quarter, and alleys were usually entrances to courtyards. If they were private courtyards, the entrances were gated and locked. If the courtyard belonged to a restaurant, he wouldn't find any privacy there.

He reminded himself that he hadn't come to the Quarter for privacy; he had come precisely because Bourbon Street was so active, and he could lose himself in the foot traffic. All he needed to do was ignore the weird feeling and get on with business. Maybe leave New Orleans entirely, now that Medina was on his trail.

Medina. Dexter thought about it and realized what felt so wrong, what had spooked him. Medina wasn't *anybody's* dog. The man had principles. Things happened to people over the years, changed them, but it would take a real sea change to turn Rick Medina into a kill-for-hire man.

Three alternative possibilities presented themselves. One: Medina had been lied to. That was the easiest explanation but possibly the most implausible because of Medina's personality. He wouldn't take kindly to being used, and if he ever found out, there would be hell to pay.

Two: Medina was definitely hunting him, but for a third, unknown party. Perhaps the secret wasn't as well kept as he had thought. God knows it would make great ammunition. This possibility was way out there on the edge of conspiracy, but as someone had said, even paranoids have real enemies.

Three: Medina was here for another reason entirely. It was mere chance that Dexter had seen and recognized him.

Yeah, sure.

Dexter reached St. Ann Street and turned down it, not looking in the windows of the voodoo shop as he walked past. That was some weird shit, and he had all the weirdness he could handle right now. Maybe he should have stayed on Bourbon; St. Ann was empty—

Medina stepped out in front of him, silenced .22 in hand.

Dexter stopped, looking into those calm blue eyes. His own pistol was stuck in the back of his waistband, and he knew he'd never be able to get to it in time. Death stared at him, and strangely he thought of Jeanette. He saw her sweet face, clearly remembered how she had hugged him so tightly the last time he'd seen her, and was humbled to realize how much she loved him.

And, looking behind Medina, he realized abruptly how it was set up. There was a fourth scenario, one he had overlooked.

"Look ou—" he began, but Medina's finger had already tightened delicately on the trigger, and the bullet punched neatly into his forehead, shutting off thought and speech and life.

Rick Medina whirled, going down on one knee, warned by the last words out of Dexter Whitlaw's mouth. He had the strong, lithe grace of a ballet dancer, but he was fifty-six years old, and his reflexes had slowed just a bit. He got off only one shot before two slugs hit him in the chest like sledgehammers. He collapsed on the uneven sidewalk, his body no longer responsive, his eyesight going even as he stared at the three shadowy figures looming over him. *Used,* he thought savagely. *Set up and used.* He felt a burst of fury, and then nothing.

A car pulled up to the curb, and the trunk was popped open. Quickly, the three men lifted Medina's body and stuffed it into the trunk. One remembered to scoop up the silenced .22 and toss it into the trunk with the body; one swiftly patted Dexter Whitlaw's pockets and shook his head at the other two. Then they all got into the car and drove sedately away, just as a man and a woman turned the corner from

Bourbon Street and began walking toward Dexter Whitlaw's body.

The couple saw the man on the sidewalk, and the woman tugged on her husband's arm. "Let's not walk by that drunk," she said. Mellowed by a couple of Hurricanes, the man agreed, and they crossed the street to avoid coming so close to unpleasantness.

It was another twenty-three seconds before four young women, teetering on high heels, clutching sequined purses so tiny as to be useless, and giggling together over the male stripper they had just watched, wobbled their merry way down St. Ann and made the discovery that the man lying on the sidewalk had a hole in his forehead.

Their shrill screams tore through the music and laughter drifting over from Bourbon. Curious heads turned. A few men broke into a run, responding automatically to the sounds of female distress. More people followed, drawing the attention of a pair of patrolmen on horseback.

Had he been alive, Dexter Whitlaw could have told them that when the action is going down, twenty-three seconds is an eon. Witnesses disappear, cars vanish, opportunities are lost, and the wash of time continues its endless scrubbing of the ineffectual marks people made.

Chapter 4

"Shit."

Detective Marc Chastain rubbed his unshaven face, feeling the bristly whiskers rasping against his hand. He yawned and sipped the hot coffee one of the patrolmen had handed him. It was three o'clock in the morning, which meant he'd had not quite three hours of sleep. He was inclined to feel grumpy but pushed the mood away. He was too controlled to let lack of sleep keep him from giving his full attention to the job. He could catch up on his sleep the next night, or the next; the poor bum lying on the uneven sidewalk didn't have that option.

One of the disadvantages of living in the Quarter—other than ancient wiring and even more ancient plumbing—was that if anything happened there, he was usually first on the scene, which meant it became his case. Hell, he had *walked* to the scene and still beat the next detective who had shown up, Shannon, by a good two minutes.

As bad as he felt, however, he was better off than the homeless man stiffening on the sidewalk. Blinking his gritty eyes, Marc surveyed the scene, scribbling notes on his pad.

The victim was approximately six feet tall, a hundred and eighty-five pounds. Age fifty to fifty-five. Gray hair, brown eyes. He lay twisted half onto his right side, his right arm having caught behind him when he fell; the arm braced him, kept him from falling over. There was a small, neat black hole in the center of his forehead but no corresponding wound in the back of his head, meaning the bullet hadn't exited. A .22, Marc thought. Without the power to punch through the skull twice, the lead had wallowed around in the brain, destroying tissue as it went. No blood to speak of, meaning the victim had died instantly. Professionals used .22s, but they were also the cheapest and most readily available handgun, making them the favorites, the "Saturday night specials" used by punk stickup kids. Despite all the outcry to ban guns completely, Marc figured he had a better chance against a poorly aimed .22 bullet than he would against an eight-inch blade or a studded baseball bat, because when a bad guy got close enough to use one of those, he was dead serious and the results far more brutal.

He couldn't rule out drugs as the motive here, but generally pushers, whether individuals or gangs, preferred greater fire power. They liked street-sweepers because they thought it was impressive to throw out all that hot lead in a couple of seconds. A single neat round in the head wasn't their style, wasn't dramatic enough.

Marc lifted his head and looked around. The blindingly bright lights of television cameras glared at him, and he narrowed his eyes to filter out the light as he surveyed the crowd that had gathered. Four young women, dressed for a night on the town, had been segregated from everyone else; one of the women was weeping hysterically, and a medic was trying to calm her. Those four had discovered the body. A patrolman was talking to the three who were coherent, getting names, taking notes. Marc would get to the witnesses in a few minutes.

All the other people had been drawn by the screams of the young women, and the crowd had drawn the television cameras. He sighed. Usually, the murder of a homeless man barely rated a mention in the newspaper, much less television coverage. If a patrolman had discovered the body, there wouldn't be any circus. But New Orleans was a tourist town, and anything that involved tourists was news. Now the newspapers and television stations would be full of more stories about New Orleans's horrific murder rate.

Never mind that most of the murders were in the drug community, that the average citizen was as safe in New Orleans as anywhere else, assuming said citizen had brains enough to stay out of certain neighborhoods; a statistic was a statistic and therefore worthy of being intoned again and again by solemn talking heads. Under pressure from a now-frightened citizenry, perhaps more frightened by the threat of losing tourist dollars than any perceived danger to their own lives, the mayor would come down hard on the police commissioner. The commissioner would then come down hard on the chief, and the shit would filter down to every detective and patrolman in the city.

Wonderful.

He looked back down at the victim, committing

25

every detail to memory. This time, he noticed a strange fold in the victim's shirt, a funny lump in the small of his back. Squatting beside the body, he used his pen to carefuly lift the shirt tail and expose the weapon tucked into the bum's waistband.

"Jesus," Shannon said, standing beside him. "Looks like an awful expensive piece for a bum to be carryin' around. Wonder where he stole it."

Marc shifted his body to block the television cameras. He took the evidence bag and, again using his pen, eased the pistol from the victim's waistband. "Glock 17," he murmured, studying the beautiful weapon. If a Glock had been stolen locally, the owner would have reported the theft, assuming he even knew one had occurred. A lot of people bought guns and put them up, and months would go by before they took the gun out again. Careless shits. If people were going to own a weapon, they owed it to themselves and their family to become proficient with the weapon, to practice regularly and keep the weapon in good condition, and to know where the hell it was.

He lifted the weapon and sniffed. It hadn't been fired; he didn't smell the stench of burned gunpowder, only the sharp, clean scents of metal, plastic, and gun oil. The weapon was in excellent condition, well cared for and maintained. He didn't check the clip, because he didn't want to blur any fingerprints, but he would bet it was full.

"Has it been fired?" Shannon asked.

"No." Marc deposited the weapon in the evidence bag, all the while studying the victim for other interesting details.

Possessing a Glock definitely raised the victim's status from ordinary street bum to unordinary street bum, which raised Marc's curiosity in direct proportion. Why would an ordinary street bum be packing a

Glock? Drugs? Not likely. Street bums were users, not dealers. That was how they got to be street bums in the first place. So, say he stole the Glock, maybe to sell for drugs; why was he still packing it around? A Glock would be easy to unload. Maybe he had felt he needed the protection, for all the good it had done him.

Why would he need protection? People who were worried about their safety made an effort not to live in the streets.

As he studied the victim, something . . . a memory . . . some sense of recognition . . . nagged at him. It wasn't the victim himself, but something about him. He let his eyes unfocus a little so he was seeing the entire body, not one detail at a time, and it hit him. Dirt.

The victim was dirty, the normal condition for street bums. But his face and hands looked as if they had been deliberately smeared. An image flashed in Marc's mind, and his head lifted sharply.

"What?" Shannon asked. He squatted beside Marc, dark eyebrows pinching together. He was a lean young black man, recently promoted to detective, sharp and tough and eager to learn.

"I think he's ex-military." Carefully, he began patting the victim's pockets, feeling for identification, but all the pockets were empty.

"Why's that?"

"Take a look at his face and hands."

Shannon studied the victim. He had done four years in the Army, so he had some experience himself. "Camouflage," he said with faint astonishment. "He was hiding."

"Probably from whoever did him." Marc studied the sidewalk and street around them. Nothing in the Quarter was new; everything was stained with age. If the television cameras hadn't been there, he might not have seen it, but the bright lights lit up the scene like daylight. Even so, the dark splotches some ten feet away blended in with the wet sidewalk so that they were barely distinguishable.

"Take a look at this." He stood and moved over to the spots, and Shannon followed.

"More blood," Shannon said.

"Yeah, but I doubt it's the victim's. The head shot killed him instantly; he didn't bleed enough to fill a thimble."

Shannon looked over at the body. "But you said his weapon hadn't been fired. Where did this blood come from?"

"Did you read the patrolmen's notes?"

"Yeah, what about them?"

"They found four shell casings, all twenty-two caliber. And the victim has how many holes in him?"

"One. But he could have been *fired* at four times and been hit the last time."

"He had a Glock seventeen in his waistband. If someone was shooting at him and had already missed three times, don't you think he would at least have tried to shoot back? He wouldn't have just stood there while the first three shots were fired, so he was killed by the first one, second one for sure; any more than that, and he would have had time to react."

"So we have two, maybe three shots unaccounted for, and blood in another location."

"Right. It follows that whoever did our victim also shot the unknown blood donor, who may or may not be dead. Another body may turn up somewhere, though I don't see the logic in carrying one body away and leaving the second one here, unless the perps just didn't have enough time to grab the second body."

"Perps? Not one guy, then?"

"He would have to be pretty damn strong to pick up a dead guy. You know how it is. They flop all over the place."

"Plus they're dead weight," Shannon said, his face straight.

Marc hid a chuckle, turning it into a cough so the television cameras wouldn't pick up the image of a callous cop laughing over the body. Cops had to laugh, otherwise they wouldn't be able to bear the carnage they saw.

"Maybe the blood donor walked away under his own steam," Shannon suggested. "There's not much blood."

"Neither is there a blood trail that I can see, though drops would be hard to spot on a wet sidewalk in the dark. What did he do, administer first aid to himself quickly enough, cleanly enough, that not even one drop hit the ground?"

Shannon shook his head in answer to Marc's question. Even a cut finger tended to drip before the blood could be staunched. "So . . . you think there were two or more perps, and the missing guy was loaded up and carried away."

"You catch on fast."

"What do you think it was, a drug deal gone bad or some bums arguing over a cardboard house?"

"I don't know. There would be at least three parties involved, and that doesn't feel right. Our victim, who was armed, didn't get a chance to protect himself, so that means he was taken by surprise. There aren't any witnesses, any weapons, any known motive."

Shannon glanced at the crowd. "So what do we do?"

"Go through the motions." It was a hard fact of life, but no police department in the country would expend a lot of effort on catching the murderer of a street bum. Marc was ruthlessly pragmatic; the city's resources were limited, so the money and effort should be spent where it would do the most good, protecting the normal, law-abiding citizens who worked and paid taxes and went to their kids' ball games. "If he's ex-military, the way we think, at least we should be able to ID him."

"Yeah." Shannon stood. "Too bad it had to be tourists who found him."

Without the tourists, this would all have been handled without fuss. With the pressure on to keep the murder rate down, there were occasional rumors that a body had been quietly taken across the river to Jefferson Parish and dumped there, so the murder wouldn't show up on New Orleans's statistics. Marc had personally never done that, never asked, so he couldn't say if it really happened or not. In New Orleans, anything was possible. It was just as possible that the rumor was the result of someone overhearing a couple of cops saying they *wished* they could dump a body somewhere. But the rumor added to New Orleans's reputation and, true or not, had become part of the local lore.

"The fuss will die down," he said briefly. "The press will make a big deal of it on the morning news, we'll identify him as homeless, there'll be a mention of it on the evening news, and then it's history."

Shannon shrugged, accepting reality as readily as Marc did. He looked around at the shabby old buildings. "You live in the Quarter, don't you?"

They walked back to the body. "Yeah, I've got a house on St. Louis."

"How'd you manage that, man?"

"Inherited it from my grandmother."

"No shit? So you're from one of those old Creole families?"

"My grandmother was. My father was shanty Irish." Marc didn't add that he had grown up in the house on St. Louis; he didn't flaunt his background. Making a big deal of his heritage would be stupid. Besides, there was nothing to flaunt. His father hadn't been able to keep a job, so, rather than see her daughter and grandson live in progressively worse dumps until they were finally homeless, his grandmother had taken them in and tolerated, reluctantly, her son-in-law's presence as the price she must pay for peace of mind. His grandmother had always acted like a dethroned queen, but the family money had long since dwindled away, and all that was left was the big house in the Quarter.

Marc didn't think of himself as Creole; he was simply an American. More than that, he was a damn good cop, hard-nosed enough to recognize there were times when he could make a difference and times when he couldn't. This was one of the times when he couldn't, and he didn't waste time beating himself up over it.

Still, as he looked down at the victim, he couldn't help wondering if the guy had any family, where they were, if they would even care that he was dead. Most of the street bums were trash, too lazy to work, into drugs and petty crimes. But some of them were mentally incapacitated, incapable of looking out for themselves, and Marc didn't have any patience with the families who simply turned these people out to shift for themselves. Yes, they were a lot of trouble, a hell of a lot of trouble, but they couldn't help it, and families were supposed to take care of their own. Maybe he was old-fashioned, but his grandmother had put family above everything, and her example had stuck.

Marc squatted by the body again, studying the dead

eyes, wondering at the scenario that had been played out here in the middle of the Quarter without anyone hearing or seeing anything suspicious. No gunshots had been reported, though at least four had been fired. Silencer? That made him think pro, and pro made him think organized crime, not street drug dealer. This guy didn't have the look of a user, anyway; under the dirt, he looked to be fairly muscular and well fed. Street bums could eat as well as anyone these days, with all the shelters and soup kitchens, but users weren't much interested in food. And dealers usually weren't homeless; they needed a base of operations.

He rubbed his nose. This didn't feel like drugs. Maybe the guy just pissed off the wrong party; maybe he was in the wrong place at the wrong time and some wiseguy took him down. Likely he'd never know, but damn, he hated mysteries.

The meat wagon boys came over. "You through here, Detective?"

Marc stood. "Yeah." There was nothing else he could do, no other details to glean from the scene. Maybe the medical examiner could come up with a name, but other than that, they likely knew as much about the victim as they were ever going to know.

In the meantime, he had four young women to interview. After watching the body being loaded and carried away, he glanced at Shannon. "You want to do some interviewing?"

The young detective looked over at the women. "As long as I don't have to talk to the one who's squalling. Man, she hasn't shut up since I got here."

"Just do some preliminaries. I'll get in touch with them tomorrow." He could request that they come down to the Eighth District, but he didn't want to make things tougher for them than he had to. The young ladies, all of whom looked to be in their early twenties, had come to the Quarter for a good time. The brutality of murder had never touched them before; he could forgive them a few tears.

"Take it easy on them," he advised Shannon under his breath as they approached. "They need a little petting."

Shannon darted a startled glance at Marc; in case the senior detective hadn't noticed, he was black, and the witnesses weren't. Pet them? Was he crazy?

But though Shannon had been a detective for only a few months, he had heard some things. Chastain kind of kept to himself, but he was well liked in the department. The word was he was the best at interrogating witnesses and suspects alike, because when he needed to be, he was cool and low-key and could calm the most hysterical witness, but he was also a real hard-ass with the bad guys.

"Chastain," one detective had said, "is the type of guy who carries a blade." By that, Shannon deduced, he was referring not to the utility pocket knife almost every man carried but to a knife whose sole function was as a weapon.

Yeah, that described Chastain, all right. A good knife fighter was smooth and controlled, sneaky and lethal.

Shannon also admired Chastain's sense of style. Man, look at him; obviously just out of bed, unshaven, his eyes heavy-lidded, but he was wearing pleated linen slacks, some kind of drapey pullover shirt, and a cream-colored jacket. Even his sockless feet looked cool, as if he'd planned it. Now, that was style.

They reached the knot of young women and introduced themselves. Shannon noticed that Chastain's voice changed, became lower, more gentle. The women subtly moved closer to him, dazed, frightened eyes fastening on his face. Even the one who kept sobbing tried to get control of herself. Smoothly, Chastain separated the group, directing two of the women a few steps away with Shannon. The girl kept weeping, though more quietly now. He heard Chastain making some low, soothing sounds, little more than rumbly whispers in his throat. Before Shannon could gather his thoughts to do more than ask names, he was aware of the girl wiping her eyes and answering Chastain's questions in a clogged, wavering, but much calmer manner.

It was a little after five before the scene was finally cleared. The witnesses were escorted to their hotel by a patrolman, the crowd dispersed, the media fed enough information for them to have their stories without giving them any salacious details, the street tidied for the next human wave. Morning brought a different set of people to the Quarter: shoppers, delivery men, tourists who felt safer during the day or simply weren't interested in nightlife.

Marc silently cursed when he thought of the paperwork he had to do. He would like to go home and fall into bed, but he'd already had all the sleep he was going to get today. He rubbed his hand over his face, beard stubble rasping. The paperwork could wait until he had showered and shaved.

"No sense walking when my car is here," Shannon said, falling into step beside him. "You going home or to the station?"

"Home first, then to the station. Thanks for the ride." They reached Shannon's car, and Marc slid into the passenger seat.

"So, did you do a hitch in the Army?" Shannon asked. "I mean, you noticed the camo."

"Marines. Right out of high school. That way I could go to college."

"Yeah." Shannon had enlisted for the same end

purpose. It felt strange for them to have that in common, a tough young black dude from a bad neighborhood and a smoothly sophisticated white guy from one of the old French Creole families.

There was no traffic to contend with, so in less than a minute they reached St. Louis. Shannon slowed. "Left," Chastain said. "That's it on the right, in the middle of the block. The blue gate."

Shannon stopped in front of the blue gate. In typical Quarter fashion, the big gate was set in a solid wall that provided privacy for the courtyard beyond. The old Creole houses were built around a center courtyard, facing inward to their own gardens rather than out toward the streets. Long wrought-iron balconies extended over the sidewalk, the third-floor balcony providing a roof for the one on the second floor. Tall white shutters framed two sets of double french doors opening onto the balcony, and Shannon could see a couple of garden chairs and a small table up there. Two lush ferns hung from the overhang.

"Ferns?" Shannon couldn't quite keep the disbelief from his tone. Chastain wasn't married. Ferns weren't normal for a heterosexual single guy.

Chastain chuckled. "Relax. They were a gift from an old girlfriend. Women like them, so I keep them. They aren't much trouble, I just water them now and then."

Shannon's mama kept ferns, so he knew there was more involved in their upkeep than occasional water. He grinned a little, imagining a slow parade of women keeping Chastain's ferns in good condition, feeding and pruning and watering. Maybe he should get some ferns.

"You want some coffee?" Chastain asked. "Or are you heading home?"

"Naw, there's no point in it now. Coffee sounds good."

"Come on in, then."

A little surprised by the invitation but anxious for a chance to do some more brain picking, Shannon slid out of the car. Chastain unlocked the gate, and they walked into a long, narrow, bricked entry. A single light fixture set into the wall lit their way. A courtyard opened up beyond them, and in the predawn darkness, Shannon got the impression of lush vegetation, and the sweet scent of flowers teased him.

Chastain turned to the right and went up a flight of stairs. "I turned the house into four apartments," he said. "It was the only way I could afford the upkeep. This one's mine."

When he reached the upper balcony, he unlocked another door, reached in to turn on a light, and motioned for Shannon to enter.

Shannon looked around, his interest keen. The ceilings were high, at least twelve feet, the floors bare hardwood except for a few scattered rugs. A lazily whirling ceiling fan hung in the center. Most of Chastain's furniture was so old-fashioned and shabby Shannon thought it had to have been his grandmother's, though here and there a few new pieces had been added. The place was clean and fairly uncluttered, though there were newspapers on the floor beside a big easy chair, a coffee cup left on a lamp table, books scattered around. "No television?" he blurted.

"It's in the armoire," Chastain said, nodding toward an immense piece of furniture. "My grandmother loved watching soaps, but she refused to leave the television out where her friends could see that she had one. The kitchen's through here."

He led the way past a small inset dining room on

the left, pushing open folding doors to enter the kitchen. It was a square, functional room, surprising in its normality. Stove, refrigerator, microwave, toaster, coffeemaker—Shannon had kind of expected a food processor or something, because it seemed Chastain was a man who appreciated fine food and would want to have all the appliances on hand for his girlfriends to cook for him. A wooden table for two was set against the wall.

Chastain expertly measured coffee and water and turned on the maker. "Make yourself at home," he said. "I'll be out by the time the coffee's done. You hungry?"

"I could eat."

"There're some pastry things in the freezer. Pop a couple in the toaster."

A moment later, Shannon heard the shower come on. He didn't want to put the pastries in the toaster too soon, so he walked over to the french doors and stepped out onto the balcony. His car was parked just below. To his left, lights were coming from the other set of doors, so he imagined that was Chastain's bedroom.

Shannon thought of his own place, with dirty clothes on the floor and dishes in the sink and dust all over everything. If he had a girl over, he had to rush around shoving clothes under the bed or in the closet, hide the dishes in the oven, try to blow the worst of the dust off, and it took a can of air freshener to cover the smell of dirty socks for a while. Chastain could bring a babe here anytime without worrying about how his place looked.

Man, this was the way to live. Nothing fancy, and just about everything was old as hell, but he bet Chastain drew babes like a magnet. The way he dressed, the way he lived . . . women liked this stuff.

Shannon settled against the railing, thinking. Maybe he couldn't own a house in the Quarter, but he could take better care of his place, clean it up, maybe buy a few plants or something. No one would have to know he got them himself instead of a girlfriend giving them to him. And he needed some new threads; nothing flashy like the drug dealers, just maybe some good shirts and a nice jacket or two. And maybe a food processor. Hell, why not?

He was so involved with his plans that he didn't hear the shower cut off. A few minutes later, he was startled when Chastain walked out onto the balcony, freshly shaven, his short black hair plastered to his skull. He was buttoning a short-sleeved white dress shirt made out of some kind of gauzy stuff.

"Ah, hell," Shannon said, disgusted with himself. "I forgot about the Pop-Tarts."

"I put them in," Chastain said.

Shannon felt embarrassed into speech. "I was just—man, this is nice, y'know? The house and everything. And I noticed the way you were with the witnesses, like you were gonna put your arms around them and say, 'Now, now,' any minute. Women like that shit, don't they? I mean, thirty seconds of that stuff, and that girl turned off the spigot and started talking. I thought she was gonna throw herself at you."

"They deserved to be taken care of," Chastain said calmly. "They hadn't done anything wrong, and they were upset. They don't see the things you and I see every day." From inside came the sound of a toaster ejecting its contents, and the two men walked in.

Chastain got two cups down from a cabinet and poured coffee into them. He had made it strong, the way almost everyone in New Orleans did, and the kitchen was fragrant with chicory. Next, he placed the pastries on two small plates, dusted them with powdered sugar, and handed them to Shannon while he got two forks out of a drawer. Shannon put the plates on the small wooden table. "These aren't Pop-Tarts," he blurted.

"A girlfriend—"

"—makes them for you," Shannon finished, and sighed.

"Yeah. They're pretty damn good when I don't have the time for a regular breakfast."

"How many girlfriends you got?"

"I have a lot of friends who are women. I don't date all of them."

Shannon got the message. A gentleman didn't brag about his girlfriends.

These few hours with Chastain had been a revelation, Shannon thought. Watching him work, seeing how he was with witnesses, how he lived and dressed and comported himself, struck Shannon all of a sudden as how a man should be. "I bet you open doors for women, don't you?"

"Of course."

Of course. That was it. The attitude. The attitude was everything. Shannon felt almost breathless. When he made a few changes, he could almost see the women lining up to be with him.

"What's your first name?" Chastain asked when the pastry on his plate was almost gone.

"Antonio."

"Well, Antonio, you have to figure witnesses are already rattled; they don't need anyone coming on tough to them. Calm them down so they can think, go low-key so they don't feel threatened and keep things to themselves." He paused to take a bite. "Say you've got a couple of kids who were someplace they shouldn't have been, and they saw something. If they're scared, they'll lie to cover their asses because they know their parents are going to be pissed. Reassure them. Talk to the parents yourself if you have to, so they don't scare the kid into shutting up entirely. You won't get anything if they do."

Shannon knew interrogation techniques: present yourself as understanding, even sympathetic. Maybe you're talking to a guy you know beat his wife to death. You say, "Man, I know how you feel. Sometimes my wife gets in my face, and I just want to punch a hole in something, you know?" Never mind that you're lying; the perp doesn't know that. He's scared, he's upset, he lost control and killed his wife, and he's looking at nothing but trouble. A friendly voice is maybe all he needs to spill his guts. Chastain gave that same friendly, sympathetic ear to witnesses, too. People probably tripped over their own feet to get to him and start talking.

"How much follow-up do you normally do on a case like this?" he asked Chastain curiously.

"As much as the lieutenant wants me to do." Chastain's voice was neutral. "If we can get an ID, I'll notify his family. They probably won't care, but at least they can take care of his burial."

"You think he was a mental?"

Chastain shrugged, indicating the odds were even. "He didn't look like a doper, didn't have that wasted look. Some of the homeless have families who send money to them. It's a lot easier than trying to take care of someone with a mental condition. Just turn 'em out on the streets."

Shannon nodded. The situation wasn't that unusual. Back in the seventies or early eighties, a bunch of do-gooders had gone to court to get patients released from mental institutions on the grounds that they were perfectly capable of functioning in society. Well, they were, as long as they took their medication. Problem was, crazy people took their medication only when they lived in a controlled environment, like a mental institution. Put them in the real world, a lot of them went off their meds and became more than their families could handle. When the stress became too much, a lot of the mentals ended up on the street, unable to hold a job or even carry on a decent conversation. They shuffled around talking to themselves, cursing people, relieving themselves in public. They were sitting ducks for mindless street violence, thrown in as they were with the dopers and the criminal element.

Something in Chastain's voice alerted Shannon, a cold undertone. "You're pissed, huh?"

"Not yet. If it turns out he had a family that could have been taking care of him, *then* I'll be pissed."

It was said mildly enough, but a chill ran down Shannon's spine. It struck him that despite Chastain's polite sophistication, when he was pissed he could be one mean son of a bitch.

Chastain gathered the dishes, rinsed them, and placed them in the dishwasher. After refilling both their cups with coffee, he said, "We'll take the coffee with us. Let's go do some paperwork." They both sighed.

Marc made a mental note. If he had time, he'd follow through on this case maybe a little more than he normally would. For one thing, he wanted to find out where this guy had got hold of a Glock .17. Little oddities like that annoyed the hell out of him.

Chapter 5

"How did you dispose of the body?"

"Drove his rental car over into Mississippi, put him in it, wiped it down. We made it look like a robbery. Someone will find him in a day or so."

"What?" The first man sat forward in his huge leather chair, which had cost almost as much as the average car. "Why in hell didn't you dump him in a bayou so a gator could get him?" He was incensed.

The man standing before him patiently shook his head. "You don't want a bunch of spooks losing one of their guys and starting to nose around looking for him. Strange shit can happen."

"Medina was CIA. The Agency isn't allowed to operate inside the country."

Like rules—and laws—weren't broken every day, the second man thought wearily. Sure, the Agency wasn't supposed to operate within its own borders. Did anyone who wasn't naive as hell think it didn't happen anyway? Unofficially, of course. He didn't even bother to reply to that nonsense, just said soothingly, "Looking for Medina isn't the same thing as running an operation. And Medina was a contract agent, not a Company guy, so he worked for other people, too. The CIA is the least of my worries. Give them the body so they know what happened to him. You said Medina was a real hard-ass, but from what I've heard, he didn't hold a candle to his son. I'd just as soon not have Junior snooping around looking for his old man."

"I haven't heard anything about a son," the first man said, frowning in concern. He glanced at the framed photo sitting on his desk, at the beloved, smiling faces. His own family was of paramount importance to him. As a young man, he had wanted nothing more than to win his father's approval and make him proud. He didn't dare expect less from Rick Medina's son.

"Not many people have. I've only heard a few whispers about him myself, and that's because I've done some work in the business."

"Can you find out where he lives, what he looks like?"

"No can do." The second man shook his head. "I don't have the contacts, and even if I did, a request like that would have me dead within an hour. I'm telling you, let it drop here. Don't do anything that will draw attention to us."

"What if you made a mistake, missed a fingerprint or something?"

"I didn't. We wore gloves, got rid of the guns, burned our clothes. There's nothing to tie anyone to Medina. If you're that nervous about it, you should have used someone else to make the hit on Whitlaw."

"No one else was even getting close to him. He was

too good. I needed someone just as good." That someone had been Rick Medina. Pity. An unencumbered piece of muscle would have been much simpler—no family who cared much; no cops who cared. Medina came with complications, but that couldn't be helped, especially now. At least he had gotten the job done, something all those other clowns hadn't managed to do. He had concocted a good story to put Medina on the hunt, but once the kill was made, Medina had had to be removed, because if he ever found out he had been used—well, it would have been nasty.

The first man sighed, getting up to pace slowly over to the floor-to-ceiling windows that looked out over the carefully manicured lawn. There was nothing in this visit to excite interest, because he normally had a constant stream of visitors, people coming and going, asking favors, performing duties. Still, this whole business made him uneasy. He had thought it was finished years ago. He had learned a lesson, though: tie up all the loose ends. Medina had been a loose end; he regretted the necessity but didn't back down from it.

"What about the men you used?" he asked, wondering if they were more loose ends.

"I can vouch for them. None of them even knew a name; they were just doing a job. I've kept everything quiet."

"Good. What about the book?"

"No sign of it."

"Damn." The word was softly breathed. As long as that book was unaccounted for, he couldn't feel safe. What sort of madness had prompted Dexter Whitlaw to record the hit, anyway? It was evidence against himself, and it wasn't as if he could include it in his body count. But Whitlaw had evidently decided he had less to lose than someone else if the truth came out, and that the someone else would pay any amount to get that book. He had almost been right. When one had other options, one wasn't bound by the rules. "Where could he have put it?"

"I doubt he would have used a safe deposit box," the second man said, thinking. His name was Hayes. He was big, stocky, unremarkable in looks, just one more slightly overweight, slightly unkempt man who hadn't kept in shape. His gaze was remote and intelligent. "He moved around too much, and he would have wanted it where he could get to it fairly easily, plus you have to pay for the boxes every year. Same thing with lockers in bus stations. Most likely, he left it with someone he trusted, maybe a friend but probably someone in his family."

"Whitlaw was estranged from his family." This was said with distinct disapproval. "He walked out on his wife and daughter twenty years ago."

"What was their last known address?" Hayes asked promptly.

"Someplace in West Virginia, but they're no longer there. I learned they moved to Ohio years ago, but I haven't located them yet."

"Whitlaw might have known where they live. He could have sent the book to them before he started trying to blackmail you. Set everything up in advance."

"That's true, that's true." Clearly disturbed by that possibility, the first man turned back from the windows.

"Have you traced their social security numbers, checked for tax records?"

"That would leave tracks—"

Hayes sighed. Yes, it would—if done officially, through the proper channels, which was the stupid way to do anything. "Give me their names and birthdays. I'll get the information—and I won't leave tracks."

"If you're certain—"

"I'm certain."

"Don't take any action without talking to me first. I don't want two women to be needlessly killed."

After Hayes had left, Senator Stephen Lake left his office and climbed the wide, curving staircase that swept in a graceful arch up to the second floor. The luxurious thickness of the carpeting silenced his steps; the polished ebony banister gleamed like jet in the summer sunlight. The air was sweet with fresh flowers cut from his own lovingly tended gardens—lovingly tended by the gardener, that is—and he paused a moment to inhale the wonderful, indefinable essence of gracious living.

He loved this house, had from the moment he was old enough to appreciate the beauty of it and everything it represented. He remembered, as a child, watching his father stoop and trail his fingers across the glossy, newly inlaid marble in the foyer, relishing the stone for both its own beauty and its testimony to his wealth and, more subtly, his power. Stephen's chest had felt full and tight with emotion as he'd absorbed his father's emotions and known he felt exactly the same way. He still did. He appreciated the lead crystal chandeliers, the exquisite furniture handmade by Europe's finest, the exotic woods from Africa and South America, the paintings in their gold-leaf frames, the ankle-thick carpeting that kept the chill of the Minnesota winters from his feet.

He had grown up playing on the beautifully manicured lawn, he and his older brother, William, taking turns being cowboys and Indians, pretending long sticks were rifles, and yelling "Bang bang!" at each other until they were hoarse. Those had been great days. The cook had always had fresh, cold lemonade to refresh them after a day of hard play in the hot summer, or hot chocolate to warm them after romping in the snow. Inside, there had been the rich smell of their father's cigars, a smell the senator still associated with power; the sweet fragrance of his mother's perfume as she hugged him and William and kissed their cheeks, and he had wriggled with delight. "My little princes," she had called them.

Their mother had loved them unconditionally. Their father had been more stern, harder to please. A frown from him could ruin the boys' day. William had found it easier to please their father than Stephen had. William was older, of course, but he was naturally more careful, more responsible. Stephen had been a little shy, more intelligent than his confident brother but less able to show that intelligence. William had often stepped between Stephen and punishment, deflecting the scoldings and loss of privileges that would have come his brother's way, because their father had often been impatient with Stephen's shyness.

Stephen had grown up wanting nothing more than to please his father, to be the kind of man of whom he could be proud. He wanted to *be* his father, a man people both feared and respected, whose smallest frown brought instant obedience but whose word could be trusted implicitly. William, however, had always been the crown prince, the heir, and so William had garnered most of their father's coveted attention. Stephen couldn't say their father's trust was misplaced, because William had been . . . wonderful. That was the only word for him. There hadn't been a mean, nasty bone in his body, and he worked doggedly to overcome his perceived failings. Even with all the responsibility on his shoulders, he had always been cheerful, smiling, ready to enjoy a joke or to play one.

William's death at the age of twenty-seven had devastated the family. Stephen's mother had never recovered from the shock, and her health began to deteriorate steadily; she died four years later. As for his father, he was shattered. Pushing aside his own grief, Stephen had tried even harder to make his father proud of him. He drove himself all through law school, studying longer and harder than his class-mates, and graduated first in his class. He married a sweet, lovely young woman from an extremely wealthy New Hampshire family and devoted himself to being a faithful, considerate, loving husband. They had two children, a boy and a girl, and Stephen watched his stern father totally melt over his grand-children.

Stephen began his political career by running for local office, as his father advised; that was how to build a base of loyal constituents. After serving a term as district attorney, he ran for the state legislature as a representative, then for the state senate. With twelve years of state and local politics under his belt, he seized the opportunity when a U.S. representative from the state retired, and he ran for his office. He discharged his duties as conscientiously as possible, and bided his time, watching the senators from his state for signs of weakness. When one became in-volved in a sex scandal, Stephen made his move and ran against him in the next election. He became a United States Senator at the age of forty-one and steadily built his power base and his reputation.

Shaking himself from his reverie, Senator Lake climbed the remaining stairs and walked down the wide upper hall to the suite of rooms at the back of the house. He knocked lightly, then opened the door. "How is he today?"

"He ate well," said the nurse with a soft smile. Cinda Blockett was a sweet creature, as tender with his father as she would be with a newborn. Her husband, James, also a registered nurse, worked the first shift with her and provided the muscle necessary for caring for a total invalid.

James had carried Walter William Lake to the huge, overstuffed recliner positioned in front of the windows, with a perfect view of the sweeping grounds and the glittering blue lake beyond, patrolled by majestic peacocks. Stephen pulled up a chair beside his father and took a gnarled, wasted hand in his. "Good morning, Father," he said gently, waited a second to see if there would be any signal of recognition such as a blink of the eye, then began to talk about the latest news, both on television and in the newspaper. He didn't restrict himself to politics but talked business, too, and science. Every time a space shuttle went up, Stephen kept his father informed. He didn't know if any of what he was saying was actually received and processed in the working portions of his father's brain, but he never gave up.

He sat with his father for more than an hour, spelling Cinda and James so they could have a leisurely meal. His father was never left alone. Three shifts of nurses cared for him, kept him fed, exercised his wasted muscles, turned and moved him so his fragile skin didn't rot with bedsores. They made his existence as comfortable as possible, playing his favorite music, turning on the television to the programs he had liked, reading aloud to him or playing books on tape. If there were any cognitive parts of his father's brain still functioning after the massive stroke that had felled him eleven years before, Stephen hoped he was doing enough to keep those parts stimulated, to make his father as happy as possible under the circumstances.

He was now one of the most powerful, most respected people in Washington, and he would never know if his father was proud of him.

When Cinda and James returned, and Stephen left his father's suite, Raymond was waiting for him just as the senator had known he would be. Raymond Hilley, sixty-nine years old, had worked for the Lake family for fifty years. Stephen couldn't remember a time when Raymond hadn't been there, his father's right-hand man, almost an uncle to him and William when they were growing up. When William died, Raymond had sat down on the floor and cried, huge tears running down his battered face.

Eleven years ago, when the stroke incapacitated Walter William Lake and Stephen became the head of the family, Raymond's skills and unswerving loyalty had transferred to him.

"Let's go down to my office," the senator said, clapping his hand on Raymond's shoulder as his father had always done, a sign of friendship and acceptance.

Coffee was waiting for them, brought in when Cinda and James finished their lunch and returned to the suite. With Hayes, the senator had sat behind his desk while Hayes took one of the chairs opposite, but with Raymond, he went over to the sitting area, and they took chairs as friends, as family. He poured Raymond's coffee first, putting in three teaspoons of sugar and diluting it with milk until the coffee barely had a tan color. He took his own coffee with a little cream, just a drop really; his father had drank it black, but even after all this time, Stephen couldn't give up that tiny drop of rich cream to mellow the bite of the coffee. Sometimes he was embarrassed by his weakness for cream in his coffee; it seemed to say he was a watered-down version of his father, a milquetoast—yes, that was a better comparison, both in sound and in image.

He knew better, of course. He had made some hard decisions in his life, not the least of which concerned Dexter Whitlaw and Rick Medina. He didn't feel good about what he had done, but neither did he doubt the necessity.

Raymond sipped the excessively sweet brew in his cup, sighing in pleasure. "I followed him to the airport," he reported in his gravelly voice, which sounded as if he had once eaten glass—and liked it. "He didn't stop, didn't use his cell phone, just went straight to the check-in counter and then to the gate."

"He could have called someone from the gate."

"He wouldn't do that. Too much chance of being overheard."

That made sense, and Stephen accepted the statement from Raymond as he would not have from anyone else.

"If you don't trust him . . ." Raymond said slowly, letting his words trail off, inviting the senator to pick up the thought just as he had done forty years ago when he was teaching the boys how to hunt and they had to anticipate what a big elk would do.

"Then don't use him," the senator said, and sighed. "I wouldn't, but I need his contacts. He's a good buffer, and I don't believe he would talk. After all, his livelihood depends on his reputation. If he couldn't keep a confidence, no one would use him."

"He has the situation handled?"

"The blackmailer has been taken care of; there are still, however, certain loose ends."

"Loose ends are like loose shoestrings; they'll trip

you up every time." Raymond sipped his coffee again, his big hands handling the transparent china cup with a certain delicacy.

"Steps are being taken."

"Good. Mr. Walter . . . well, I wouldn't want anything to come out that might hurt him. He's a great man. He did some things people might not understand, not knowing the whole story. He doesn't deserve to have people saying bad things about him, especially now when he can't protect himself."

"No," the senator said, and sighed. "He doesn't."

"Caucasian male, seventy-one and three-quarter inches tall, weight one hundred eighty-two pounds, age fifty to fifty-five. Gray hair, brown eyes. Distinguishing marks: a 'Semper Fi' tattoo on the left forearm, a surgical scar four inches in length on his lower right abdomen, a two-inch keloid scar diagonally on the right quadriceps—"

Marc tuned out the assistant medical examiner's detailing, for the record, of the victim's many scars. None of the scars looked like a bullet wound, but several of them did look as if he'd had some close encounters with sharp blades. Most of the scars, though, were the sort people collected just going through life: childhood falls that cut the knees, various nicks and scrapes. The most important detail, for purposes of identification, was the tattoo. Not only had he been in the military, but the tattoo narrowed down the branch of service for them. They would soon have a real name for this John Doe.

As predicted, the morning television news announcers had waxed eloquent, and in rounded funereal tones so listeners would know how serious the issue was, about the early-morning murder in the Quarter. The New Orleans murder statistics were trotted out again, followed by a noncommittal statement from the police department, followed by a passionate statement from the mayor to the effect that the citizens—and tourists—of New Orleans *must* and *would* feel safe in the city. It was a good campaign slogan; he had used it before.

Marc dispassionately watched the autopsy. He had a strong stomach and had never puked the way some detectives did. Like the medical examiners, he could ignore the smells and concentrate on what the body told them. Working homicides, it was a handy knack to have.

This body wouldn't have much to say. A bullet in the brain was pretty obvious. The where, when, and how weren't in question, just the who and why.

The young women who had discovered the body hadn't been any help. None of them could remember seeing anyone else, period, either walking or driving. The shooting had to have happened just minutes before, but no one, not even anyone living close by, had heard a thing.

The victim's personal effects, such as they were, hadn't yielded anything except a wedding ring, carefully sewn inside the cuff of his pants. Maybe he had stolen it, but it had fit his ring finger, and he had kept it carefully hidden, which told Marc he had valued the ring beyond what money it would bring in a pawn shop. The guy had once been married, maybe still was.

"You're getting on my nerves, Chastain," the doctor said testily, clicking off the microphone so he could speak off the record. He was a busy man, impatient and harried, and he seldom spoke personally to the detectives who attended the autopsies.

Marc lifted one eyebrow in silent question.

"That's what you're doing." A stained scalpel was

jabbed in his direction. "You just stand there, quiet as a rock and about as active. You don't interrupt me to ask questions, you don't turn green and gag, you just watch. Damn it, you hardly even blink. What do you do, go into a trance?"

"If I have any questions, I ask them when you're finished," Marc said mildly.

The scalpel jabbed once more. "You're still doing it. You didn't even change expressions. Do me a favor; do something human before I start thinking you're a robot." Behind him, his assistant smothered a laugh.

"If you're in doubt, when you're finished, I'll let you watch me piss." The offer was made totally deadpan, and this time the assistant didn't manage to control the laugh.

"Thanks, but I'll pass on that wonderful opportunity."

"I don't make the offer to just anyone. You're the only man who's ever heard it, so you might want to reconsider. Just don't get any wrong ideas about my sexual orientation."

Behind her mask, the assistant's eyes were sparkling. The doctor shot her a sour look. "Don't even think about volunteering for the job."

"Too late," she admitted cheerfully.

Marc winked at her.

"Forget I said anything," the doctor muttered, and switched the microphone on again, putting an end to the discussion. Pity. Marc had enjoyed needling him, and evidently the assistant had enjoyed the exchange, too. It was the first time Marc had seen the brusque doctor interrupt any autopsy to make a personal remark.

Just for the pure hell of it, he stuck his hands in his pockets and began jingling the change. After two minutes, the microphone was clicked off again. "Forget I said anything," the doctor snapped again. "And stop jingling your change, damn it! You sound like Santa Claus."

Marc shrugged and took his hands out of his pockets, but his eyes were glittering with amusement.

Sometime later, the body of the victim had told them that except for being dead, he was in remarkably good shape. No sign of disease in any of the major organs, no blockage in his veins, good muscle definition, no needle marks on his arms or between his toes to indicate intravenous drug use. The toxicology report wasn't back, and it might indicate some other type of drug use, but overall the victim looked too healthy to have been a user.

Cause of death was a gunshot wound to the head, fired at medium range, no exit wound. The penetrating missile was a .22-caliber bullet, which had also sent several bone fragments through the soft brain tissue. The kinetic energy of the tumbling projectiles had destroyed massive amounts of tissue, like a tidal wave rolling through the brain and smashing everything it touched.

X rays and photographs of the victim's teeth had been sent to the Marine Corps for identification. Depending on how efficient they were, the victim's identity should be forthcoming within a few days. Marc would begin trying to locate any family, and maybe, just maybe, within a week or two the poor guy could have a burial.

He was surprised when the identification came back the next day. Someone in the vast tangle of military and civilian bureaucracy was on the ball; either that, or by pure chance the victim's teeth had been in the first batch checked for a cross-match. There was a name now: Dexter Alvin Whitlaw, from Keysburg, West Virginia. Next of kin was a wife,

Shirley Jeanette Allen Whitlaw, and a daughter, Karen Simone Whitlaw. Marc had their social security numbers and their last known address. He could find them.

The message light was blinking when Karen got home from work. She was tempted not to listen to the messages, just to take a quick shower and fall into bed. Since she'd sold the house and moved into an apartment four months ago, the nights had seemed even more lonely; after working all day, she hadn't had either the energy or the interest to do much unpacking, and a lot of her things were still in boxes, which made her feel as if she were living in a sparsely furnished motel room—or a warehouse. The rooms seemed to echo, intensifying her sense of being alone, of missing Jeanette.

She hadn't been sleeping or eating well, either, and was losing weight. In an effort to jar herself out of her depression, she had switched shifts with one of the other nurses and was now working nights. The strategy had worked, to some degree. She was so tired when she dragged home early in the mornings that she literally fell into bed and slept like a log. After the first disastrous day, when she had been awakened eleven times by telemarketers and wrong numbers, she learned to turn off the phone.

Lately, she had been trying to stay up for several hours after getting home, to mimic the routine of daytime jobs, but not today. This was the morning after the night from hell. She wanted nothing more than to get off her aching feet and just sleep.

She worked on the surgical floor, where noncritical patients were placed after surgery. They were all in pain, but everyone had a different tolerance for pain. Some were so stoic only their blood pressure would indicate whether or not they were hurting; others screamed bloody murder at the least discomfort. Tonight had been a night for the screamers. They *hurt,* damn it, and wanted something *now:* another pill, turn up the morphine drip, anything. Of course, the nurses couldn't exceed the doctors' prescribed dosages without authorization; all they could do was take the heat. Tracking down a doctor in the middle of the night to authorize more pain medication was usually an exercise in futility; the nurses practically needed a team of bloodhounds to track down the doctor on duty, who had a genius for being somewhere else and not hearing his page.

Then a patient, a thirty-two-year-old mother of two, had gone sour on them. She was in for a ruptured appendix and had been very sick for several days but was recovering. Tonight, just after supper, she had been walking to the bathroom and suddenly slumped to the floor. A blood clot had lodged in her pulmonary artery, and she was gone, despite all their efforts. It happened sometimes, but the shock never really lessened. The only thing that had changed was that Karen had learned how to work through the shock, to keep going, to push it away. All nurses and doctors had to learn that, or they couldn't function.

But the kicker was when some idiot let a nineteen-year-old boy, wacked out on drugs, escape from the psych unit, where he had been taken because of the security. Some security. And where had the kid headed? Straight to the surgical floor, where all the good dope could be found.

He had shed his hospital gown somewhere along the way. Stark naked, his pupils so contracted he looked like an alien, hair standing out in wild tangles, he had wrecked the desk looking for drugs. Finally, he had found the locked cabinet, but Judy Camliffe, the floor charge nurse, had the key in her pocket. Security got there as he was trying to tear the metal doors apart. Unfortunately, subduing a naked man is tricky; there are no clothes to grab, and bare skin is slippery. The kid fought free so many times Karen lost count. They wrestled in the halls, upsetting carts, dumping files and charts everywhere, waking patients who then either became alarmed or decided they needed more pain medication. By the time the kid was finally subdued, the surgical floor was a wreck. By the time the nurses finished with their shift, so were they.

The message was probably from a salesman or a charity; she hadn't had time yet to make friends with any of her new neighbors, and all of her other friends were nurses who knew what shift she worked and wouldn't call to chat. She couldn't think of any remotely urgent reason she should listen to her messages, but still she dropped her bag and went over to the machine. She wouldn't be able to sleep knowing that red light was blinking.

Out of habit, she picked up the notepad and pen she always kept by the phone, just in case there might actually be a call she needed to return. She punched the play button and listened to the tape rewinding.

After some whirring and a couple of clicks, a drawling baritone voice broke the quiet of the room. For some reason, her breath gave a little hitch. The voice was somehow beguiling, with warm, dark, pure masculine tones that quivered along her nerve endings, almost as if she had been touched. Even disguised by the drawl, there was a hard edge of authority evident as well. He said, "Miss Whitlaw, this is Detective Marc Chastain with the New Orleans Police Department. I need to talk to you concerning your father. You can reach me at—"

He recited the number, but Karen was so taken

aback she didn't write down a single digit. Hastily, she punched the stop button, then replay. When the whirring and clicking stopped, she listened again to the brief message and once again was so distracted by his voice that she almost missed the number a second time. She scribbled it down, then stared at the pad in a fog of fatigue and bemusement.

Dexter was evidently in trouble and thought she would bail him out. No, he thought *Jeanette* would bail him out; he couldn't know his wife had been dead for six months. Had the detective said *"Miss* Whitlaw" or *"Mrs.* Whitlaw"? His drawl had slurred the word.

She couldn't resist. She replayed the message one more time, as much to hear that voice as to determine if he had thought he was calling her or her mother. Listening closely, she thought he said "Miss," which was politically incorrect of him, but she still wasn't certain.

She didn't want to call. She didn't want to hear about Dexter's troubles, and she had no intention of bailing him out of anything, anyway. All she wanted to do was get off her feet and go to sleep.

She thought of her mother, how Jeanette had taken him back time and again, how she was always there if he needed her. *He* had never been there for *them,* but Jeanette had never wavered in her devotion.

Suddenly, Karen felt swamped by an exhaustion that had nothing to do with physical tiredness and everything to do with a lifetime of bitterness, of wariness, and these last lonely six months of grieving for her mother. She was tired of being dragged down by her father's desertion. It was done, and nothing she could do would change it. She didn't want to be one of those people who spent their entire lives whining about their past troubles, as if that excused them from responsible behavior in the present. She had loved her mother dearly, still loved her and would continue to grieve for her, but it was time to get on with life. Instead of letting the empty apartment depress her, she should get her things out of the boxes she had packed them in to move, and make a home here.

Maybe she would take more classes, get her master's degree in nursing. She might go into the critical care field. It was challenging but fascinating for those who could stand the pressure. She was calm during emergencies, able to think fast on her feet, both necessary characteristics in a good critical care nurse.

She took a deep breath. For the first time since Jeanette's death, she felt in control of herself, of her life. She had to deal with Dexter, if only for her mother's sake, so she might as well make the call. Without giving herself any time perhaps to change her mind, she picked up the receiver and punched Detective Chastain's number.

Unconsciously, she held her breath, bracing herself to hear his voice. How silly of her, to let herself to be affected by a man's voice on the telephone, but recognizing the ridiculousness of her reaction didn't mitigate the strength of it.

The phone rang several times, but no one answered it. Surely detectives didn't keep bankers' hours, she thought.

She glanced at her wristwatch. Seven forty-five. "Idiot," she muttered under her breath, and hung up. Louisiana was in the central time zone, an hour behind Ohio. Detective Marc Chastain was definitely not in his office at six forty-five in the morning.

She couldn't stay awake until a reasonable time for him to be there. She couldn't stay vertical another five minutes. Dexter would have to wait.

But she would call. When she woke up this afternoon, she would call.

That decision made, she stumbled into the bedroom. Fatigue made her clumsy as she undressed. Yawning again, she stretched out between the cool sheets and sighed with bliss, arching her aching feet and wriggling her toes. She tried to imagine how Detective Chastain looked. Voices almost never matched appearances; the detective was probably a pot-bellied good old boy, edging toward retirement, with a couple of grown kids. But he had a voice like dark honey, and it was with her as she drifted to sleep.

The shrill ringing of the telephone jarred her awake. Confused, startled, Karen bolted upright in bed, then groaned as she realized she had forgotten to turn off the ringer before she went to sleep. The digital clock taunted her with big red numerals: nine-thirty.

She grabbed the receiver just to silence the obnoxious noise. "Hello," she said, her voice foggy with sleep.

"Miss Whitlaw?"

That voice. Just two words, but recognition tingled down her spine. She cleared her throat. "Yes."

"This is Detective Chastain, New Orleans Police Department. I left a message for you yesterday concerning your father."

"Yes." She started to say she had intended to return his call this afternoon, but he was already speaking again, the warm tones noticeably cooler.

"I'm sorry, Miss, but your father was killed two days ago in a street shooting."

Shock made her go numb. Her hand tightened on the receiver until her knuckles turned white. "Two days?" Why hadn't someone called before?

"He didn't have any ID on him. We identified him by his military dental records." He kept talking, saying something about her coming to New Orleans and verifying Dexter's identity. He was brisk, businesslike, and Karen fought to organize her scattered wits.

"I'll try to catch a flight today," she finally said. "If not—"

"The airlines have special arrangements for emergencies," he cut in. "You can be here this afternoon."

If you want to. She heard his unspoken accusation in his clipped tone, and resentment stirred. This man didn't know anything about her; who was he to stand in judgment on her relationship, or lack of it, with her father?

"I'll call you when I get there," she said, anger making her voice tight.

"Just come to the Eighth District on Royal Street."

Karen repeated the address, then said, "Thank you for calling." She hung up before he could say anything else.

She pulled her legs up and rested her head on her knees. Dexter was dead. She tried to absorb the news, but it was too unreal. She knew she should be feeling something other than shock, but she was empty. How could she mourn a man she barely knew? It was his absence, not his presence, that had shaped her life.

Throwing the sheet back, she got out of bed. She felt like a walking zombie, but she had to make some calls, arrange a flight, pack a bag. Only duty drove her, but duty carried a big whip.

Her father was dead. The thought kept reverberating in her mind as she stood under a cold shower. She hadn't really known him, and now she never would.

Chapter 6

"Karen Whitlaw, Karen Whitlaw." A man named Carl Clancy stood at the pay phone—it had taken forever to find one with a directory—and ran his finger down the tissue-thin page. It was just after noon, and the sun was baking him. He shifted position so his body blocked the glare from the paper. No Karen Whitlaw was listed, but he found a K. S. Whitlaw. He would bet that was her. Single women always used their initials; the practice was so common they might as well go ahead and have their full names printed, except for the simple precaution of protecting their full names.

He dropped some change into the slot and dialed the number. After four rings, he heard the click of an answering machine, and a pleasant female voice said, "You've reached 555-0677. Please leave a message."

Smart girl, he thought with approval. She hadn't

given out her name to any jackass who happened to dial her number. People did that all the time, gave out their names on their answering machine messages, even put signs on their mailboxes or in their yards announcing "The Hendersons," or whatever. Fools. All some burglar had to do then was look up Henderson in the phone book until he came to that address, then call to see if anyone was home. If no one answered, he could waltz right in, secure in the knowledge he was alone.

In this case, however, Carl already knew her name. The call had just verified her address. She was probably at work; the information he'd received on her said she was a nurse. He could take his time, give the house a thorough toss, find the book Hayes wanted. If he couldn't find it, Hayes said, torch the house, just to be on the safe side. Maybe the book was in a safe deposit box, but people were seldom that cautious with valuable items; they just found what they thought was a clever hiding place somewhere in their home.

Returning to his car, he took out the city map he had bought and located Karen Whitlaw's street. He could be there in fifteen minutes, max; plenty of time to do the job and catch his late-afternoon flight.

He drove through the neighborhood, looking for Neighborhood Watch signs and neighbors who were out gardening or mowing their lawns. The houses were smallish and past their prime. He saw only a few children playing, and most of the cars in the driveways were older sedans, which told him that the majority of the houses were owned by old people whose kids had long since grown up and left or young couples who had bought their first houses and hadn't yet started their families. The houses with no cars in the driveway would belong to the young couples, who were at work.

That was both good and bad. There weren't many people at home in the neighborhood, but those who were would likely be old people. Old folks were nosy. They knew what cars belonged in the neighborhood and what cars didn't, and they didn't have anything better to do with their time than peer out windows.

Well, a few old folks couldn't keep him out of a house he wanted into. The trick, if he was seen, was to look as average as possible and to act as if he had every right to be there. Even better was if no one saw him. He was good at not being seen; that was why Hayes had picked him for the job.

He drove around until he found a convenience store and parked the rental car as far to the side as he could. In case the clerk was watching out the window, he went inside and bought a soft drink, taking care not to make eye contact or do anything that would make him memorable. Leaving the car there, he briskly walked the three blocks to Karen Whitlaw's house.

When he reached her street, he began cutting through backyards, using shrubbery and fences for cover. People put all sorts of junk in their backyards, which was great for concealment. Generally, his biggest problem was dogs. Dogs were a pain in the ass. He could hear one of the little bastards now, yapping its head off inside the house he was now behind. Carl settled into place behind a bush, remaining motionless until the yapping ceased.

Finally, he reached the Whitlaw house. Getting in was a piece of cake. The lock on the back door wouldn't keep out a determined ten-year-old; he opened it within seconds. God, if people only knew.

He did a walk-through of the house first, checking the most obvious hiding places: the freezer compartment of the refrigerator, on top of cabinets, under chairs. He didn't know exactly what the book looked like; no one did. Just look for a little notebook, Hayes had said. It'll be old and dirty.

There weren't any old, dirty notebooks in any of the obvious hiding places. Methodically, Carl began tossing the house. He looked in every drawer, took every drawer out and checked for anything taped behind or underneath. He felt the curtains to see if anything had been sewn into the hems, examined all the cushions and pillows for a resewn seam or any suspicious lumps. He didn't wreck the place; that was for malicious amateurs. The real art was to get in and out without leaving a trace of his presence. He didn't slash the furniture, and he put everything back in place after he had examined it.

There were framed photos sitting around, some of them of a smiling young couple. He assumed the pretty little blonde in the pictures was Miss Whitlaw. He wouldn't mind having her as his nurse, especially if she sat on his lap the way she was doing with some grinning idiot in one of the photos. The grinning idiot was the guy in the other pictures; evidently, he was the man of the moment.

In the bedroom, he found men's clothing in the closet and shaving gear in the bathroom. He clucked his tongue. Miss Karen had a live-in boyfriend, or at least one who stayed over regularly enough to leave some of his clothes here. Maybe she had even married him, recently enough that the number in the phone book was still listed in her name.

The house was small; he was efficient. Within two hours, he had covered it, and the book wasn't there unless she had gotten real clever and hidden it under the house or, somehow, in the ceiling. He found the trap door into the attic area and peered around, but everything was dark and dusty, and it was more than a hundred degrees up there. Nor was he inclined to crawl around under the house; that wasn't a good hiding place, because it was so dank. The moisture ruined everything.

He was certain the book wasn't on the premises, but Hayes's orders had been to burn the place if he didn't find the book. He shrugged. Orders were orders, and Hayes was a careful man. Carl set about following those orders.

In his opinion, the best way to burn down a house was a grease fire in the kitchen; there weren't any accelerants to raise suspicion, and it always looked like an accident. Fires started in kitchens all the time.

He whistled softly as he set to work. Bless her, Miss Karen had fried up some bacon that morning and left the pan of grease sitting out to cool. Using a towel, he turned on the gas burner and set the pan on top of it, then arranged the towel so that it was close enough to catch fire when the grease blazed up. He made a silent bet with himself, then opened the cabinet door closest to the stove. Yep, that was where she kept the cooking oil, in both bottles and spray cans, right where they were closest to the heat and were most likely to catch fire. She couldn't have made it any easier for him if she had tried.

Professional that he was, he didn't leave without knowing he had done his job. While he waited for the grease to flame up, he took a battery out of the smoke detector and reversed it, then put the detector back in place. He hated listening to that damn shrill noise.

Smoke was filling up the kitchen pretty good now. He opened all the doors in the house so the fire could get good air flow and spread more quickly. He didn't enjoy burning the house; he even regretted upsetting the pretty little blonde. It would hurt her to lose all her pictures and things. But a job was a job, and this wasn't personal.

Crouching on the floor to stay out of the deadly smoke, he waited until the pan on the stove flamed with a sudden *whoosh*. The towel caught fire immediately, and tongues of flame leaped up the cabinet. Carl quickly left the house then and took his usual precautions returning to the car. He glanced back occasionally and at last was rewarded by the gust of black smoke that meant either the roof or a wall had been breached by the flames. It was tempting to drive by the house to make certain it was engulfed, but that was a bad idea, and he knew it. Never go back. As old as the house was, and the way he had opened up all the rooms, the fire would spread too quickly for anything to be saved.

He checked his watch when he heard the first siren in the distance: ten minutes. Too long. Houses burned much faster than people realized; they thought they would have several minutes in which to rescue their treasured possessions. Wrong. By the time most fires were noticed, the people inside had about thirty seconds in which to get out. The only way he had been able to remain as long as he had was because he had been aware of the fire from the beginning, he had stayed low, and he had been near the door. By the time the fire department actually got to the house, every room would be involved. They would concentrate on keeping the flames from catching the trees on fire and spreading to the other houses.

He gave a mental shrug as he drove away. He had both failed and succeeded. He didn't have the book, but if it had been anywhere in that house, it was now totally destroyed. He had carried out Hayes's instructions, though they seemed excessive to him. He'd tell

Hayes he didn't think the book was there, and what Hayes did then was his own business. Carl had done his job.

The dented, rusted pickup rolled to a stop at the end of the narrow dirt road, and two lanky teenage boys bailed out. The dead end widened into a large open area, the left side of which was a rocky pit. Two rough-hewn sawhorses were positioned in front of the pit, a plank placed across them. On the plank sat an assortment of tin cans, and the ground beyond was littered with more.

From the gun rack behind the seat, the two boys took a pair of .22 rifles. "Man, Shavon was all over Justin last night," one said, shaking his sandy head. "She was so shit-faced I bet she ain't woke up yet."

"And if she has, I bet she wishes she hadn't," the other boy replied, and they both laughed as they expertly slotted .22 longs into their rifles. "Does her daddy know she drinks?"

"I don't see how he can help it, considering she goes home from her dates drunk all the time." Disapproval colored the boy's voice. "I ain't got nothing against drinking, but Shavon stays drunk as much as she does sober. She's gonna wreck that car of hers one day and kill somebody, and then there's gonna be trouble."

"Her daddy's just as bad. I guess she comes by it honest."

The two positioned themselves, their sneakers toeing a shallow rut in the dusty red ground that revealed how often they indulged in tin can plinking. They began firing methodically, and one by one the tin cans went spinning. When all of the cans were down, the two trudged to the sawhorses and began resetting the cans for another round. As they walked back, the sunlight glared on something shiny just beyond the clearing, making one boy squint his eyes. "Damn, that's bright! There's something behind that big bush."

"Looks like a car," the other replied, craning his neck. He was the taller of the two. "Let's go see."

"Reckon somebody's back there making out?"

"If there is, bet his pecker lost its starch when we started shooting." They snickered at the idea. A quick look darted between them, and the taller boy held a finger to his lips. They tiptoed toward the bush, barely containing their snorts of laughter at the thought of catching some of their friends doing something they shouldn't be doing. Or maybe it was some of their friends' *parents,* which would be even better.

The two boys moved with the silence of longtime hunters. When they got closer to the huge bush, they could make out the roof outline of a car, and the tall boy made a motion with his hand indicating they should slip around to the rear. They did, and when the rear of the car came into view, they stared in disappointment at the Louisiana plates. Even more disappointing, no one was visible in the car.

"Shit, all this sneaking for nothing."

"Shh! Maybe they're layin' down in the seat."

"No way." The boy straightened. "Look, the windows are rolled up. Ain't nobody making out in a car in this heat with the windows up."

"Maybe the car's stolen, and somebody stashed it out here." They looked around, strong young hands tightening on their rifles. Making no effort at stealth now, they walked up to the car. It was a white Pontiac four-door, coated with a layer of red dust. The tall boy leaned down and peered in the driver's-side window, then jerked back so violently he stumbled and almost fell.

"Shit! There's a dead man in there!"

* * *

Karen felt the heat as soon as she stepped from the jet into the extended accordion of the jetway. The air was heavy with humidity, and sweat popped out on her forehead as she lugged her carry-on bag up the slight slope. She had dressed in a short-sleeved summer suit that felt too cool while she was on the plane, but now she was sweltering. Her legs were baking inside her panty hose, and sweat trickled down her back.

Detective Chastain had been right about the airlines; she had made one call, spoken to a sympathetic, calmly efficient reservations agent, and found herself scurrying in order to get packed and to the airport in time to catch the flight. She hadn't had time to eat before getting on the plane, and her stomach had clenched in revolt at the thought of eating the turkey sandwich served during the flight. She disliked turkey anyway; there was no way she could eat it with her stomach tied in knots and her head throbbing with tension.

The headache was still with her. It throbbed in time with every step she took as she followed the signs to the baggage claim area. She had never felt the way she felt now, not even when her mother died. Her grief then had been sharp, overwhelming. She didn't know what she felt now. If it was grief, then it was a different variety. She felt numbed, distant, oddly fragile, as if she had crystallized inside and the least bump would shatter her.

The weight of the bag pulled at her arm, making her shoulder ache. The air felt clammy even inside the terminal, as if the humidity seeped through the walls. She realized she hadn't called ahead to reserve a room. She stood in front of the baggage carousel, watching it whirl around with everyone's bags except hers, and wondered if she had the energy to move from the spot.

Finally, the conveyor spit out her bag. Keeping a tight grip on her carry-on, she leaned over to grab the other bag as it trundled past. A portly, balding man standing beside her said, "I'll get it for you," and deftly swung the bag off the belt.

"Thank you," Karen said, her heartfelt gratitude evident in her voice as he set the bag at her feet.

"My pleasure, Ma'am." Nodding his head, he turned back to watch for his own bags.

She tried to remember the last time a stranger had been so courteous, but nothing came to mind. The small act of kindness almost broke through the numbness that encased her.

Her taxi driver was a lean young black man wearing dreadlocks and an infectious smile. "Where you goin' this fine day?" he asked in a musical voice as he got behind the wheel after stowing her bags in the trunk.

Fine day? Ninety-eight degrees with a matching percentage of humidity was a fine day? Still, the sky was bright blue, unclouded, and even over the reek of exhaust in this island of concrete, she could catch the scent of vegetation, fresh and sweet.

"I don't have a room yet," she explained. "I need to go to the Eighth District police department on Royal Street."

"You don't wanna be carryin' your bags around in no police station," he said, shaking his head. "There's a bunch of hotels on Canal, just a few blocks from where you want to go. Why not check into one first, then walk on down to Royal? Or I can take you to a hotel right in the Quarter, but it might be hard to get a room there if you don't have a reservation."

"I don't," she said. Maybe all taxi drivers gave advice to weary travelers; she didn't know, not having traveled much. But he was right; she didn't want to lug her bags around.

"The bigger hotels, like the Sheraton or the Marriott, are more likely to have vacancies, but they're gonna be more expensive."

Karen was so exhausted that she cared more about convenience than cost. "The Marriott," she said. She could afford a few nights in a good hotel.

"That's just two blocks from Royal. When you come out of the hotel, turn right. When you get to Royal, turn right again. The police department's a few blocks down, you can't miss it. Big yellowish place with white columns and all the patrol cars parked out by the fence. It's in all the TV shows about New Orleans, looks like one of them old Southern mansions. I reckon cops still work there, since the cars are still there."

She leaned back and closed her eyes, letting the flow of words wash over her. If she could make it through the next few hours, she would go to bed early and get a good night's sleep, and tomorrow she would feel normal again instead of so unnervingly fragile. She didn't like the feeling. She was a healthy, energetic, calm, and competent young woman, known on the surgical floor for her level head. She was *not* an emotional basket case.

Within the hour, she was installed in a room with a huge king-size bed and a view of the Mississippi River and the French Quarter, which to her disappointment looked ramshackle, at least from the vantage point of fifteen floors up. She didn't take the time to unpack but did splash cold water on her face and brush her hair. It must be fatigue making her so pale, she thought, staring at her reflection over the sink. Her dark brown eyes looked black in comparison with the pallor of her cheeks.

The taxi driver's directions made it sound easy enough to get to the police station, no more than five or six blocks, too short a distance to bother with another taxi. The walk would help clear her head.

She almost changed her mind about walking when she stepped out into the heat. The afternoon sun burned her skin, and the thick air was difficult to breathe. She would have taken a taxi after all if the sidewalks hadn't been buzzing with people who didn't seem to notice the heat. Usually, heat didn't bother her this much, either, and the nineties weren't uncommon in Ohio during late summer.

Her stomach roiled, and she fought back a rise of nausea. Maybe she was coming down with something, she thought. That would explain how awful she felt.

But even with all her present stress, practically from the very moment she turned right off Canal onto Royal Street, she felt the charm for which the French Quarter was famous. The streets were narrow, and Royal was clogged with cars parked on both sides. The sidewalks were cracked and uneven, the buildings old and, for the most part, dilapidated. But the doors were painted with bright, festive colors, flowers bloomed in boxes, ferns and palms turned second- and third-story balconies into gardens. Intricate wrought-iron railings and gates drew the eye, and alleys were lined with lush vegetation, hinting at the gardens beyond. She caught a variety of accents and languages as she passed other people. If the circumstances had been different, she would have loved to go into some of the exotic-looking shops.

But today she didn't have the energy to do more than place one foot in front of the other and hope the police station wasn't much farther down the street.

Even on the shady side of the street, the sidewalks held the day's heat, and it was burning through the soles of her shoes.

Finally, she saw several police cars parked in front of a stately mansion; when she got close enough, she saw the sign on one of the white columns: "New Orleans Police 8th District." The building was a creamy shade that was too golden to be salmon and too pinkish to be tan. Black wrought-iron fencing surrounded the building and its immaculate landscaping. A genteel garden party wouldn't have looked out of place there.

Karen went inside the open gates and up a couple of wide, shallow steps. A massive door opened into an enormous room with blue walls and a ceiling that looked at least fifty feet high. Globed lighting fixtures, pamphlets for tourist attractions, and the general air of a museum made her wonder if she was in the right place after all.

A female police officer was sitting behind a raised desk. She seemed to be the only other person there. Karen looked up at her. "Does a Detective Chastain work here?"

"Yes, Ma'am, he does. I'll call and see if he's in. What's your name?"

"Karen Whitlaw."

The officer spoke quietly into the phone, then said to Karen, "He's in, and he said to come to his office." She pointed in the appropriate direction and recited instructions. "Take a right, and it's the third door on the left."

Ceiling fans whirled overhead as Karen followed directions; the stirring air raised chills on her arms after the furnace of the streets. She had never been in a police department before. She expected something approaching mayhem; what she found was ringing phones, people sprawled in chairs, clouds of cigarette smoke, and the odor of strong coffee. It could have been any busy, disorganized office, except for the fact that most of the people there were armed.

She found the appropriate door and knocked on it. That smooth, dark voice she remembered so well said, "Come in."

She opened the door, and her stomach twisted again, this time with pure nervousness, as she looked at the man rising to his feet. Detective Chastain wasn't what she had expected. He wasn't middle-aged, pot-bellied, or balding. Mid-thirties, she guessed. He looked like a man who had seen too much ever to be surprised by anything again. Thick black hair was worn cropped close to his head, and he had thick eyebrows arching over narrow, glittering eyes. His skin was olive-toned, and his five o'clock shadow was heavy. A couple of inches over six feet, broad-shouldered, muscled forearms; he looked tough, maybe even mean. Something about him scared her, and she wanted to run. Only the years of discipline learned on the job kept her from doing so.

Marc stood as Karen Whitlaw stepped into his cramped office. He had the usual cop's talent for sizing up people, and he used it now, studying her with eyes that gave nothing away while he noted every detail about her. If she was distressed in any way by her father's death, she didn't show it. Her expression said that she thought this was all bullshit, but she'd get through it and then get on with her life.

Pity, he thought, assessing her again, and this time with a man's eye instead of a cop's. He didn't have much use for coldhearted people, but she was a pretty woman. Mid- to late twenties, with a face that managed to be both exotic and all-American, clearly shaped but with a slant to her cheekbones, an intriguing sultriness to her dark, slightly deep-set eyes. Better than pretty, he thought, revising his opinion. She was understated, so her looks didn't jump out at a man, but she was definitely worth a second look.

Nice shape, too; medium height, slim, with high round breasts that hadn't jiggled at all when she walked. That meant they were either very firm or she wore a killer bra. On a purely physical level, he would like to find out which it was. Steadily increasing pressure in his groin told him he would like that very much. He gave a mental shrug. It happened sometimes; he'd have a strong sexual reaction to a woman he didn't even like. Mostly he ignored the urge, because the payoff wasn't worth the cost.

He held out his hand to her. "I'm Detective Chastain."

"Karen Whitlaw." Her voice was a little throaty but as composed as her face. Her fingers were cool, her hand delicate in his, her handshake brief and firm. She had beautiful hands, he noticed, with long tapered fingers and short, unpolished, oval-shaped nails. No rings. No jewelry at all except for a serviceable wristwatch and a pair of small gold balls stuck in her earlobes. Miss Whitlaw obviously didn't believe in gilding the lily, but then she really didn't have to.

Her hair was as dark as her eyes, brushed back simply from her face. It hit her shoulders with a slight undercurl. She was neat. Businesslike. Unemotional.

It was the unemotional part he didn't like. He hadn't expected her to be sobbing, but people usually exhibited some sign of grief or shock, however controlled, at the death of a family member, estranged or not. Regret usually caused a few tears even if there was no genuine grief. He couldn't see either in this self-possessed woman.

"Sit down, please." He indicated a chair, the only chair in the tiny office other than his. It was straight-backed and didn't invite people to relax and linger.

She sat, her skirt positioned to fall at the middle of her knee. She kept both feet on the floor. She was so still she reminded him of a porcelain doll. "You said on the phone that my father's death appeared to be the result of random street violence."

"Not random," he corrected, sitting down and closing a file that had been open in front of him. "Whoever killed him meant to do it. But the rea-son—" He shrugged. The reason could be anything, from drugs to a dispute over a cardboard box. With no witnesses, no murder weapon, no leads of any kind, the case was dead, and no one was going to put out any more effort on it.

She sat in silence for a moment. Though he would have respected at least some show of emotion or remorse, at least she wasn't yelling at him, demanding that he find her father's killer, as if she really cared what had happened to him. Marc toyed with the idea of finding out if by chance she had taken out a large insurance policy on her father. The possibility wasn't remote; money was at the bottom of a lot of murders, though it could just as easily be over something as mundane as how a steak was cooked.

"How long has it been since you saw your father or heard from him?"

"Years." She looked as if she were about to say something else, but instead, she pressed her lips firmly together and let the single word stand.

"Are there any life insurance policies on him?"

"Not that I know of." Shocked, she realized what he was thinking.

"You didn't know where, or how, he was living?"

Karen sensed his hostility, though he kept his face

impassive, his eyes hooded. Detective Marc Chastain definitely disapproved of her for some reason, but if he pursued the insurance angle, he would hit a dead end. Maybe he expected her to start screaming at him because he obviously wasn't working very hard to find out who had murdered her father. But she hadn't expected an all-out effort. She was a nurse; she saw all too often what happened when a homeless person was the victim of a crime. Police departments nationwide worked with limited resources, and they couldn't waste their precious time or money on useless causes. Hospitals did it all the time. Triage was necessary, or everyone lost.

She could have told him that, but she was too hot, too tired, and too stressed to care what he thought. Her head was pounding. She felt as if she were about to fly apart in all directions, her emotions roiling, and the only way to handle it was to stay in control. That was the way she did it at work, when a patient died no matter how conscientious she was in her care, no matter how good the doctor was, no matter that it was a sweet-faced child or a lively old lady with a sparkle in her eye. People died all the time. She had learned how to handle it.

"He didn't keep in touch," she finally said.

"He was a Vietnam vet." Statement, not a question.

"Yes." She knew where this was leading. The disturbed vet, in need of psych care, cast out and ignored by his family because he was too much trouble, too much of an embarrassment with his moods and rages and unpredictability.

But Detective Chastain didn't say it; he didn't have to. Karen read it in his cool, narrow-eyed gaze.

"He walked out on us when I was a child," she said sharply, more sharply than she had intended. She could feel her control frazzling, feel the jagged edge of some pain she refused to let herself identify, and sternly fought her emotions back in line. There would be time enough for that later, when she was alone and this hard-faced, dark-browed man wasn't looking at her with veiled contempt.

She didn't owe him any explanations. She didn't have to reveal the pain and anger and fear of her childhood, just so he would think better of her. All she had to do was get through the next couple of days, then return to Ohio and go back to work, to the silent, empty apartment that wasn't home yet despite having lived there for four months.

"What do I have to do to claim the body?" she asked after a moment, her voice once more cool and composed.

"You have to identify him, sign some papers. I'll walk you through it. Have you made arrangements to take him back to Ohio?"

Karen sat there, stunned. She hadn't thought of that. She had been focused on getting through the funeral, but not *where* the funeral would be. She didn't have a plot in Ohio where she could bury Dexter. There wasn't room next to her mother's grave—not that she wanted that, anyway, but Jeanette would have.

Karen's hands twisted together as she tried to control the sharp jab of pain. She had let her mother down. Jeanette had asked very little from her and had given everything, but Karen had let her own resentment of her father prevent her from doing what her mother would have wanted.

"I—I didn't even think—" she said, then wished she hadn't. His expression was as lively as a rock's, but again she sensed that wave of disapproval.

Regret speared through her, not because of what Detective Chastain thought of her but because she had wasted so much time feeling bitter, letting it cloud her thinking. No more.

Chastain gave a brief shrug, broad shoulders moving in a gesture that was oddly Gallic. Karen thought that maybe because she was in New Orleans, she expected everything to have a French flavor. And maybe she was even more stressed than she had realized, if she was letting unimportant details distract her. She had been trained to keep her mind on the job in front of her, not on trivia such as how a New Orleans cop shrugged.

"If you can't handle the expense of taking him back, I can help you find a burial plot here," he offered, though she could tell he hoped she would refuse. "Not in the city, that would be impossible, but a few miles out of town. Or you might consider cremation. It would be cheaper."

Cheaper. He thought she would have her father cremated because it was cheaper. She didn't have anything against cremation, if that was what someone wanted, but she couldn't help thinking of Jeanette again. Dexter should be buried beside her. She had to deal with this now, but when she got back to Ohio, she would start making arrangements to have her parents buried together. She would have to locate two plots side by side, deal with the legalities and technicalities of moving the bodies—oh, God, she couldn't think of her mother as a *body*.

She couldn't think at all; her mind was growing number by the minute. And whatever Detective Chastain's private opinion of her, he had at least offered his assistance. She was uncomfortable accepting his help, knowing he didn't like her, but right now she desperately needed it. "Thank you," she forced herself to say, her voice unusually husky. "I'm not usually so disorganized. My mother died just a few months ago, and I'm still not—" She stopped, looking away, appalled that she was making excuses for herself.

He stood and retrieved his jacket from the back of his chair. "I'll drive you to the morgue now, if you feel up to it."

She didn't, but she stood anyway. She stared at him, wondering how he could stand wearing a jacket in this heat. She felt dizzy, both too hot and too cold at the same time, sweat trickling down her spine and raising a chill. The lazily turning ceiling fan merely stirred the warm air. She didn't understand it; she had dressed in the coolest suit she owned, but she might as well have been muffled in wool instead of cotton.

Then Detective Chastain's hand was on her arm, a warm, hard hand. She felt the calluses on his fingers, smelled the light lemony tang of his aftershave, and she had the blurred impression of a big body standing very close to her, too close, almost as if she were leaning on him. An arm was around her back, and the hand holding her arm forced her back down onto the chair, the strength in his grip somehow reassuring. "Sit here," he ordered quietly. "Put your head down, and take deep breaths. I'll get you something cold to drink."

She did take the deep breaths, but she thought that if she bent over to put her head down, she would just keep going until she was on the floor. So she sat motionless, her eyes closed, as he left the small office. From beyond the open door, she could hear people talking, telephones ringing, papers rustling. There was a lot of cursing, some of it sharp and angry, some uttered in lazy, liquid accents that almost made her forget the content of the words.

Cops. Nurses who worked the emergency and trauma units were around a lot of cops, but except for some periods of training, she had always been a floor nurse, so the world of a cop was alien to her. Her mind drifting, she listened to them talk: hard, profane, callous, and yet curiously concerned. Cops and nurses had a lot in common, she thought sleepily. They had to harden themselves against heartbreaking details but still care about the overall situation.

"Here you go."

She hadn't heard him return, but suddenly an icy soft drink can was pressed into her hand. She opened her eyes and blinked at it. Usually, she drank decaffeinated diet soda, but this was the real stuff, chock full of sugar and caffeine.

"Drink it," he said. Evidently, it was an order, not a suggestion, because he lifted her hand and tipped the can to her mouth.

She was forced to swallow, childlike, and flashed him a look of resentment. He met it with a sort of bland insistence that once again made her think of a rock. Detective Chastain was about as yielding. With a flash of insight, she thought that he would be relentless when going after something he wanted. She would hate to be a criminal with Chastain on her trail.

The soda fizzed on her tongue, tart and sweet at the same time, and it was so cold she could feel it slide down her esophagus. He made her take another swallow before deciding she could manage on her own, but even then, he moved less than a foot away to prop against the edge of his desk. He stretched out long, muscular legs clad in lightweight olive slacks, his loafer-shod feet just inches from her own much smaller shoes. She pulled her feet back a little, oddly disturbed, her stomach clenching in a reaction that was almost like fear, which was ridiculous. She didn't fear Chastain; despite his attitude, she was even grateful to him.

"Drink all of it. The humidity's kind of like altitude," he said easily. "Both of them can sneak up on you and knock you flat. For a minute there, your eyes weren't focused. Feeling better now?"

She was. Karen realized she had almost fainted at his feet. She was a nurse; she should have recognized the signs. By not eating that day, she had all but set herself up for a faint, and the heat and humidity certainly hadn't helped. Every thread on her felt clammy. How embarrassing it would have been if she had sprawled on her face.

Given his veiled dislike, she wondered why Detective Chastain hadn't let her do just that. But he'd been both alert and unexpectedly kind, and she remembered that swift sense of security she had felt at his supporting touch.

"Thank you," she said, looking up at him again. This close to him, she realized with surprise that his eyes were a pale, crystalline gray, with dark charcoal rings around the outer rims of his irises. Given the darkness of his hair and brows, his olive complexion, she had thought his eyes would be dark, too. Or maybe she had been on the verge of fainting before she walked into his office, because how else could she not have noticed such a glittering color? Her stomach clenched again, and she took a deep breath to calm herself. "I'm ready to go to the morgue now."

Whatever his thoughts, she couldn't read them on his face. "You don't have to actually view the body," he explained. "The medical examiner's office uses videotape for identification purposes. It's easier on families."

Evidently, he thought the prospect of the morgue, of viewing her father's body, had gotten to her as much as the heat and humidity. "I'm a nurse," she heard herself saying. "The sight of a body isn't likely to make me go to pieces, but still—" Still, she was glad it would be on videotape.

He put his hand on her arm again, cupping her elbow in an old-fashioned gesture. "Then we might as well get it over with, hadn't we?"

Chapter 7

Dr. Pargannas, the assistant medical examiner, slid the cassette into the VCR. While Karen watched the small television screen, Marc watched her. It wasn't a hardship; her profile was delicate and clear-cut, completely feminine. Viewed from the side, her mouth looked tender and tremulous. He settled back, his lids lowering over his eyes as he studied her, analyzing her as intently as if she were the prime suspect in a murder.

Dr. Pargannas spoke quietly to her. Marc knew the drill, so he didn't bother listening. Sometimes shaken family members needed to be prepared, bolstered, for what they were about to see. Miss Whitlaw squared her shoulders and in her cool, calm voice said, "I'm ready." No squeamishness about her, no sir.

He gave a mental shrug. Of course, she wasn't squeamish; she couldn't be, and do her job. He'd bet she was a real treasure in an emergency, but he had doubts about her bedside manner afterward. He'd been a patient in a hospital twice, both times courtesy of the job, and he thought it must be a hospital rule that one nurse per shift, per floor, had to be a coldhearted bitch. Maybe Miss Whitlaw wasn't a bitch, but he sure hadn't seen any signs of warmth in her. He wouldn't want her jabbing needles into *his* ass.

No doubt about it, though, she turned him on, with those dark bedroom eyes and that deceptively tender mouth. He shouldn't have touched her, but hell, he couldn't let her pass out at his feet. So he had held her against him, supported her, felt the softness of her body under his hands, smelled the sweet musk of her skin—and he wanted her. He didn't know if there was any passion in her at all, but he'd sure like to get her in bed and find out.

Get your mind out of her pants and back on business, Chastain, he chided himself. This wasn't the time or the place for horny thoughts, and besides, he was getting hard thinking about it.

Dr. Pargannas clicked on the tape, and the victim's pallid, waxy face filled the screen.

If he hadn't been watching Miss Whitlaw so closely, Marc would have missed her reaction. He saw the barely perceptible flinch, quickly controlled, and her graceful hands twisted together in her lap. "Yes, that's my father," she said, still calm, but her knuckles were white.

Marc looked from those betraying hands to her calm face, and the shock was like a slap in the face. Abruptly all the little details clicked into place. God, how could he have missed it? He felt like a fool, because he should have seen it from the beginning. His gaze sharpened as he studied her.

No, she wasn't as untouched by this as she wanted to be. He had noticed in his office that every time her composure cracked, she would quickly recover, her shoulders squaring, her chin going up. She didn't like being out of control, and she definitely wouldn't like breaking down in front of strangers, but suddenly he knew she was far from being unfeeling.

Maybe she felt too much. His gaze went again to her hands, locked together as she literally held herself in a tight grip. Maybe she had learned to protect herself by pretending she didn't care, by holding people at a distance so she wouldn't be hurt. In a flash of insight, he thought she must be lonely, aching with grief, but at some time in her life she had learned to hide behind a mask of unconcern, maybe when her father had walked out on his wife and daughter. Kids learned to act tough even when they were terrified inside.

If he read the signs right, she was just trying to hold herself together right now but would cry her eyes out when she was alone.

That wasn't good. A woman needed a shoulder to cry on. In this case, a man's shoulder. His, to be specific.

His reluctant sexual attraction suddenly coalesced into something much sharper, more urgent, and this time he didn't even try to talk himself out of it.

Without conceit, Marc knew he was a damn good cop. He made his living taking snippets of information and piecing them together to form a picture. His instincts were usually on target, but in this case he'd let a few misconceptions get in the way, and she had picked up on his initial hostility. Hell, if he was right about her, she was so sensitive she had probably felt blasted by his attitude. She had reacted, typically, by pulling even deeper inside herself. To get her to trust him now, and he fully intended to, he would have to overcome not just her normal wariness but her protective reaction to his wrong impression and his initial coolness.

But he wanted her, and the wanting increased every time he looked at her, every time she breathed. Getting her was something else; doing it would take all his skill. She was skittish and, given her father's example, probably didn't trust men very much. Still, there had never been a woman he'd wanted whom he hadn't gotten, and he had no intention of letting Miss Karen Whitlaw be the exception.

Marc had two big advantages when dealing with women. First of all, he respected their differences from men, and whenever he became involved with a woman, he devoted himself to discovering what she needed. Of course, the needs varied from woman to woman, but for the most part they all wanted the attention and caring that said they were important to him. When Marc was with a woman, he was hers; it was that simple. He gave each one the respect of fidelity while their affair lasted, he learned their moods and quirks, and he lavished them with attention—in short, babying them. He loved doing it, loved seeing a woman glow with happiness.

Given her background, he thought Karen was desperately in need of babying. She had spent her life being a tough little soldier, and she deserved the chance to relax, to let someone take care of her for a change. He was just the man for the job.

His second big advantage was that he was both ruthless and relentless.

He would have to move fast, because she wouldn't be here long, probably no more than a couple of days.

He didn't have time for a leisurely seduction, disguised as dinner and dancing, stretched out over several weeks. She had a job and a home to return to, and unless he forced the issue before she left, she wouldn't have any reason for continuing the relationship.

He had no doubt there would *be* a relationship. He was absolutely certain, more certain than he had ever been before. The shock he had felt a moment before had gone all the way through him, deep into his bones. And he was, suddenly, uneasy in a way he had never been before, because having a woman had never before felt this important, this *necessary*.

He didn't know how they would work out the details, with her in Ohio and him in Louisiana, but they could settle all that later. The most important thing right now was to stake his claim, and to do that he had to win her trust.

Beginning now, he thought, flicking a glance from her hands to her composed expression, then to the television screen. Despite her immediate identification of her father, Dr. Pargannas was painstakingly showing her the "Semper fi" tattoo and other identifying marks, perhaps wanting to make certain she hadn't spoken hastily, perhaps because Marc had been lost in his thoughts and hadn't moved to end the session. He swore silently to himself; he should have stopped this the second she spoke.

"Thanks, Doc," he said now, putting one hand on the back of her chair and bracing the other on the table in front of her, effectively embracing her without touching her. He saw her stiffen a little, an instinctive reaction to the subtle possessiveness of his position, but she was too upset to be consciously aware of what he had just done. Those somber dark eyes glanced at him, then quickly averted when they made eye contact, but not before he saw the relief in them.

She hid it well, managing to shift so she could slide out of the chair away from him, standing and saying briskly, "What do I have to do now?"

"Sign some papers so we can release the body," Dr. Pargannas replied, then blinked at the narrow look Marc gave him. "Ah . . . that is, your father's remains." The doctor seemed bewildered; if she had been more visibly upset, he could have understood such tact, but he plainly considered it a waste of time with such a businesslike woman.

Marc had stood when she did. Noting the tension in her shoulders, he quietly said, "I'll call a funeral home for you, then take you to a couple of small cemeteries so you can pick out a plot—if that's what you want?"

"Yes, thank you," she said quickly.

"Okay, we'll get the paperwork wrapped up here. Doctor?" Damn, those dark eyes of hers were really getting to him, twisting his guts into knots. He wanted to cradle her, hold her close so she would know she wasn't alone in this, but it was too soon; such a blatant move would panic her. He had to keep it low-key until she relaxed enough with him.

Instead, he put his hand on the small of her back, feeling her warmth through her dress, knowing the heat of his hand on such a sensitive area would comfort her. On a normal day, she would probably jump away and give him a frosty look, but this wasn't a normal day. She was tired, heat-stressed, and was going through an emotional wringer. She was too tense even to notice the touch, except perhaps to feel relief that he was there and that he was helping her.

Dr. Pargannas was staring bemusedly at him. "Hmm? Oh—of course. Take Miss Whitlaw to my office, and I'll be there in a minute. Would either of you like a cup of coffee?"

Marc felt Karen's small shudder at the thought. "I'll get us something cold from the drink machine," he said as he ushered her out of the conference room and into the cramped, cluttered office across the hall.

Thirty minutes later, he was walking her back to the car. The second soft drink had steadied her once again, but the effects of the sugar would wear off soon; she needed food. He thought for a second. A leisurely sit-down meal in a cool restaurant would be best, but likely she would balk at the idea. Not only would she consider it an intolerable delay when they had so much to do, but the surroundings would make her feel as if they were on a date. Less beneficial but more likely to be accepted would be if he picked up something in a drive-through and they ate as he drove.

"Would you mind if we got something to eat?" he asked in an easy tone. "I didn't get a chance to eat lunch." That was a lie, but so what, if it accomplished his purpose. In retrospect, he was angry with himself for missing the signs when she first walked into his office. She was brittle with stress, on the verge of shattering, and only her self-discipline held her together. He wanted to kick his own ass; he usually read people better than that.

"Eat?" Her tone was vague, as if she had only the faintest idea what the word meant. Then she visibly shook herself and said, "Of course, I don't mind."

"We'll pick up something from a drive-through. Do you like Mexican, hamburgers, fried chicken, red beans and rice, pizza—"

"Mexican is fine," she said, because it was the first thing he had listed.

A cop knew every restaurant in town, and he drove

to a tiny, ramshackle place that had once been a barbecue hut. There were no tables inside, just the drive-up window through which the owner dispensed tasty burritos and enchiladas. Soon they were on their way again, and he watched the color seep into her face as she slowly chewed on a burrito.

"How long is the drive?" she asked.

"About half an hour, in traffic." A half-smile quirked the corners of his mouth. "I could put the blue light on the dash, but I try not to use it unless I'm hungry, or really need a bathroom."

A startled little laugh spurted out of her. She covered her mouth with her hand, blinking as if she couldn't believe he'd actually joked with her, and she had laughed in any case. Those big dark eyes were owlish with surprise.

Because of those eyes, he decided to push it a little further. "You'll notice that I cleaned up my language in deference to you, instead of saying something about really needing to take a piss."

She laughed again and looked just as startled as she had the first time. "Ah . . . yes, I noticed," she managed to say. "Thank you."

Marc veiled his satisfaction. That harmless, teasing little exchange had firmly shifted their relationship from strictly business to subtly personal, relaxing her. She needed to relax; from the looks of her, she needed to *sleep*. When she had finished eating the burrito, he took the wrapper from her, brushing her fingers in the process, and stuffed it in the bag with his own discarded wrapper. "Why don't you lean back and close your eyes until we get there?"

"I'm afraid I'll go to sleep if I do." She watched the traffic. "I work third shift, so I—"

She stopped, and he continued the sentence. "So

you hadn't had more than a couple of hours' sleep when I called." That explained a lot. She was truly exhausted.

"I returned your call when I got home, but it was too early for you to be in."

"Didn't the voice mail pick up?"

She shook her head. "No, and I let it ring for a long time."

He smothered a curse and reached for his cellular phone, jabbing in a number with his thumb. Karen watched nervously; she constantly saw patients who had been in car accidents because their attention wandered while talking on the phone while they were driving. Detective Chastain kept his eye on the traffic and his left hand firm on the wheel. He was a very good driver, she thought, his driving style so smooth she scarcely noticed how fast they were moving.

He broke the connection with another jab of his thumb. "Voice mail isn't working. Sorry about that. I'll check into it when we get back; a detective can't afford to be unreachable. In the meantime, grab a nap if you want. I'll wake you up when we get there."

She wanted to refuse, but she was too tired, and the temptation too irresistible. She leaned her head back on the headrest of the seat and closed her eyes against the late-afternoon sun, which was glaring through the windshield straight into her eyes. Cold air poured out of the air-conditioning vents, though, washing over her wrists and throat, and she felt her tight muscles slowly ease.

Sleep evaded her, but still it felt good to rest. Though she had been braced to endure the identification process, she hadn't expected it to be so difficult. Surely the years of separation and the lifetime of desertion and broken promises should have given her as much emotional detachment as if she had been identifying, say, a neighbor. It hadn't worked that way.

Though she hadn't seen Dexter in several years, she had recognized him immediately, without a single doubt. His hair had grayed more, but his face, which should have been craggier, had been smoothed by death. She had seen that before, as if the end of life erased some of the lines it had worn into the flesh, giving death a peaceful mien. His broken nose hadn't changed, still listing slightly to the right. That was his jaw, long and narrow, and the straight line of his brows. There were the deep-set eyes and high cheekbones she had inherited, as well as the tapering fingers.

The neat hole in his forehead was new.

She had tried to look at it clinically, but everything in her had recoiled. She had wanted to bolt from her chair, get out of that room, go somewhere, anywhere. Instead, she had clenched her hands hard enough to dig her nails into her palms and forced herself to speak calmly. She had hoped identifying him would bring the session to an end, but instead, the doctor continued running the videotape, making comments in a dry monotone.

Thank God Detective Chastain had stopped him. The tape couldn't have gone on more than a couple of minutes, but it had felt like hours to her. She had been frozen in her seat, unable to speak or move, until Chastain broke the spell by speaking. Dizzied by a flood of relief, she had actually leaned toward him; she hadn't been aware of swaying, but suddenly his face was much closer, his arms opened to catch her if she toppled out of the chair. After she had almost fainted in his office, he apparently wasn't taking any chances. Embarrassed, she had scrambled to her feet to show him she was perfectly all right.

He must not have been convinced, though, since he had poured yet another soft drink down her. She wondered if she had completely misread him before, if her own frazzled state had led her to see dislike where none had existed, because now he seemed like a perfectly nice man. If he disliked her, he was hiding it well now, and she was so tired she didn't care. She had needed to eat, and she needed to sleep. Tomorrow, after she had done both, she would be her old self again, but for now she was grateful for Chastain's help.

Burying Dexter here was the most logical thing to do, until she could get everything arranged back home. She supposed there were places where his body could be stored, but whatever Dexter's failings, and they had been many, he had still been a person, a man, a husband, and a father, not just a lump of dead flesh. He deserved the ritual of a funeral, the prayers said over his remains.

She felt a sense of relief and knew she was doing the right thing.

The detective's radio crackled, rousing her from her drifting, half-asleep reverie, though she didn't open her eyes. He spoke quietly into the radio, and it was like hearing his voice again for the first time. She didn't notice his voice as much when she was looking at him, she realized; he was a physically compelling man, not so much because of his looks as because of the forcefulness of his character. He controlled his intensity, but it was revealed in those narrow, glittering eyes.

Now, though, his voice poured over her like dark honey. She didn't listen to the words, just the tone. The slur of his drawl was relaxing, as if there was no hurry to go anywhere or do anything. The way he said "where" gave the word two, perhaps three, syllables.

If he took as much time making love as he did talking, he must be— The sexual thought shocked her, and her eyes flared open. She didn't dare glance at him, though she was abruptly, acutely aware of him sitting no more than a foot away.

Her cheeks felt hot. Where had *that* thought come from, and now, of all times? She wasn't in the habit of speculating about a man's sexual skills. She wasn't in the habit of speculating about men, period. In her view, sexual freedom was stupid from the beginning, and now it was dangerous as well. She had never dated much, and not at all since Jeanette's death.

The truth was, she had always avoided getting emotionally involved with a man because she hadn't trusted any of them. She had been afraid to risk her heart the way her mother had done; she didn't want to waste her life loving a man who never returned that love. Instead, she had been wasting her life not loving a man at all.

She felt stupid and angry at herself. All men weren't alike; she *knew* that. Yes, her father had abandoned them, but she also knew men who loved their wives and families, who were faithful and dependable. But emotionally she hadn't moved beyond the quiet fear and desperation of her childhood. Only yesterday . . . no, this morning—God, the day felt as if it had been a year long, and it wasn't over yet—she had decided not to let the past drag her down. She had started making plans for the apartment, for her career, but those plans hadn't included a man.

How dumb could she be? Why hadn't she seen this before? She refused to cheat herself out of a husband, a family, just because of her father's miserable example. When this was over and she was home again, she would start accepting some of those invitations that occasionally came her way. She knew some nice men, and it was time to give one of them a chance to be more than just a casual friend.

In retrospect, she was glad she'd had such a spicy little thought about Detective Chastain, because it had sparked that burst of self-examination. And he probably *was* good in bed, she thought, feeling defiant. Whatever his personal opinion of her, he was going out of his way to smooth the path for her. One of her friends on the surgical floor, Piper Lloyd, said you could always tell if a man was a good lover or not just by watching him at work. Some of the male doctors—okay, most of the male doctors—thought they were God's gift to women, but according to Piper's theory, they were too arrogant and in too much of a hurry. If they didn't pay attention to their patients, they weren't likely to pay attention to a lover.

Piper would approve of the detective, Karen thought drowsily. She would already be batting her eyes at him and fluffing her cap of black curls, but then Piper was a battle-scarred veteran of the love wars. She was careful about sex but not shy about going after what she wanted.

Karen wasn't anywhere in Piper's league. Just dating occasionally, giving a guy a chance, would be a big step for her.

"Are you married?" Her eyes popped open when she heard the words come out of her mouth. She hadn't meant to say that; she hadn't intended to say anything at all, because it had felt too good to sit there with her eyes closed. Instead of looking at him, she stared at the passing scenery, where Burger Kings had given way to trees and grass as they left the city behind.

"No, never have been," he replied, his tone easy, surprising her. "How about you?"

"No, I—no." She had started to go into a long explanation about being too busy but decided to leave the answer as it stood. She hadn't been too busy, she had been too wary.

"Engaged?"

Well, one nosy question deserved another, she thought. "No."

"I was, once, but we both thought better of it." He flashed her an oddly veiled look. "Cops have the highest divorce rate in the country. Some women can't handle kissing their husbands good-bye in the mornings, knowing it might be the last time."

Karen clucked her tongue, irrationally amused instead of sympathetic. "Shallow," she pronounced in judgment. "Imagine being upset over a little thing like that."

A quick grin lightened his expression. He had what she thought of as the typical cop look, slightly remote, definitely cynical. The military-short black hair made him look even harder, so the flicker of amusement was as brilliant as a jag of lightning in a sullen sky.

"You could marry another cop," she suggested.

He grunted as he turned on his left signal, slowing as he approached an intersection, then taking a secondary road. "Yeah. Like you'd marry a doctor or another nurse."

She made a face. Some people married within the profession and made it work, but Karen wanted some freedom from the hospital. She immersed herself in the work while she was there, and she loved her job, but she didn't want to take it home with her.

"What type of nursing do you do?"

She gave him points for actually knowing there were different types. "I work on a hospital surgical floor, but I'm thinking about going back to school and getting my master's, maybe specializing in trauma."

Saying the words aloud, however, seemed to solidify them, and she knew she was going to do it.

One eyebrow quirked. "Isn't that like ditching a desk job for front-line duty?"

"You're in the trenches yourself," she pointed out. "Besides, I want to know more, do more." She tucked a curve of hair behind her ear, half turning toward him, her normally serious expression bright with intensity. "I want to know what the latest procedures are, the newest drugs and treatments. I don't want to change a surgical dressing, I want to apply the pressure that stops the bleeding." She didn't know why she was telling him, a virtual stranger, all of this, but there was something about him that made it easy to talk. Odd, because they certainly hadn't started off in a buddy-buddy mode. Maybe it was because he seemed really interested, or maybe it was just a relief to get her mind off Dexter. Maybe she was punch-drunk with fatigue or riding a sugar high from all the soft drinks he had poured down her.

He pulled into the parking lot of a small country church, empty and dozing in the fierce afternoon heat. To the side, beneath the sheltering limbs of massive live oaks, was a well-tended cemetery. Karen looked at the graves and felt her insides tighten again. She had managed to forget for a few minutes, but the respite was over. She squared her shoulders and got out of the car.

"Someone will be here in a few minutes," Chastain said, slipping on a pair of sunglasses as he walked beside her toward the cemetery. "If you like the plots, you can do the paperwork this afternoon."

She drew in the thick, heavy air, feeling as if there wasn't enough oxygen in it. She was already dewed with sweat, and she thought longingly of another one of those icy soft drinks, sugar overload or no. Chickens *cooked* at a lower temperature than this. She was at least half done herself.

Chastain's hand settled on her back again, as hot as a brand. This wasn't real, she thought, staring at the fuzzy tangle of Spanish moss draped from the trees, swaying in a nonexistent breeze. Just this morning, she had been sleeping in her darkened, air-conditioned bedroom. Now she was roasting in New Orleans, picking out a burial plot for the father she hadn't seen in years until the ME had popped in a video of him on an autopsy slab, and she was being baby-sat by a tough-looking cop who didn't like her but who, for reasons of his own, was being very helpful.

No, it wasn't real. It was a nightmare, but nightmares, like all dreams, eventually came to an end.

Langley, Virginia

Franklin Vinay, the deputy director of operations, habitually worked late. He enjoyed the hours at his desk when his staff had gone home, the phone mostly stopped ringing, the demands on his time lightened. It was then that he plowed through the mountain of papers that landed on his desk every day, trying to stay one step ahead of the country's adversaries—whoever the hell they were.

It had been easier during the Cold War; everything had been clear-cut, the enemy known. He was afraid the fragmented former Soviet Union was more dangerous now than it had been before, without experienced hands at the many helms. China worried the shit out of him, but the current administration was more interested in making money than in protecting the country's security. Any jackass with half a brain now could find out how to make a bomb, America's so-called allies were happily selling arms and technology to anyone who could raise the money, and military capability was at an all-time low. It was a recipe for disaster, and he spent the long hours at his desk trying to keep the mixture from boiling over.

A quiet knock on his door interrupted him, and he sighed, closing the file he was reading. "Come in."

He expected the door to be opened by a junior staffer pulling long hours, too, but instead, a familiar homely face poked into view. "Thought you'd still be here," Jess McPherson said, easing into the room and closing the door behind him. "I've got some bad news."

Jess and the DDO went back a long ways, so long that there was no formality between them. He knew the look on Jess's face, and his guts tightened. "What happened?"

"Rick Medina's dead. His body was found in Mississippi." McPherson folded his long, lanky body into a chair.

"Ah, shit." Profound sadness was in Vinay's voice. Rick Medina was a legend in CIA circles, but more than that, he had been a personal friend. There weren't many of the old group left; everyone now was into technology, forgetting that the best satellite and the best computer couldn't replace that most basic of sources, a man in place. Human intelligence, HUMINT, was at the core of every good decision Vinay had made. "What happened? Was he working?"

He hoped to hell not. Rick had never been regular CIA; instead, he had been a contract agent, which meant he regularly hired his services out to other customers, meaning other countries. With Rick, though, Vinay had always had faith none of his other jobs had jeopardized the security of his country. Other agents weren't as particular, but Rick Medina was, simply, a patriot. Then, too, there were other considerations.

"Nothing for us," McPherson said. "The buzz I'm getting was that he was handling something personal. The local cops have tagged it as a robbery/murder, but shit, I can't see Rick getting caught flat-footed by a punk with a cheap twenty-two."

"That's what killed him? A twenty-two?"

"According to the report. Two shots in the heart. A couple of kids found him in his car, hidden behind some bushes in an old abandoned quarry. His wallet was lying on the seat beside him, empty. Cash and credit cards gone."

"Convenient, for identification purposes." Vinay chewed on his lip. "Almost too convenient."

"Yeah, I know. It doesn't feel right to me, either, but like I said, he wasn't working for us, so I don't have a clue what he was really doing. For all we know, this was nothing more than pure damn bad luck, and a sorry-ass punk accidentally got off some good shots."

"What about Rick's weapon? Was it found?"

McPherson shook his head. Vinay hadn't really expected an affirmative answer. No piece of street shit would pass up an expensive weapon such as Rick Medina carried. Nor would they be able to pick up a thread on the serial number, because Rick would have made certain no weapon could be traced back to him.

"Where's John?" McPherson asked softly.

"On assignment."

"You gonna tell him or leave him in place?" Any assignment John Medina was on was, by definition, crucial.

"Tell him. I trust his judgment." Not only that, only a fool would withhold from John the news of his father's death.

"Tell him to give me a call," McPherson said, rising to his feet.

Vinay gave his old friend a searching look. "Jess? You know something you haven't told me?"

"No, but John might. And if he goes after whoever did Rick, well, I'd consider it an honor to help."

Chapter 8

Karen slept so deeply that when she woke the next morning, she felt slow and thick-headed, unable to get stirring. Her eyes felt gritty, and her pillowcase was damp. Dimly, she remembered crying during the night, surfacing briefly from sleep and feeling overwhelmed with despair and loss.

Finally, she dragged herself out of bed and stretched, feeling every muscle pull and reluctantly come awake. She opened the curtains and stared out at a blindingly bright day; she could already feel the heat pulsing against the window. Thanking God for the efficiency of the Marriott's air conditioning, she stumbled to the shower and let cool water pelt down on her, dispelling more of the mental cobwebs.

She had just finished blow-drying her hair when she heard the phone ringing. Pulling her robe around her, she dashed into the bedroom. "Hello?"

"Good mornin'." The warm, dark voice in her ear

instantly identified the caller. "I hope I didn't wake you?"

"Good morning, Detective. No, I was already awake. I just got out of the shower." Twisting, Karen peeked at the digital alarm/radio bolted to the nightstand. She blinked, but the red numbers remained the same: ten twenty-three. "I can't believe I slept so late," she blurted, surprised. "Is it really almost ten-thirty?"

He chuckled, the sound so warm her stomach began to melt. "Yes, ma'am. You were so tired yesterday, I thought you might sleep late, so I waited to call. I need to turn over your father's effects to you, if you feel like doing it today. If not, it can wait."

It could wait until tomorrow, he meant, but she had scheduled the funeral for tomorrow, and she didn't think she could handle both ordeals in the same day. "No, I'll come down there as soon as I've eaten."

"If I have to leave on a call, I'll let you know, save you the walk down here."

"Okay," she agreed. After breaking the connection, she called room service and placed her order, pushing away the dread that settled in the pit of her stomach like cold oatmeal. Dexter's effects would be shabby clothing and worn shoes, perhaps with holes in them. She hated to think of him without adequate clothing, without a safe place to sleep or shelter from the weather. She had always imagined him living a carefree, rootless life without his wife and daughter; she had never imagined him in need of the most basic requirements of life.

It hurt. He could have lived a normal life with his family, but he had rejected them in favor of . . . *nothing*. No home, no job, sleeping in cardboard boxes, getting his meals in missions and soup kitchens or what he could dig out of a garbage can. Had he stolen a shopping cart from a supermarket and trundled his worldly goods around in it? He had turned his back on them for *that?*

How could a man do that? Didn't he feel any connection, any responsibility, to his family? How could he have hurt her mother that way and still feel free to show up or call her whenever he got the urge? What was it about him that Jeanette had loved until her last breath?

"Oh, Mom," Karen whispered, aching for her mother, whose pain had been the greatest. She, at least, had never known her father that well, and so she hadn't suffered so much on her own account but rather in sympathy for her mother. She was grateful Jeanette hadn't had to see that videotape and wouldn't have to claim a pitifully small pile of possessions.

She had just dressed, as comfortably as possible, in a sleeveless peach sheath and sandals, when room service arrived with her breakfast. Her appetite had faded, but she forced herself to eat. The coffee was scalding hot and impossibly strong; after one sip, she pushed it aside and drank the glass of ice water instead. Perhaps if she cooled her insides, the heat wouldn't seem so oppressive.

At least Dexter hadn't been cold. At least he hadn't died somewhere in the dead of winter, with snow on the ground and holes in his shoes, newspapers stuffed inside his shirt for warmth.

Her stomach heaved, and Karen pushed the thought away, along with the tray. Swiftly, she brushed her teeth, put on lipstick, and secured the room key in the zippered section of her shoulder bag. "Ready as I'm going to be," she whispered, and left the room.

The morning was hot but fresh. New Orleans was a

city of food, and a multitude of scents filled the air: pastries baking, spices simmering, chicory-flavored coffee brewing. The aroma was especially strong when she walked past Brennan's, renowned for its exotic breakfasts. Everything was so different from what she was accustomed to in Columbus that she could have been in another country. Even the people looked more exotic, more dramatic in both coloring and dress, almost gypsyish. She heard a multitude of accents and languages around her as she briskly walked past strolling tourists and lingering shoppers. She saw sequined Mardi Gras masks in shop windows and glittering harlequin faces draped with strands of colorful beads. An enormous leopard, carved from a single piece of wood, watched from one shop window as she passed.

The ambience of New Orleans sucked at her, trying to slow her steps to the accustomed pace. Sweat beaded between her breasts, trickled downward, telling her how silly she was to hurry. Everything would wait, would still be there if she stopped to look in a shop window. She resisted the urge.

She could see the Eighth District ahead on the right, the mellow, gracious building drawing her with its promise of coolness. She knew there were the ordinary municipal buildings in the city, she had seen some of them yesterday when Detective Chastain had taken her to the morgue, but the Eighth District building was like New Orleans itself: seductive, stylishly old and gracious, lazily sinful. What had those old walls seen? What scandals and murders had been unraveled under that roof, what torrid love affairs had been conducted there? One didn't normally associate a police department with love affairs, but this was New Orleans, this was the Quarter, and anything was possible.

A different police officer sat at the desk in the huge front room, where the ceiling fans ceaselessly paddled in circles in the thick air. Karen gave her name and was allowed to proceed past the desk. She wound her way through the warren, the old floor creaking under her feet.

Detective Chastain was on the phone when she reached the tiny, cluttered office. He looked up when he saw her standing in the doorway and motioned her inside.

Her heartbeat jumped, then settled into a rapid tattoo. Karen sank onto the straight-backed chair, clutching her shoulder bag on her lap. There was a sack on his desk, an ordinary brown grocery sack, and she tried not to look at it. Instead, she looked at him, desperately focusing on details such as the contrast of his gold wristwatch against his tanned wrist, the short dark hairs on his forearms, revealed by his rolled-up sleeves. He was wearing a plain white collarless shirt and black slacks, a simple, stark outfit that made him look more like a choreographer than a cop, except for the holstered pistol he wore on his belt at his right hip.

She consciously tried not to listen to his conversation, but she was nevertheless aware of his growing impatience. He began scowling, his dark brows pulling together. He glanced at her, then abruptly switched languages, unleashing a barrage in Creole French that she was glad she didn't understand, because the tone of curses was unmistakable no matter what language he used.

Finally, he growled something and slammed down the phone. Gray eyes narrowed to slits, and he swiveled his chair to face her fully. "I hope you don't speak French."

"I don't," she assured him.

"I know all the cuss words. Most of the time, that's

enough." He ran his hand over his close-cropped hair, the abrupt gesture revealing his irritation. He took a deep breath and let it go. "Do you want a cup of coffee or a Coke?"

"No, thank you." She essayed a smile. "I just ate, so I'm not in danger of collapsing at your feet. You don't have to pour sodas down me today."

"Our motto is 'Serve and protect,' so it was in my job description." The corners of his eyes crinkled in a smile that almost reached his mouth, then faded as he gestured toward the brown grocery sack. "I wouldn't normally handle this, but something you said yesterday made me think . . . well, this might hit you harder than you anticipate."

The dread she had felt earlier passed from the consistency of cold oatmeal to that of set concrete. Her hands clenched on her purse. "In what way?" She kept her voice calm, but the stiff upper lip she was maintaining took more and more effort.

He was silent a moment, then he left his chair and came around to sit on the edge of his desk, the way he had the day before. "You were very close to your mother, weren't you?"

The question took her off balance. "Yes, of course. When my father left us, she was . . . devastated. He had left the military, so she didn't get a monthly check anymore. She had me to take care of, and she didn't have any job skills, so she took any job she could get: cleaning houses, taking in ironing, waiting tables."

"Those don't pay much," he commented. His gaze never left her face.

"No. She worked two or three jobs, until I was old enough to get a job and help. The day I was hired at the hospital, she quit work. She had worked herself into the ground all those years, so it was my time to take care of her."

He regarded her silently for a moment, his expression enigmatic. "Not many people would feel that way," he finally said.

"Then something's wrong with them." Karen flared. She would have done anything she could to make her mother's life easier.

He held up his hand in a calming gesture. "I agree, I agree."

"Why are you asking? What does my mother have to do with you turning over my father's effects?"

He hesitated. "He kept something that was important to him. He could have hocked it, but instead it was sewn into the hem of his pants leg."

Puzzled, she stared up at him, trying to think what on earth could have been important to her father; certainly his wife or daughter hadn't been.

Detective Chastain reached behind him and took a small brown envelope out of the sack containing her father's clothes. He opened it and poured the contents into his hand. "It meant something to him," he said quietly, squatting down in front of her and opening his hand, palm up so she could see what he held.

Karen stared at the gold ring lying on the detective's callused palm. For a moment, she didn't recognize it for what it was, then she went numb all over. Her mind somehow separated from her body as if reality had abruptly altered. His wedding ring. He had kept his wedding ring. The simple presence of that plain gold band challenged everything she had thought she knew about her father. "That isn't fair," she whispered, and she didn't mean the detective's perception but instead her father's unexpected sentimentality. She didn't want to know this about him; she didn't

111

want to think that perhaps he had regrets, and pain, and broken dreams. It was easier just to think of him as unfeeling.

But nothing was ever easy. Not death, and certainly not life.

Chastain didn't say anything, just continued squatting there with the ring lying on his palm like an offering.

What would have happened if she had been on her own? Surely there was a list of items, and she would have signed a receipt stating that she had received everything on the list, but she wouldn't have known her father had kept the ring sewn into the hem of his pants to keep it safe. The busy medical examiner wouldn't have done this personally, a clerk would have handled the chore, and she would never have known. Detective Chastain had gone out of his way to do this, as he had gone out of his way the day before to help her.

She saw herself reach out, the movement involuntary, as if her hand didn't belong to her. Her fingers were trembling. Slowly, she touched the ring, tracing the circle with one fingertip, then withdrew her hand to rest it once again in her lap.

Detective Chastain took her hand in his, his touch gentle as he opened her hand and placed the ring on her palm, then folded her fingers over it. The ring was warm, his hand even warmer. "He cared," he said. "I don't know why he left, but he didn't stop caring."

She couldn't look up at him. Instead, she stared at their hands, his hard and strong, tanned, much bigger than hers. His clasp was light, as if he were aware of his strength, as many men were not, and took care not to hurt her inadvertently.

Desperately, she struggled to hang on to her control, but his nearness and understanding undermined her. And he seemed to understand that, too, because he released her hand and stood, returning to his seat behind the battered desk.

"Thank you," she said, almost inaudibly. His distance was a relief, yet she found herself yearning for his support.

"You're welcome," he said, and left it at that.

"The rest of his things . . . are just clothes?"

"Yes. There's a list."

"At least I'll know what size suit to buy for him," she said, though she cringed at the idea of going through the shabby garments looking for tags. It was too much, too soon.

Detective Chastain paused a moment, watching her, then said quietly, "Forty-four long."

She swallowed and nodded, looking down at her hands. She had to ask him something, just to be certain, and though the answer would be difficult for a cop, she somehow knew he would be honest with her. "Detective . . ."

"What?" he asked gently after a moment, when she didn't continue.

She raised her eyes to him, squarely meeting his gaze. "Are—are you still working on the case?"

He paused, then said, "No."

Karen flinched, though it was exactly what she had expected. He squatted down in front of her again and took her hand in his, rubbing his thumb across her knuckles. The slight roughness of his callused skin scraped her, a warmly masculine sensation.

"I'm sorry," he murmured.

"I understand," she said, though with difficulty. "You have to put your effort where it will do the most good. It's the same in an emergency department."

"Reality's a bitch."

His tough sympathy, his honesty, meant more to her than if he had mouthed all the right platitudes, if he had tried to soothe her with well-meant lies. She squeezed his hand, then straightened her shoulders. "I have a lot to do today, so I'll get out of your way." He moved back, giving her room to stand. "Thank you," she said as she left.

Marc sighed as Karen left his office, her face colorless but calm. His chest felt tight. Damn it, her father had been murdered, and he couldn't do anything about it. As soon as he had gotten an ID on the body, the word had come down to move on to a more productive case. There wasn't any percentage in trying to solve a homeless murder, not that he had jack shit to go on anyway. It was just so damn frustrating.

God, he had wanted to hold her, just pick her up and hold her on his lap and let her know she didn't have to do this alone. But he hadn't, both because it was too soon and because to do so would have shattered her hard-won calm.

She had probably been acting calm and responsible since she was a child, forcing herself to become a little adult when she should have been carefee, playing with dolls and skipping rope. He saw it all the time: when there was only one parent left, and the child saw that parent struggling, the child would in effect *become* the parent, taking on responsibilities far beyond the child's age. She had probably taken over the housekeeping chores, made sure her tired mother had food waiting for her when she got home from work, done everything she could to lighten the load.

Karen had even gone into nursing, taking on even more responsibility. It was telling that she had then become her mother's sole support, completing the role reversal. She had probably called her mother by her given name rather than "Mom," at least part of the time, for the little girl had become the mother, and the mother had become the dependent. It was obvious she had adored her mother and so had been that much more protective.

She had spent her life taking care of others, and now he wanted to take care of her, wanted it with a fierceness that shook him. He was normally protective of women, but he had never before felt like this. Something inside him had altered, shifted, and he couldn't regret the change.

Did she have any idea how valiant she was? Her dry comment the day before about women being shallow for having trouble committing to a cop because of the danger factor had been amusing, but she had meant it. Karen Whitlaw wouldn't walk away from a commitment because she was scared; she would be there, through the bad times as well as the good.

Whenever he had been in a relationship, Marc had kept his work out of it. Being called away on a case was unavoidable, but he hadn't brought the details home. He had always shielded his lady friends from the ugliness he saw, partly because of his own protective nature but also because he had never thought they would understand or be able to accept the part of his nature that made it possible for him to deal with the things he did. Perhaps he had underestimated the ladies in his life, but he had seen a lot of relationships destroyed by the pressures of the job, and he hadn't wanted to take the chance.

He *knew* Karen wouldn't flinch. She would brace her shoulders and lift her chin, as he had seen her do several times when the pain and stress would almost overwhelm her. Most people would have broken down under the emotional burden she was carrying, but she had faced the situation squarely and controlled her tears until she was alone.

He knew she had cried; her eyelids were swollen. She had cried, and he hadn't been there to hold her.

He would be, he thought fiercely. From now on, he would be.

Chapter 9

The day was overcast, with rain threatening any minute, and so muggy Karen felt as if she would melt. Sweat gathered in a pool between her breasts, trickled down her sides. Her dress was thin and short-sleeved but still *black;* she could feel the fabric absorbing the heat. She concentrated on her physical misery and on the distant sullen rumble of thunder. She thought about how lush the grass was, listened to the birds singing, and let herself be annoyed because her heels kept sinking into the soft black dirt. She'd never before seen dirt so black, and she marveled at its richness.

She looked at the massive trees, the flowers. This small country cemetery was prettier and more peaceful than the large, manicured "garden of rest" where Jeanette was buried. Perhaps she should move her mother down here, rather than have Dexter taken to Ohio.

Her stomach clenched. She had tried so hard not to think about what was happening, but her wayward thoughts had led her to the funeral anyway. She didn't want to think about the man in the casket. Dexter Whitlaw. Her father. Whatever his failings, whatever devils had driven him, at this moment she admitted that her memories of him weren't all bad.

There had been a few times when he sat on the floor and played dolls with her, folding his long legs as if he didn't even notice his cramped position, listening with apparent raptness as she spun elaborate stories about what the dolls were doing. Usually, they were sick, and she was taking care of them, an early manifestation of her nursing tendencies. And a couple of times, Dexter had taken her with him on walks in the woods and showed her how to hide in a bush and sit very still so that even the squirrels and the birds forgot they were there. Did those few bright moments outweigh a lifetime of darkness? Was she supposed to remember only them and forget the nights when her mother sobbed into her pillow, longing for a man who wasn't there?

What a waste of life, both Jeanette's and Dexter's. Regret swelled in her chest, suffocating her, or maybe it was just this damnable humidity making it impossible for her to breathe. It couldn't be regret; why should she cry for a man who had never given her a second thought, who bothered to call or visit only when *he* needed something? And yet he had kept his wedding ring, sewed it into his cuff to keep it safe. It had been important to him, as Detective Chastain had pointed out. Whether it was the life the ring represented, the normal life he had walked away from, or the people in that life, she couldn't begin to imagine.

She wouldn't cry for him. She refused to. But the

outline of the casket was blurred, the minister's words were nothing more than background noise, and the pressure in her chest was so great she could barely contain it.

The trees stirred and rattled, breathing. A surprisingly cool gust of wind hit the backs of her legs, breathed down her neck. A chill rippled down her spine. The sensation was refreshing, though, and she sighed as the sweat evaporated on her body. She was grateful for the reprieve from the heat, even when a fine mist of rain closely followed the wind.

In only moments, she went from overheated to downright chilly, as the wind picked up and the rain began to pelt down. Detective Chastain opened an umbrella and held it over their heads, moving closer so they were both sheltered. She didn't know what she would have done without his assistance these past two days, she thought numbly. He had done more than walk her through the necessary procedures, much more; he had stepped in and taken care of arrangements, cut through red tape, smoothed over glitches before they became real obstacles. He had even remembered the flowers for the casket and helped her arrange for them.

She couldn't think why he had done it. She was a commonsense person, but she was beginning to think she had imagined his dislike the first time they met, because not even a glimmer of hostility had shown since then. Maybe fatigue and shock had made her hallucinate. Still, Chastain had gone above and beyond duty, even if she had been mistaken in her initial impression of him. Maybe this was an example of the courtesy toward women for which Southern men were so famous, but he had gone a great deal farther than opening doors for her or standing when she entered the room.

Yes, that was it. Think about the detective, or about regional differences in general; think about anything but the fact that the minister was pressing her hand and murmuring condolences, and the funeral director was waiting for her to leave so they could lower the casket into the grave and begin shoveling dirt over it. The grave was even disguised by a green felt carpet, as if the sight of it would be too much for the bereaved.

But she couldn't leave. She couldn't walk away from Dexter now, not in his last moment above ground. He deserved to have someone there for him, someone whose memory would record these details, so that he wouldn't vanish without a trace. Whatever his failings, he was her father, forever linked to her through shared genes.

"Go ahead," she said hoarsely. It was an effort to speak. Her arms roughened with chill bumps, and she hugged them against the bite of the wind, wondering where the heat had gone. The rain drummed down on the umbrella, spattered her legs and her back, and a shiver seized her.

She saw the funeral director glance at Detective Chastain, as if the final decision was his. Perhaps it was. If he chose to drag her away from the graveside, she didn't know if she would be able to protest, or to resist. If she tried to argue, the tenuous control she was maintaining would shatter, and she would collapse into a sobbing heap. A sobbing heap was not a good position from which to assert authority.

But he gave a brief nod, and she tried to tell him with her eyes how grateful she was, not just for this but for everything. The funeral director turned aside with a quiet word to the waiting men. Chains creaked, and the casket was slowly lowered into the grave.

Karen shivered again and found she couldn't stop. Was she shivering or trembling? She couldn't tell, didn't care. All she knew was that she was shaking from the inside out, her teeth clenched hard to hold back the sob that was choking her.

Silently, Chastain stepped behind her, blocking the wind and rain from her with his body. She stood stiffly, locked rigid with the effort of control, but he moved closer, so close that he pressed against her, strong and solid and warm. As if it were the most natural thing in the world, he opened his jacket and enfolded her inside the sheltering wings. The cloth draped over her shoulders, her bare arms, wrapping her in warmth. He still held the umbrella in his left hand, but his right arm slid around her and held her anchored to him, tight against his hard chest.

The gesture stunned her. Except for her mother, no one had ever put themselves between her and the world. Chastain's action was so unexpected and intimate . . . and protective. The protectiveness was what destroyed her, even while it supported her.

Hot tears blurred her vision once more, washing out the images of the men bending and digging their shovels into the mound of dirt, but she heard the sound of dirt spilling into metal. They worked methodically, despite the pouring rain, as if the job was too somber to be hurried. She stood until they were finished, and all the while Chastain stood at her back, warming her, lending her his strength so she could continue to stand upright.

Karen was accustomed to standing alone. Even as a child, she had tried not to bother her mother with her problems, because she had always sensed Jeanette carried enough burdens. Nursing school had only enhanced her independence by giving her even greater responsibilities. She hadn't leaned on anyone in years, and she was shattered to find herself doing so both emotionally and physically with a man who had been a total stranger a mere two days before. She tried to blink away the tears that kept burning her eyes. She tried to say something and found the pressure in her chest was too great to allow the words to escape. She straightened, though something in her cried out at the sudden cold, the loss of contact. She turned to face him, but his face swam before her eyes, and suddenly she couldn't bear it any longer.

The sob that tore out of her throat sounded like the wail of a wounded animal. She didn't know if she collapsed against him or if he reached for her, but abruptly she was in his arms, her face buried in the curve of his shoulder. She wept convulsively, her entire body shuddering as she clung to him, her fingers digging into his back.

Chastain let the umbrella drop to the soggy ground. He bent his head over hers, murmuring soft, consoling sounds that didn't seem to be words at all, but just the sound was enough. She tried to burrow closer, vaguely appalled at her own neediness yet helpless to stop herself. One big hand closed over the nape of her neck, massaging, cradling, hot on her tender bare skin.

The pain was almost more than she could bear, grief and regret and a piercing sense of loneliness tearing at her. Despite her deep resentment, while Dexter lived, there had always been the possibility that one day he would work out whatever problems he had, get rid of the demons that rode his shoulder, and want to forge a relationship with her. That couldn't happen now. He had died still largely unknown to her, all the bright possibilities at an end. She mourned that loss of hope as much as she mourned him, a father she had never really known but whose absence had shaped her life. Now she would never be able to tell him how angry she was, how hurt, never reach out to him and feel the connection of family. She wept for that, and for her mother, and for him.

But such extreme emotion was exhausting, and gradually she quieted, still held securely in Detective Chastain's arms, her wet face still buried in his shoulder. She heard him speaking quietly over her head to someone, perhaps the minister, and a few moments later, she heard footsteps moving away, squishing on the wet ground. They were alone, and now she was grateful to him for yet one more thing; she needed privacy and he had provided it.

The rain had stopped beating down, dwindling to nothing more than a lukewarm mist as the storm moved on. The wind had died, and already she could feel the heat of the day rebuilding, steam forming on the ground. His heart thumped steadily under her ear, his chest rose and fell with the cadence of his breathing, and the warm, musky odor of his body mingled with the faint, fresh, lemony fragrance of his aftershave. He smelled delicious, she thought dimly, just the way a man should smell.

Her mind drifted. She tried to think of the last time she had been this close to a man, but the memory eluded her, and somehow she didn't think she had ever before been so close. Other men had held her, of course, but not like this. She had never accepted comfort from a man, never let any of her few boyfriends see her weep. She had never let herself need them, but somehow, in this moment, she needed Chastain. She needed to feel his arms around her, just for now. She needed the physical strength so evident in his tall, muscular body, a strength that effortlessly supported her weight, and she needed to be held as tightly as he was holding her. She needed to hear his dark-honey voice murmuring to her, needed the reassurance that right now, just for a few minutes, she wasn't alone.

The emotional storm had left her drained, exhausted, oddly detached. "I'm sorry," she said in a sodden voice, muffled against his shoulder.

"You're entitled." He shifted a bit, holding her with one arm while he reached into his pocket. "Here's a handkerchief."

She groped for it without lifting her head, wiping her eyes and blowing her nose, and then wondered in acute embarrassment how she could possibly give it back to him after blowing her nose on it. She crushed the cloth in her hand. "I'll wash it," she mumbled.

He gave a quiet chuckle, then wrapped his arms around her again. She resettled her head on his shoulder, sighing, feeling the dampness of his coat under her cheek. In the trees overhead, birds began to twitter and sing again with the passing of the rain.

"I never really knew him," she whispered, feeling compelled to talk. "He'd drift back into our lives every other year or so, and Mom would start hoping this time he would stay, but then he'd leave again, and she would cry for days. I hated him for that."

Those strong, comforting arms tightened, squeezing. "Did *you* want him to stay?"

"At first. Every time he came back, I ran to my room and prayed as hard as I could that he wouldn't leave again, and that Mom would be happy and not cry anymore. That never worked for long. Then I started making wishes. I wished on falling stars, on wishbones, I tossed pennies into any pool of water I could find. I didn't know any officially designated wishing wells, but I figured any water would do."

He chuckled again, and she found herself somehow smiling into his coat. The smile was wavery, but it was there. He rocked her back and forth a little, as if she were a child. "Feeling better?"

She nodded. "Crying causes endorphins to be released into the body, automatically lifting the mood."

"Then you must be slap full of endorphins right now," he teased, and this time she laughed. It shocked her, and she went still. How could she laugh? She was standing by her father's grave.

"Don't worry about it," he said, shaking her a little, understanding without being told why she had gone rigid in his arms. "People always laugh at funerals, sometimes even the families. My grandmother always said it was the angels' way of easing the burden. It isn't disrespectful, it's healing."

He was right. She thought back to other funerals she had attended, the bouts of muffled laughter, and she relaxed again. "When I was about eleven, we went back to West Virginia for my grandfather's funeral—my father's father. I remember Granny sitting in a rocker, holding this little lace handkerchief, reminiscing about Gramps with some of the older people. They all started laughing at some tale, trying to hold it back at first, but then Granny started actually *whooping,* rocking back and forth, holding her stomach and laughing 'til she could barely breathe. They all laughed like maniacs."

"It helps to remember the good times. So, you're really a West Virginia girl? I thought I heard a drawl sneak into that Ohio accent a few times." He imitated her accent, saying "Oh-Hi-uh," instead of "Oh-Hi-oh" the way Southerners did. As he spoke, he subtly released himself from her clutches, though not her from his. Moving to her side, he started her walking by the simple means of walking himself, holding her close with an arm around her waist. She had to walk or be dragged.

Karen hadn't wanted to show her face yet. She knew her eyes were swollen, her nose red, her makeup ruined. She only hoped she had been able to blot up the worst of the destruction. But Detective Chastain had decided it was time for her to leave, so, willy-nilly, she was leaving. Perhaps he had work to do and had to get back to New Orleans. She felt guilty about the way she had monopolized his time.

"Am I keeping you from something?" she asked, embarrassed all over again. He had offered his help, but perhaps it had only been a courtesy offer and he hadn't really expected her to accept.

"Of course not." He squeezed her a little as they reached the graveled little path that led to the car. "I'm off duty, and I don't have any appointments."

"Or a date?" she asked, disliking even the idea. She was surprised at herself. Had she suddenly become so needy that she couldn't bear losing his support? She had better snap out of it fast, because she was flying home the next morning.

"No date," he said easily. "Why don't we walk around the Quarter for a while, then have dinner? You haven't seen anything of New Orleans, really, and you need to relax."

Her sudden tension seeped out of her. He wanted to spend the rest of the day and the evening with her. Well, perhaps he didn't really *want* to, perhaps he merely felt responsible for her, but she was too grateful for the chance to avoid a long evening spent alone with only her melancholy thoughts for company that she felt a flood of relief at the invitation. "Thanks. I'd like that."

The afternoon sun suddenly blazed full on her face, the rain clouds gone for now, though ominous dark clouds were building again in the southwest. The heat and brightness of the sun were incredible, and she felt herself beginning to sweat again, as rapidly as she had grown chilled before. Squinting her swollen eyes against the glare, she misjudged her distance from the edge of the path and brushed against a shrub. The stubby branches snagged her hose and held fast.

"Darn it!" She stopped, looking down to assess the damage. The nylon was tangled on one of the branches. A hole the size of a half-dollar had been torn in the fabric, and an ugly run laddered both upward and downward from the hole. A run in black hose was particularly ugly, she thought, looking down at her pale leg peeking through.

She started to lean down and release herself, but he squatted beside her and curved one hand around her calf, using the other to work the nylon free. A small red scratch from the branch marred her skin, shining brightly through the gaping hole in her panty hose. He rubbed his thumb over the scratch, soothing the sting.

"You can take them off at the car," he said, rising, his task accomplished. He smiled down at her with those brilliant gray eyes. "I'll stand on the other side and not look, I promise."

The prospect of taking off her panty hose in his presence, even when he was on the other side of the car, seemed almost too daring and intimate. *Intimate.* There was that word again. All day—well, actually since the first day—it seemed as if he had wrapped her in a blanket of intimacy without actually doing anything sexual. He had touched her constantly; he put his hand on her arm or her back, held her, supported her, and perhaps she couldn't have made it through the ordeal without those touches that let her know she wasn't alone.

Perhaps the sense of intimacy was all on her part; perhaps Southern men were normally this solicitous toward women. She hadn't known any Southerners before, since they didn't exactly flock to Columbus, Ohio, so she had no means of comparison. If Detective Marc Chastain was typical of the Southern male, she thought, then the women in the rest of the country didn't know what they were missing.

They reached the car, and Marc went to the driver's side and turned his back, just as he had promised. The brutal sun beat down on their heads, and he shrugged out of his jacket, holding it in one hand while he waited.

His black hair was rain-wet and gleamed in the sun. His white shirt was thin, letting the warmth of his skin show through the fabric as it draped across his broad shoulders. Karen looked across the car at him, and the bottom dropped out of her stomach. For a moment, she stood paralyzed, unable to look away from him. Every detail was suddenly overwhelming in its clarity: the size of him, the set of his head on his shoulders, the neatness of his ears, the black hair that tapered to a point on the back of his neck. That big pistol was still clipped to his belt, and she wondered if he ever went anywhere without it.

She had never before been so acutely, physically aware of a man as she was in that moment, almost breathless from the impact on her senses.

"May I turn around now?" he asked lazily, and the moment passed.

"Not yet," she said. He settled against the side of the car, still patient.

Karen looked down at her leg. The torn nylon sagged, looking much worse than bare legs would. Vanity, if nothing else, inclined her to do as he said. Faintly amused, at both him and herself, she lifted her skirt and hurriedly peeled off the ruined panty hose, then wadded the nylon into a ball and stuffed it in her purse.

To her surprise, she instantly felt better. As hot and muggy as the air was, she was immeasurably more comfortable without the hot nylon wrapping her from waist to toe.

Almost as soon as she straightened, he was around the car, opening the door for her. There was that touch again, this time on her back, gently guiding her into the car. From out of nowhere surged a longing to be in his arms again, comforted and protected, to be able to rest her head on his shoulder. Such weakness was so alien to her that Karen automatically straightened her shoulders, mentally recoiling. Yes, she had been under a lot of stress, and while maybe it was okay to lean on that strong shoulder for a little while, she wouldn't allow herself to make a habit of it.

As he slid behind the wheel, he gave her his habitual half-smile, the one that crinkled the corners of his eyes and just barely curled his lips, the one that made him look sleepy and . . . something else; she wasn't certain just what.

"On second thought, it looks like it's going to rain again, so walking in the Quarter is out," he said. "We'll go to my house. We can sit on the balcony, drink a glass of wine, people-watch. You don't need to mope around a hotel room all by yourself."

An afternoon walk and dinner were one thing, but going to his house was quite another. "I've imposed enough—" she began.

"Don't argue."

"It's your day off, and I—"

"I said don't argue."

The easiness of his tone kept her from taking umbrage but didn't blind her to his determination. He had decided she was going to his house, so go she would.

It was because he was a cop, she thought, letting her

head drop back against the seat. When he gave an order, he expected it to be obeyed. Doctors were like that, too. A nurse didn't have to agree with the order, as long as she carried it out. But that was her job, and this wasn't. Nor was it police business. She could tell him no. The problem was, she didn't want to. She wanted to sit on his balcony and sip a glass of wine; it seemed so Southern, so *New Orleans.* She wanted to amuse herself with a little people-watching. She definitely didn't want to face that empty hotel room right now.

They didn't talk much during the half-hour drive back to the city. She felt limp, oddly detached, almost dreamy. She recognized it as the aftermath of her emotional storm and relief that the funeral was over, as if she had accomplished some herculean task and now could rest. The sense of drifting was pleasant.

She didn't realize he lived in the Quarter until he turned onto St. Louis. Until then, she had just thought he was taking a shortcut through the Quarter, though when she looked at it logically, she knew that was ridiculous. Why wind his way through the narrow, crowded streets of the Quarter to get anywhere except *in* the Quarter? He slowed and punched the button on his garage door opener, and a wide blue door began sliding upward. He wheeled the car into the opening when there was barely enough room for it to fit under, making her gasp and duck her head.

He chuckled. "Sorry. When you pull in here enough times, you learn how to judge it down to the inch." He cut off the car engine, got out, and walked around to her side of the car. Karen felt awkward just sitting there and making no attempt to open the car door herself, but she waited anyway. It took only a few seconds, and he seemed to expect to perform the courtesy. He opened the door, and she got out. He put his hand on her back again, a warm, light pressure that guided her toward a flight of stairs. At the top of the stairs, he unlocked a wooden door and opened it outward, ushering her through.

She stepped out onto a wide balcony that overlooked a luxurious courtyard. An old stone fountain occupied the middle, serving as a focal point around which plants of all kinds flourished. Enormous ferns and tall palms waved their lacy fronds; roses and geraniums and other flowers she couldn't name filled the air with perfume. She was certain she caught the scent of jasmine, though she didn't see any of the little starry white flowers. Enchanted, she stepped forward and rested her hands on the wrought-iron railing. This was wonderful. She looked down at a stone bench almost hidden among the foliage and wondered if he used the garden to escape from the stresses of his job.

"It's beautiful." She drew the delicious scent deep into her lungs.

"Thanks. One of the tenants keeps the place looking like a greenhouse, and I give her a break on the rent. The courtyard's nice, but I don't have time to take care of the plants. It would be just rock and dirt down there if it wasn't for Mrs. Fox."

"Then bless Mrs. Fox," she said, reluctant to leave the small paradise.

"Amen." He unlocked a door as he spoke, opening it inward and holding out his hand to her. She left the railing and walked inside, and felt as if she had also left the twentieth century behind. This house was from a different era, a different world. The plastered ceilings were at least twelve feet high, and the furniture was antique, but it was the kind of antique that was used every day, not put behind glass. The faded rug beneath her feet was still thick and luxurious, marvelously cushiony. The only modern note was a big easy chair, large enough to accommodate his height.

She started to ask how he could afford a place like this on a cop's salary, but the question was too rude, and she bit it back.

"I inherited the house from my grandmother," he said, watching her look around. "The attic is full of pieces of furniture that are two hundred years old. The fabric rots, of course, but I take care of the wood and every so often have a piece reupholstered."

"It must be wonderful, living in a place like this."

"I grew up here, so sometimes I take it for granted, but yeah, it's great." He held out his hand again, beckoning her forward. "This way." He led her through a small dining room and into the kitchen, then through double French doors leading out onto another balcony, this one overlooking the street. "Have a seat," he invited. "I'll get us something to drink. Are you hungry?"

"No, I—"

"I bet you didn't eat lunch," he said, his eyes narrowing. "Did you?"

"No," she admitted.

"You're a nurse," he said evenly. "You should know better. Sit."

Karen sat. He went inside, and she relaxed in the cushioned wrought-iron chair, watching the activity in the street below with a sort of fuzzy curiosity. She was tired and empty and still a little numb. Sitting here was just about all she felt she could manage right now. She looked at the hanging baskets of ferns, at the French doors on either side of her, and again felt herself in another world. The hot afternoon sun had cranked the temperature up into the nineties again, making steam rise from pockets of rainwater on the sidewalks, but the shade kept the heat tolerable. She needed a fan, though, just to be in keeping with the atmosphere. Smiling at the thought, she closed her eyes.

She must have dozed, rousing only when he set a tray on the table beside her. The tray held sandwiches of shaved ham, a plate of cookies, two empty glasses, and a bottle of red wine. "A domesticated man," she said, and heard the dreaminess of her tone as if she hadn't quite awakened yet.

"Don't give me too many points," he said in the lazy tone he seemed to have patented, sitting down on the other side of the little table. "The cookies are from a bakery, and any fool can make a sandwich."

He had changed clothes, she noticed, shedding the tie and exchanging his slacks for a pair of threadbare jeans. He was barefoot, and though he still wore the white shirt, he had left the tails hanging out, wrinkled from where it had been tucked in before. He had also opened a couple of buttons, so that it was fastened only to the middle of his chest. A broad, hairy chest, she noticed, still drowsy. Nice.

He propped his bare feet on the balcony railing, sighing as he relaxed. "Kick your shoes off," he invited.

She did, because the idea of being barefoot in this steamy weather sounded so wonderful. And she propped her feet on the railing, too, reasoning that passersby below wouldn't be able to see more than a few inches up her skirt, assuming anyone even looked. There was too much going on at street level for anyone to be concerned with whether or not she showed a little leg. She sighed just as he had, because it felt wonderful to be free of the hot, restricting shoes, to put her feet up, to feel her spine loosening. She so seldom just *sat* that this was a luxury.

Without sitting up from his relaxed position, Marc

stretched out an arm and expertly poured two glasses of wine. "Eat," he said, and waited until she took one of the sandwiches before snagging the other for himself.

Silently, she munched on the sandwich, sipped the wine, and watched the tourists strolling below. From somewhere drifted the sound of a street band, and she could also hear someone expertly playing show tunes on a piano. Snippets of conversation floated upward, mere background to the moment. She couldn't imagine any other place in the world like New Orleans, with its casual, exotic magic.

Their feet were propped side by side on the railing, and she surveyed them with interest, struck by the differences. Hers were much smaller and more slender, delicately formed, definitely feminine. His feet were big, bony, a little hairy on top: masculine. Interesting.

"Do you know," she murmured, still dreamy, "why men's feet look so different from women's?"

He moved his left foot over so it was touching her right one, eyeing them. Cocking his head a little, he said, "Nail polish."

If he had been within reach, she would have elbowed him. "Nooo. It was all that running around barefoot, chasing antelope and woolly mammoths."

He laughed, actually laughed aloud, a deep and deliciously male sound that made her toes curl. "So women's feet stayed dainty because all they had to do was wander around and pick berries."

"*And* carry the kids around." She wanted to hear him laugh again. She almost shivered again, this time with delight.

He settled his broad shoulders more comfortably in the chair. "Well, it would have been tough chasing woolly mammoths while carrying the papoose as well as spears."

"Excuses, excuses. Anything to get out of baby-sitting." The wine was good, she thought. She usually didn't care for red wine, but this was mellow and rich. She finished the glass and set it on the table, sighing with contentment.

Nothing was said for quite a while. The sizzling heat made conversation somehow unnecessary. A bass rumble of thunder announced the approach of more rain, and clouds began inching their purplish mass over the blaze of the setting sun. Marc carried the tray inside but left the plate of cookies on the table. He returned after several minutes. Music drifted from inside, a lazy blues instrumental. Everything drifted down here, she thought, closing her eyes. Anything else required too much effort.

"More wine?"

"Mmm, yes."

"Then eat a cookie."

"Slave driver." But she smiled as she picked up a cookie and bit into it. The flavor exploded on her tongue. "Ohh, that's good," she moaned. "What is it?"

"White chocolate. Pecans. Other stuff. They're my favorite kind." He ate one with gusto, then another.

What a mixture he was, she thought in amusement. Almost Old World in some ways, typical modern American male in others. He would feel perfectly at ease stretched out in his chair in that marvelous old living room, wearing jeans and a T-shirt and watching a ball game. Plus, he was a cop, adding to his complexity. What other qualities would surface on longer acquaintance? It didn't matter, she realized; she wouldn't have a chance to find out, because she was leaving tomorrow morning. An odd pang tightened her stomach.

They killed the plate of cookies and their second glasses of wine. Thunder rumbled again, edging closer. Rain began to spatter on the street, and the tourists below began hurrying for shelter. Within minutes, the street was deserted, and the silvery rain increased in steadiness, hurrying twilight.

Karen felt slightly chilled on the outside, but the wine had created a warm glow inside. A single saxophone mourned, the pure notes reaching to her soul. She hugged herself, aching inside.

"Dance with me," he said softly, standing up and holding out his hand to her.

She stood and went silently into his arms. She closed her eyes, and her head found her personal resting place on his shoulder. There couldn't be anything more perfect, she thought, than slow dancing, barefoot, on a balcony in New Orleans, while the rain poured down and twilight wrapped around them. He was so marvelously warm, she wanted to sink into him, and she actually caught herself pressing closer. Immediately, she started to pull back, but he stopped her with a firm hand on the small of her back, urging her even closer.

"It's okay. Just rest against me." The words were barely a murmur, as if he didn't want them to intrude on the moment.

So she relaxed again, so readily that she felt a flicker of guilt in the far recesses of her brain. She was shamelessly using him, for comfort, for support, for . . . for pleasure. Yes, this was pure pleasure: the strength of his arms around her, the hardness of his chest and belly rubbing against her breasts, her own belly, as they swayed to the hypnotic wail of the sax. His thighs slid along hers, his feet brushed hers, and occasionally she even felt the bulge of his genitals, though she thought he was being careful about that—his perfect manners again. She found herself waiting, almost breathless, for the next time their movements brought her hip against him. She wanted to curl into him, press herself fully to that intriguing bulge.

Her heartbeat was slow, heavy. The chill was gone; she felt deliciously warm, almost boneless, all thought suspended.

One strong hand slid up her back to close lightly over the nape of her neck, and the other moved down to her bottom. She didn't think of protesting. Somehow the touch wasn't demanding anything of her. He was just gently kneading her bottom, that was all. She had never before realized how good that could feel.

He tilted her head back, his hand firm on her neck. She saw the sensuous curve of his mouth, then he was kissing her, and even that wasn't demanding. Her eyes drifted shut again. His lips were soft, shaping hers, and he didn't use his tongue.

Abruptly, she wished he would. She wanted more of his taste. But she enjoyed what he was giving her, more than she had ever enjoyed any other man's kisses, so she let herself get lost in those light, brushing kisses. And she realized she had curled into him, after all, her hips arched toward him.

His hand left her bottom, almost drawing a protesting moan from her. But she heard the click of the door handle behind her and realized he was guiding her back into the kitchen. It was dark inside; he hadn't left a light on. She didn't bother opening her eyes, merely sighed with dreamy pleasure as he continued kissing her and his hand returned to her buttocks. Both hands, she dimly realized, and she was clinging to his shoulders with both hands. Her breasts were tight, achy; her loins were full. It felt good, better than good. She wanted his tongue, she wanted it so much that she rose on tiptoe and deepened the kiss herself, tentatively probing. And she wanted to stretch against him, so she did that, too, pressing her breasts to him and feeling her nipples pinch with pleasure.

He gave a low growl, deep in his throat, and took the initiative from her. This time, the pleasure was sharp, splintering, and she moaned aloud. Oh, yes. He tasted wonderful, like cookies and wine and himself. His tongue moved deep and sure, taking, and hers danced around it, softly teasing. She had never before realized kisses could be so subtle, so full of meaning, so varied.

He grasped her skirt and worked it up to her waist, then slid his hands beneath the waistband of her panties to clasp her bare bottom. Her buttocks were cool, his hands hot; the contrast had her arching forward, gasping. Her breasts throbbed; her hips undulated a little, reaching for and finding the hard ridge of his penis, rocking against him, instinctively seeking relief. She had gone beyond warm; she felt feverish, her skin too tight, her clothes too binding.

He stooped a little, tugging at her panties. They slid down her thighs, dropped to her ankles. "Step out of them," he whispered, and mindlessly she did so. Her heart was pounding, her body caught in a fever of need.

"Open your eyes."

She did that, too, staring up at him in the rain-washed dimness of the room, his face lit by the watery light seeping through the french doors. His expression was set, his eyes narrow and piercing, his mouth fiercely sensual.

They weren't in the kitchen after all, she realized with a sort of distant surprise; he had danced her through the other set of doors. They were in his bedroom.

The bed hit the backs of her knees, and he eased her down onto it, his hands firm and sure. She barely had time to register the coolness of the sheets beneath her bare bottom, then he was on her, heavy and solid, kneeing her thighs apart while he opened his jeans.

She breathed deeply, her eyes half closed, watching him through the fringe of her lashes. She still felt dreamy, as if none of this were real, yet she had never wanted so intensely as she did now, never hungered for another man as she did for him. The power of her need surprised her; she wasn't quite certain how she had come to this moment, lying on a bed with a man she barely knew, her panties on the floor and her skirt around her waist.

The first touch of his penis to her was startling, a stark intrusion of reality. Her eyes flared with shock, and her fingers dug into his shoulders. He held her gaze, his big body pressing her into the mattress, and entered her with a hard, steady thrust, sheathing himself to the root with one movement. Her body arched in feminine shock at the force of his penetration, at this searing invasion. His penis was smooth and hard, thick, impossibly deep, and she writhed around him.

He steadied her, holding her firmly as he withdrew a little and thrust again, his gaze intent on her face. She couldn't stop her gasping cry at the resulting sensation, the pleasure that was almost torment. Her heart pounded violently against her ribs. She clung to him with desperate hands, feeling as if she were about to be torn apart by an internal force she couldn't contain. He whispered soothingly to her, words of masculine reassurance she couldn't quite grasp, but the dark honey of his voice was more effective than any words.

"Please." She heard herself begging, for mercy, for relief, for anything and everything.

He understood her urgency even better than she. He pulled back and thrust deep, hard, then again, and she began climaxing.

He rode her hard through the waves of sensation, pounding into her, holding her thighs spread wide so she had no control, no protection. He showed her no mercy as she convulsed and arched, nor did she want any. She wanted only him, the fierce intimacy of his body locked into hers.

When her spasms eased, she lay sprawled limply beneath him. She was exhausted, emptied out, barely conscious. His powerful body bucked when he came, and her flesh quivered from the impact of his thrusts.

He lay heavily on her, his chest heaving as he gasped for breath, his heart thundering against her own. He felt damp with sweat through his clothes, but a slight, cooling breeze wafted through the open French doors, bringing with it the freshness of the rain. Karen turned her face into his neck, breathing in the hot odor of his skin, and felt herself sink toward sleep.

She roused a little when he withdrew, instinctively protesting the loss of his weight, the comfort of his animal warmth in the rain-cooled night. "Shh," he murmured, soothing her.

Enough light came through the windows and open doors that she could sleepily watch him remove and discard a condom, and she was alert just enough to ask, "When did you put that on?" She would swear his hands had never left her after they had entered the bedroom.

"When I put on the music." He turned back to her,

still kneeling between her spread thighs. His eyes were heavy-lidded with concentration as he began removing her clothes. Karen let him unzip her dress, his hands working under her; her sluggish thoughts still centered on the condom. He had planned this, then. Even before they had begun dancing, he had intended to make love to her.

The significance of this seemed important, but why eluded her. He tugged her dress off over her head and tossed it aside, then deftly unclipped her bra and removed it, too. Her attention was caught by her nudity, which, despite the intimacy of the act they had just shared, made her feel far too vulnerable. She shocked herself, lying there naked and spread in front of a man who was still clothed, even though his jeans were down around his thighs. He should have been soft, but his swollen penis jutted out from under his shirt, twitching with arousal.

Her hands moved; perhaps he sensed her intention to cover herself, for he caught her wrists and pinned them to the pillow beside her head, and took his time looking her over. Her nipples drew into tight little points under his inspection, and he smiled. Leaning over her, he licked her left nipple, circling the point with his tongue before gently catching it between his teeth and applying delicate pressure.

Prickles of heat shot through her. She gasped, fruitlessly wrenching her arms in an effort to free them—not to push him away but to hold him close. He sucked at her, pressing the nipple hard against the roof of his mouth while his tongue worked at it, and she writhed helplessly. She hadn't known her breasts were so sensitive, but the way he was sucking her aroused her so sharply she felt herself, impossibly, building toward another climax.

Bending forward as he was, the tip of his penis

nudged at her swollen folds, prodding her opening. Her breath snagged, caught. Her hips arched.

He swore softly, his breath ragged, and reared back from her. He fought his way out of the shirt, tossing it aside, and quickly sheathed himself with another condom. Leaning over her again, he caught her wrists in one hand and stretched her arms over her head, arching her breasts upward in tender offering. He took full advantage of her position, sucking both nipples, gentle and ruthless at once.

His free hand moved over her belly, down between her spread legs. She was swollen and sensitive from their lovemaking, barely able to take the two big fingers he worked up inside her. She quivered, gasping, and her head tossed restlessly back and forth within the frame of her upstretched arms.

A shudder of arousal rippled over him. "You're tight," he murmured, kissing her throat. "Am I hurting you?"

"N-no." She could barely speak. His fingers reached deep inside her, pressing upward. His thumb rasped over her clitoris, circled it enticingly. "Oh, my God." She cried the words, arching tautly. Heat poured through her, drawing her upward like a bow. She could feel another climax building, even stronger than the last. Her shaking thighs were spread achingly wide again as he shifted close to her, taking his fingers out of her and replacing them with the long stroke of his shaft.

The spasms boiled swiftly upward. He felt them begin and pressed himself deep. Rhythmic cries shook from her, and her body convulsed. He controlled his own urges and slowly, carefully, rebuilt her desire until she climaxed yet again, and only then did he let himself come.

She slept, and woke to his hands on her again.

Night had completely fallen, and he had removed his jeans. Rain still pattered down outside, and the French doors were still open, letting in the damp air. Nothing else in the universe existed but the confines of the bed and man who held her close to his heat and hardness. She didn't think, simply *was,* for the first time in her life, lost to pure physical pleasure. He could have done anything to her, and she wouldn't have protested.

He slid down her body and pressed his mouth to her, the caress so tender and intimate she almost wept, would have if desire hadn't risen again, throbbing insistently in her loins. He mounted her, said, "I'm going to do you hard this time," and did, ruthlessly driving for his own pleasure and making her come, too. She thought she would faint this time, the spasms were so intense. She clutched his sweaty sides and completely gave herself up to him. This savage lovemaking in the dark, rainy New Orleans night was more intensely carnal than anything she could have imagined doing, and she didn't want it to end.

This time, he slept, too, holding her so close that sweat formed between their bodies, sealing them together.

The night felt endless. She woke to the same rain and darkness, the hot damp air, the contrasting coolness of the rain-laden breezes. She couldn't see a clock anywhere, wouldn't have looked at it in any case. She kissed her way down his body. By the time she reached his groin, he was awake, erect, groaning. She kissed his shaft, licked the length of it, and felt it grow even more, then she took him fully in her mouth. Torment was a two-way street, and she wanted him to enjoy it as much as she had.

She didn't know how many times they made love

that night. Her mind was in a fog, her body completely turned over to him. When she was so exhausted she simply couldn't respond again, he cradled her in his arms and brushed a tender kiss across her eyes. "Sleep, darlin'," he whispered in that black magic voice, and it was as if she only needed to hear the words before she let go of consciousness.

Chapter 10

Hayes was a careful man. He hired competent people, but when someone told him a job was done, he didn't necessarily take it for granted that the job had been done to his satisfaction.

He made it a point to double-check everything. His caution paid off, letting him catch and deal with irritants before they became major problems. The people who worked for him considered him a major pain in the ass, but the people for whom *he* worked were eternally grateful for his attention to detail.

When Clancy called and reported he had taken care of his assignment, Hayes believed him; Clancy was damn good at what he did. But he still contacted another source to have a copy of the police report on the house fire, as well as the newspaper account, faxed to him on a private, untraceable line. He was competent with computers but more comfortable with older technology; he thought the security was better. With computers, who knew what little puke in Hoboken or somewhere was taking a peek at everything he sent or received?

His source called back the next day. "I can't find anything about a Karen Whitlaw's house burning," he said. "There was a house fire, but the house belonged to a couple named Hoerske."

Hayes cursed. It wasn't like Clancy to burn the wrong house. "Do me a favor," he said. "Look in the phone book, and see what Karen Whitlaw's address is."

"Okay. Just a minute." The sound of riffling pages came through the phone line. "Whitfield . . . Whitfield . . . Whitlaw. There's no Karen Whitlaw listed, but there is a K. S. Whitlaw."

"Hold on." Hayes checked the file he had on Dexter Whitlaw's wife and daughter. The daughter's middle name was Simone. "That would be her."

"Okay. The address is . . . hell, the address is the same as the Hoerskes' house."

Hayes felt a headache forming behind his eyes. He pinched the bridge of his nose. "Fax everything you have to me."

"Sure."

Twenty seconds later, the fax machine was humming as it spit out the requested documents. Hayes didn't bother with the police report; he picked up the copy of the newspaper account: "A fire yesterday morning destroyed the residence of Nathan and Lindsey Hoerske. According to the fire marshall, the flame began in the kitchen. The Hoerskes, who bought the home only four months before, were not at home at the time of the blaze."

Hayes tossed the sheet down. It didn't take a genius

to figure out what had happened; the Whitlaw woman had sold the house. Probably Clancy had looked up her address in the phone book, but phone books were only updated once a year.

He called Clancy. As always, he got voice mail. "Leave a number," Clancy's voice instructed, without identifying himself. "If I know you, I'll call back."

"You fucked up," Hayes said, also not identifying himself.

"The hell I did," Clancy said, picking up the phone. He sounded pissed; he wasn't used to customer dissatisfaction.

"She didn't live there, asshole. She sold the house four months ago."

"Well, sonofabitch. I hate that, burning down a house for nothing."

"Find her. And this time, do the job right."

Senator Stephen Lake expected to be the next president; a lot of other people expected the same thing. He and his older brother, William, had been groomed for public office from the time they were born, but when William died, Stephen had become the heir apparent. The Lakes were lawyers and judges and politicians, and Stephen was the fourth generation to follow that path.

Senator Lake had always been acutely aware that William was his father's first choice, the apple of the old man's eye, and after William's death, Stephen had tried even harder to be the perfect politician, to make up to his father in some small way for the pain of losing his favorite son. He had set a sure and steady career course, building a reputation over the years as a man who always took the high road; an admirable position, Franklin Vinay thought, but the chair of the

Senate Intelligence Committee, not to mention the agencies involved, would be better served by pragmatism than idealism.

The DDO didn't like being summoned to the senator's office like a schoolboy ordered before the principal. He went anyway, and none of his distaste was revealed in his expression as he sat in the beautifully appointed office. He did wonder, though, what had brought the senator back to the capital during August; the last Vinay had heard, Senator Lake had been happily settled at the Minnesota estate he so loved. Vinay couldn't imagine anything less than a national emergency luring any of the politicians from their vacations during the worst of the summer heat. Since he would have known before any congressman if there was a national emergency, perhaps even before the president, Vinay knew that wasn't the case.

That made Senator Lake's presence all the more curious, and Franklin Vinay wasn't a man who ignored curiosities.

"Coffee, Frank?" the senator asked, gesturing toward a pot.

"No, thanks. I'm not tough enough to drink coffee during this heat."

The senator laughed genially and helped himself to a cup, perhaps to prove *he* was tough enough. Vinay smiled, watching as the senator poured a single drop of cream into his coffee, wondering how many cups the senator would drink before he felt his manhood sufficiently established.

He didn't ask why the senator had summoned him. Vinay had been in the game a long time; he knew the power of silence, how to play the subtle game of position: force the other side to come out first. He didn't betray any anxiety, or any secrets, by rushing into speech. That they were ostensibly on the same side didn't matter; Vinay let no one force him into unguarded speech. When he knew what the senator wanted, then he would know how to react.

Unfortunately, Senator Lake was a great one for small talk, rather than getting to the point. "This is the hottest summer I can remember," he said, leaning back in his butter-soft leather chair. "Miserably hot. Normally, I take August for vacation—"

Like every politician in D.C. didn't, Vinay thought.

"—maybe get in a little trout fishing. Do you fish, Frank?"

"Not in years." He'd been too busy trying to contain some noxious *isms,* such as communism and terrorism.

"You really should try to get away more. Fishing puts a man back in touch with nature. You get to see unspoiled parts of the country, and you remember that most of America doesn't live in big cities. Our media is so dominated by what happens in the cities that we tend to forget the concerns of the rest of the country."

Vinay opened his mouth to agree, but the senator waved a hand. "Here I am rambling on, and I know you're busy. I'll get to the point. One of my aides informed me that one of your contract agents has been killed in Mississippi. Reassure me, Frank, that he wasn't on an assignment for you, and don't give me the standard quote that the CIA is forbidden to operate within our own borders. Being forbidden to do something and *not* doing it are two different things."

Vinay looked blank, but inside he was furious. The only way one of the senator's aides could find out about Rick Medina was from an inside source in Vinay's department. "Senator, there are no operations inside our borders, period. If a contract agent has been killed—and I haven't heard anything about it—then it was something unconnected to us."

"You haven't heard?" Now the senator looked blank. "But—"

"We use a lot of contract agents. They also work for other countries, as you well know, whenever they aren't working for us. Perhaps this person was on assignment, but not for us, and if that were the case, I wouldn't have any information on him or her. Which is it, by the way?"

"Which—?"

"A man or a woman?"

"Oh—a man. You truly haven't heard?"

"Like I said, if it doesn't concern the Agency, I would have no reason to be informed."

"I was informed this man's son is one of your people."

The senator had been informed of too goddamned much, Vinay thought grimly. And if he really thought Vinay would identify one of his most important operatives, then the senator also expected too goddamned much. "It's possible, but unless the death affected operations . . ." He shrugged, to show how unimportant it was to him that a contract agent had been killed.

Senator Lake consulted a file. "The agent was Rick Medina. Does the name ring a bell?"

"Rick Medina!" Vinay managed a credible look of shock. "Are you sure of that?"

"My source is very reliable," the senator said stiffly. He wasn't accustomed to having his word questioned.

"I've known Rick for years—not well, no one knew him well, but he was one of our most reliable contract agents. Damn!"

"Are you also acquainted with his son?"

"Rick didn't have a family," Vinay lied. "He was a complete loner."

"I see." For some reason, Senator Lake seemed nonplussed. "Well."

Vinay stood, his patience at an end. He was glad he was able to tell the truth about Medina not being on assignment for them when he was killed, but the senator knew too much, details of information that should not have come his way. Already, the deputy director was planning how he would bring the mole in his department out into the sunlight—and then fire his ass.

"Was that all you wanted, Senator?" he asked politely. "I assure you Medina wasn't running anything for us. If you want more detail, I'll be happy to check into his death and get back with you on anything I find."

"Oh, no, that won't be necessary. I was just worried about—well, you know the situation in the country these days, with militia groups looking for any detail, no matter how far-fetched, that they can find to prove our government has run amok. It's best to head these things off at the pass."

It was a fairly legitimate concern, but something about the way it was stated struck Vinay as a little too pat, as if the answer had been rehearsed. "Yes, sir," he said. Something wasn't right here; he couldn't put his finger on it, but he trusted his instinct. Why would Senator Lake feel he had to come up with a plausible excuse for asking about Rick Medina?

Maybe Rick wasn't the focus of his questions. Maybe he had really been trying to get information on John. Suspicion struck Vinay hard in the gut. He couldn't think of any good reason why the senator would want or need to know anything about John

Medina, but several bad reasons occurred to him, and they all needed to be investigated. He hadn't reached his present position by being gullible.

After Vinay had gone, Senator Lake sat down at his wide, hideously expensive desk, absently rubbing his fingers along the glassy finish while he stared thoughtfully at the door through which Vinay had passed. Something very disturbing had happened in that meeting. There were two possibilities, and he didn't like either of them. Either Hayes was mistaken in his information, or the deputy director of operations had just lied to him.

Slowly, Senator Lake reached for the phone, then with swift decision punched in the number for a private line in his house. It was answered on the second ring, and a comfortingly familiar, rumbly voice soothed his sudden anxiety. "Raymond, could you catch the next flight to D.C.? I may need you."

Chapter 11

Dragging her suitcase, Karen let herself into her apartment. Grimly, without letting herself look at the answering machine because she knew the little red light would be blinking like a caution light, she went into the bedroom and completely unpacked. She took her time about it, hanging what she hadn't worn back in the closet and separating everything else into two piles, one for the laundry and one for the dry cleaner.

She watered her plants, put the laundry in the washing machine, then called her floor supervisor. "Judy, hi, it's Karen. I'm home, and I can go back to work tonight if you need me."

"If I need you?" Judy Camliffe echoed in heartfelt relief. "Marletta's been out with strep throat for two days, and Ashley called in sick today, too."

"What's wrong with Ashley?"

"The brown flu. So hell, yes, I need you. The

question is, do you need to come back so soon? I'll manage tonight, somehow, if you need another day."

"Thanks," Karen said, meaning it. Judy was under a lot of pressure to keep her floor running smoothly with fewer nurses than ever, since the hospital wasn't immune to cutbacks. Five years ago, there were twelve registered nurses on the surgical floor, four per shift. Now there were eight whom Judy had to juggle among three shifts and two off days per nurse each week. Some nights there was only one RN on duty. The rumor was they would be going on twelve-hour shifts before the end of the year. "But I'm okay; the funeral was yesterday, and I flew home this morning."

"Really? I looked for the obituary, but I didn't see it."

"He's buried in Louisiana. I didn't have a plot for him here, and one of the detectives suggested I bury him there for the time being. Mom would have wanted them to be buried together, and there's no room beside her, so I'll have to find another place and have them both moved . . ." Her voice trailed off. She was vaguely surprised at herself. She liked Judy, considered her a friend, but she wasn't in the habit of rambling on about her private problems even to Piper, who was her closest friend. But mentioning Marc even indirectly rattled her so much she could barely think coherently; her heartbeat jumped into overdrive, her stomach clenched, her breasts tightened, her mouth watered. The symptoms of panic and sexual desire jumbled together, just as they had that morning when she had awakened in bed with him.

"Gee, that's tough," Judy said. "Uh, I hate to ask, but did you get a copy of the death certificate or maybe an obituary in the New Orleans paper? You have to have one of them to get paid for the days you were off."

"I have a copy of his death certificate." Marc had gotten it for her. She didn't know how long it would normally have taken, but he had sweet-talked someone in the medical examiner's office into processing the paperwork. Her heartbeat did another sprint. He wouldn't have had to do any sweet-talking; all he had to do was ask, in that midnight voice, and if the clerk was a woman, he would have his paperwork.

"Good. That'll minimize any hassle with payroll. Are you sure you feel like working?"

"I'm sure."

"Then I can definitely use you tonight. Come in at your regular time."

That settled, Karen looked around for something else to do. When she went into the living room, the message light flashed insistently at her. She ignored it, went into the kitchen, and made a sandwich, then did something she rarely had time for: she sat down in front of the television and put up her feet. There was an interior decorating show on Discovery. Since her apartment was badly in need of decorating—unpacking would help—she watched the show while she ate her sandwich.

She had run. Literally. Like the biggest coward on earth, she had sneaked out of the house while Marc was in the shower. Her feet still ached from running in high heels the nine or so blocks to the hotel. She had thrown her clothes in the suitcase, called the desk, and checked out, then prayed he wouldn't be waiting in the lobby for her. She couldn't face him; she had never been more embarrassed. Of course, there was a strong possibility he might not bother to come after her, that he would be relieved to get her off his hands, but she didn't want to take that chance.

She got off the elevator on the mezzanine, then carried her bag down the final flight of stairs so she wouldn't run into him at the bank of elevators. She went out the side door of the hotel, into the big parking bay, and got into a taxi.

She was lucky; he didn't know what airline she was flying. He also had to work. Still, when the loud-speaker at the airport requested that Karen Whitlaw please pick up one of the courtesy phones, she didn't, just in case he was actually in the airport instead of at work.

She didn't breathe a sigh of relief until the plane backed away from the gate. Not that Marc would use his badge to get on board the plane for a face-to-face; after all, she wasn't a criminal, just a woman he had slept with the night before.

It wasn't the sleeping part that embarrassed her. It was what they had done when they weren't asleep.

She wasn't a prude, or frigid, or innocent—two of those were an impossibility in her profession, as far as she was concerned—but nothing like last night had ever before happened to her. She thought of herself as careful and responsible, two qualities that precluded sleeping around. Piper said she was picky and para-noid, which wasn't as flattering but had the same result. She had never, *never,* been as reckless, as thoughtless, as she had been last night. Whatever Marc had wanted to do to her, she had let him, and he had wanted to do a lot. Let him? She had actively participated, and climaxed more times than she could remember. She had been like a bitch in heat.

She stared sightlessly at a demonstration of a paint-ing technique that involved dabbing a ball of plastic wrap in paint, then blotting it on the wall. God, how stupid could she be? Maybe if she'd had more hands-on experience, so to speak, she would have seen him coming.

She winced at the pun, her cheeks burning. The

truth was, she had been humiliatingly easy for him. She had been seduced, and by a master. He hadn't made a single wrong move.

The cheerful woman on television was single-handedly turning a blank wall into a masterpiece of designer painting. Karen scowled at her and clicked the television off. She was fairly certain she was never going to paint her walls with a wad of plastic wrap. How could she concentrate on decorating, anyway, when she had some serious brooding to do?

There was no single point she could use to salvage any pride. She had been very willing, and she couldn't salve her conscience by pretending otherwise. On the other hand, there was no denying his skill. The degree of her willingness was testimony to that.

She leaned her head back on the sofa, staring at the plain white ceiling. Marc's ceilings were high, with fancy crown molding, and yummy ceiling fans everywhere.

She punched the cushion. Damn it, she did *not* want to think about him!

How could she stop, though, when her insides still throbbed? If any of her friends at the hospital had bragged about having sex that many times in one night—with one man—Karen wouldn't have believed her. Well, now she knew there really were men who could get it up that often. She felt raw and swollen between her legs, proof of the excesses of the night in case she doubted her own memory.

Looking back, she saw how he had led her, inevitably and without a pause, straight to his bed. Hindsight wasn't worth a damn, though. She hadn't felt even a tingle of warning at the time. Using means both swift and subtle, he had fostered a sense of intimacy between them and then capitalized on it. The man knew his stuff.

The day before had been one long seduction. Her entire acquaintance with him had been a seduction. She had studied human sexuality, knew the signals, and still she had missed them; only in retrospect were they crystal clear.

First had come the concern, the solicitousness for her well-being, the touches disguised as courtesy. She remembered his hand on her arm, sliding down her back, resting on her waist. He had won her trust, lulled her into accepting his constant touch without suspecting the sexuality behind it, and then aroused her to the point where she hadn't even thought about calling a halt to their lovemaking.

And yesterday . . . oh, yesterday. She remembered the way he had put his hand on the back of her neck while she wept, a gesture so sexually possessive she didn't know how it had slipped under her radar, but at the time she had been aware only of being comforted. By then, she was so used to having his hands on her that it had felt . . . right.

He had even managed, with perfect logic, to talk her into taking off part of her own clothing, and she had felt relaxed enough with him to do it. He couldn't have arranged for her to snag her panty hose, but he had been quick to take advantage of it. Just her panty hose, just her shoes . . . it had all felt so casual, so relaxed, and had set the stage for her to lose all her clothes.

He had further softened her with wine, though she couldn't use even that to excuse herself. She hadn't been tipsy. He had seen to that, carefully feeding her, not giving her any grounds on which she could later excuse herself, or accuse him. She had been sober but warmed by the wine and his care, his touch. She remembered the brush of his bare feet against hers while they danced, and her toes curled, her nipples tightened.

What could be more romantic than a hot sax and a slow dance on a balcony in New Orleans on a rainy summer night? She had been completely in his arms then, under his spell, so subtly aroused she had been almost at fever pitch and hadn't even realized it. She remembered the fleeting contact with his erection while they danced, and knew now it hadn't been accidental. He had teased her with it, letting her surreptitiously seek out another brief touch, making her feel everything was still casual while subtly intensifying her arousal.

He had orchestrated every touch, gentling her, bringing her to the point where she not only would accept him sexually but was eager for the act. He hadn't put one step wrong; he hadn't grabbed her breasts or shoved his hand between her legs, moves that would have startled her into pulling away. She didn't know why having his hands on her bottom hadn't warned her, but all her alarms had been silent. Maybe she had already been past the point of no return. He had bypassed all the usual foreplay, except for those wonderful kisses; when he was ready, he had simply tossed her skirt up and taken her, except that the entire day had been foreplay and she had been more than ready for him, climaxing with embarrassing speed.

The memory of it had her face hot, her breath rushing in and out of her lungs. Damn it! One night with him had turned her into a sex kitten, evidently. She wanted him. Still. Now.

The man knew more about sex, and women, than should be legal. He had been so sure of himself, and of her, that he had put on a condom even before asking her to dance. She should be grateful for that, at least, because she had been so far gone that the thought of protection had never crossed her mind, and she was a nurse, for God's sake. She hadn't thought of pregnancy or disease, only of completing the act for which her body was clamoring.

He had certainly destroyed another of her assumptions, because she had always thought people who claimed to be swept away by passion were exaggerating to cover their own stupidity and carelessness. Now she was the newest member of the Stupid and Careless Club.

So much for her vaunted caution and self-control; Marc Chastain just hadn't gotten his hands on her, yet. Well, now he had, and now she knew that she had no caution or self-control where he was concerned.

There were so many levels of foolishness to her behavior that she could scarcely believe what she had done. She had gone straight from her father's grave to a stranger's bed. She didn't think she could have made it through the ordeal of the past few days without Marc's aid, but he was still, essentially, a stranger. She didn't know anything about him except that he was a cop, he could seduce a statue, and he had screwed her brains out.

The deliberate crudity of the thought didn't make her feel better, it made her feel like crying.

If she thought he had been wildly attracted to her from the beginning, she would still be embarrassed by having slept with him, still be mortified by her carelessness, but she wouldn't have run like a scared rabbit. But he *hadn't* been attracted to her; in fact, he had taken an instant dislike to her. Lying in the cool of the early morning, pinned to the mattress by his muscular arm, all she could remember was when she had first met him, and she knew she hadn't been mistaken. So, if he disliked her so much, why had he immediately launched his seduction tactics? The awful possibility that occurred to her was what sent her running.

Maybe he was guilty of nothing more than horniness. Maybe he had made love to her casually but not maliciously, taking the opportunity when it presented itself. Maybe. She didn't believe it. For one thing, he hadn't left anything to chance, not even the condoms. He had set out to take her and accomplished his aim with ridiculous ease. His actions bespoke a deliberation that frightened her, and hurt her beyond measure.

Given his immediate dislike, what if his entire seduction campaign had been aimed at taking her down a peg? Screw her, use her, walk away from her.

One of the residents at the hospital had even said something like that to her, after she had turned down his invitation for the third time. "One of these days, some slick stud is going to get your panties off," he had said, sneering, "and when he gets through with you and walks off, you'll find out you're not any better than the rest of us."

She didn't imagine studs came any slicker than Marc Chastain.

She winced, wishing she would stop thinking in those awful puns.

Now she thought of an even worse possibility. What if his actions had been motivated by *pity?*

She groaned, covering her eyes. Great. Just great. She was that most pitiable of creatures, a mercy fuck.

Karen rolled her head and looked at the blinking light on the answering machine. She didn't have to listen to the messages; she could walk over there and erase them. She wouldn't have to hear that dark velvet drawl again or, worse, *not* hear it. Maybe he had just said to hell with it and walked away, and there was no message from him to erase.

"Damn it." She said the words aloud. "Damn it, damn it, *damn* it." The repetition didn't help. She had to face the truth she had been trying hard to avoid, but her own inability to stop thinking about him made avoidance impossible. She had done something far more stupid than sleeping with him; sometime during the past three days, she had fallen in love with him.

She had told herself it was only because he was being so helpful at a time when she really needed it, but her heart had given a big thump every time she saw him. She had told herself it was just his voice, that marvelous, deliciously male voice, that attracted her. She had told herself a lot of things, but the truth was her insides had jolted in primitive recognition the first time she had seen him. Call it chemistry, call it biology—hell, call it voodoo—for whatever reason, she had gravitated to him like a nail to a magnet, and everything he had done after that had only intensified her feelings.

How could she not love him? He had fed her, sheltered her with his own body, warmed her; such simple, even primitive actions, things a caveman might have done for his cavewoman of choice when he wanted to get under her bearskin with her. Funny that they were as effective now as they had been thousands of years ago.

She couldn't put her finger on any one moment when her initial feelings had crystallized into something more serious, but neither could she discount what she was feeling. It was real, it was fierce, it was terrifying—and it was painful.

If all he had wanted was casual sex to while away a rainy night, then he shouldn't have been so damn courteous and gallant, she thought furiously, tears stinging her eyes. And if he disliked her so much that he had deliberately tried to make her care, so her hurt would be worse—

She didn't know what to do. She didn't have the experience to deal with this kind of situation. She had never loved a man before, never let herself even get close to loving one. It was ironic that she had just decided to begin giving men more of a chance in the romance field, and then Marc had come in under her radar and laid her flat, quite literally.

She should have stayed and faced him. It would have been the smart, dignified thing to do. Just lay it all out, like an adult—no game playing, just honest talk.

Well, it was too late to act like an adult. The least she could do now was apologize for her behavior and let him worry about his own.

The blinking light on the answering machine was driving her crazy. Swearing, tears burning her eyes again, she stalked over to the machine and punched the play button.

There was a hang-up, then a recorded message trying to sell her cleaning products, three more hang-ups, a message from Piper saying, "God, Karen, I'm so sorry about your father. Why didn't you call?" The next message was an aluminum siding salesman, then another hang-up, and all at once a deep, furious voice: "God damn it, Karen—" He stopped, and when he spoke again, it sounded as if his teeth were clenched. "What the *hell* did you mean, running away like that? You call me the fucking minute you get home, or by God I'll—"

She didn't get to hear the rest of the threat, because he slammed down the phone. Her knees went weak, and she grabbed the edge of the desk for support. No velvet in his voice now; all she could hear was steely rage. The force of it took her aback. She hadn't expected rage. Disgruntlement, maybe, but she had expected the phone call to be something along the lines of "Are you all right? Running away wasn't necessary." She had expected him to *check* on her, nothing more, and the very mildness of his response would make her feel even more cowardly for running.

She hadn't heard him curse before—those perfect manners again. She hadn't been naive enough to think he didn't swear at all; she had heard him, though he had been speaking French. He was a cop, after all, and under the courtesy was a toughness that in normal circumstances would have made her keep as far away from him as possible. Her father had been a tough man, too. But she had needed Marc, and she had never in her life felt safer than she had with him. It wasn't just the pistol in his belt holster, it was the man himself, big and confident, with his hard, glittering eyes. He was tough, all right, and she didn't doubt he could be mean when the situation warranted.

With her, however, he had been gentle. Courteous. He had used sex words in bed with her, of course; she closed her eyes as she remembered some of the things he had said, and done. Arousal curled low and warm inside her, making her squeeze her legs together. She shivered and groaned aloud.

Just as she had the first time he called, she rewound the tape and played his message again. She winced as the force of his fury hit her ears. She had run from him as if he were a rapist, insulting him after he had gone to a great deal of trouble on her behalf, regardless of what his private opinion of her was. Being a cop, he would also have tried to catch her, to make certain nothing was wrong. She hadn't even had the courtesy to answer his page. No wonder he was furious; she was furious with herself. Yes, she'd had a rough few days, a rough *year,* but she couldn't excuse herself on those grounds. She couldn't excuse herself at all.

She picked up the phone and dialed before she could do something else childish, such as chicken out.

"This is Chastain. Leave a message."

Voice mail. Damn voice mail. Karen clenched her teeth. He deserved a personal apology, deserved the chance to swear at her some more, but it might take her days to catch him in the office. "This is Karen. I'm at home. I'm sorry for running out on you this morning. It was childish of me, and I—I don't have any excuse. I thought—never mind. I acted like an idiot, and I'm sorry."

There didn't seem to be anything else to say. She bit her lip and hung up. The pit of her stomach felt cold. Maybe he would call so he could tell her she was a jerk and an idiot, but likely she would never hear from him again.

On impulse, she took the microcassette out of the answering machine and put it in a drawer. Even if he was swearing at her on the tape, at least it was his voice. She could listen to it occasionally to remind herself she was a fool.

She put a new tape in the machine, then stood uncertainly. She could sit waiting for the phone to ring, or she could finish the laundry, do some chores, and try to get some sleep. She had to work that night, and she hadn't had much sleep the night before. Marc had been on top of her, and inside her, most of the night.

She closed her eyes, breathing deeply as memory curled around her. No matter what, it had been a night to remember. She regretted a lot of things about what had happened, but for a few hours she had been lost in sheer physical ecstasy. Marc had given her more pleasure than she had known it was possible to feel. It was impossible to regret that.

And she loved. She, who thought she had blocked out all love except that for her mother, found that she hadn't blocked anything. Despite everything, she loved her father. There was peace in finally admitting it, in no longer fighting to keep herself closed off. She loved him, ached for the life he had wasted, the love *he* had rejected. She was more like him than she had ever thought, in her reactions, her efforts to seal herself off, and like her mother in that despite all her efforts, she loved anyway.

She suspected this meant she would love Marc for the rest of her life.

Marc was still in a savage mood late that afternoon when he entered his office. He was hot, sweaty, tired, and so pissed off he wanted to tear something apart with his bare hands.

Karen had run from him.

He had expected her to be nervous this morning, maybe a little shy, a little embarrassed. Knowing he was short of time and opportunity, he had taken their intimacy to deeper levels, faster, than he had ever done with a woman before. There wasn't an inch of her body he hadn't touched or kissed in his effort to stake a claim on her that she wouldn't be able to easily dismiss. He had left her asleep in the bed and taken a shower, intending to waken her with kisses, hold her on his lap and pet her, tease her, bring a smile to those too-serious dark eyes—and then make love to her again. But she hadn't been asleep after all; instead, when he came out of the bathroom, she was gone.

She must have run all the way to the hotel; that was the only way she could have avoided him. By the time he got there, she had already checked out by phone, and he hadn't been able to cover all the exits. She had slipped past him again, and a valet in the transportation bay remembered getting her a cab to the airport.

He paged her at the airport, but she hadn't answered. By then, he was so angry she was lucky he *hadn't* been able to catch her. Instead, he called her home phone and left a blistering message; probably not a smart thing to do when he was trying to gentle her out of her skittishness, but her running had rattled him.

The relative coolness of his office washed over his damp skin, wringing a sigh of relief from him. He shed his jacket and rolled his shoulders, unsticking his shirt from his back and raising chill bumps at the sensation. He ran an impatient hand over his hair and the back of his neck. God, he hated child murders. He would rather work a hundred other cases than investigate the death of a child. The helplessness and fragility of the little bodies got to him, hit him hard.

He had a five-year-old little boy in the morgue, dead from a fall down the stairs. An accident, his mother said. But the kid's legs had been covered with small, half-healed burns that she had tried to pass off as mosquito bites, and yellowish bruises had blotched his skin. Yellow bruises were old bruises, healing bruises. He had had an accident on his bicycle, his mother said.

The woman had been terrified. She had sat motionless at the kitchen table, as if she were afraid to move. Once she did turn her head, when her husband said something, and Marc thought he had seen a dark mark on her neck, just under the edge of her collar.

He knew the signs: the blouse buttoned up to the throat, the long sleeves even in sweltering weather, slacks instead of shorts.

Marc no longer wasted time wondering why a woman would stay with an abusive man, or how a mother could be cowed into silence even when her child was killed. He'd been a cop long enough that nothing surprised him. He did know he had to be careful on this case, because the husband was a lawyer and would know if there was a *t* left uncrossed or an *i* undotted. He was also a criminal defense lawyer, which made Marc all the more determined to nail his ass.

The ME would likely discover other evidence of abuse, such as previous fractures. He would determine the marks on the child's legs were from cigarette burns, not mosquito bites, and his report would provide reasonable grounds for arrest. Marc only hoped he would be able to get a warrant before the son of a bitch panicked, knowing his wife would be able to testify against him, and killed her, too.

Marc sat down to listen to his voice mail and leafed through the pile of papers that had accumulated on his desk during his absence. Most of it was routine stuff, notices, memos, reports he had requested.

He had a lot of contacts in the city, a lot of snitches who would gladly roll over on their buddies rather than get on his bad side. Most of the stuff he heard was penny-ante, but sometimes all it took was a detail that fit into an overall picture he already had, and his case was made.

He didn't expect Karen to call, because of the message he had left rather than despite it. It was probably for the best, at this point. When he was completely calm again, he would call her and try to get this courtship back on track.

Her message took him by surprise. He stopped and leaned back in his chair, listening grimly. She sounded subdued. ". . . I thought—never mind. I acted like an idiot, and I'm sorry."

She thought . . . what? She thought too damn much, that was the problem. He could almost hear the worry going on behind the words. The woman didn't know how to relax and have fun, she had to shoulder the responsibility for everything—

"Shit," he growled, puffing out his cheeks. He should have guessed she would wake up kicking herself for what she would consider wildly irresponsible behavior. He'd been so careful not to spook her before he could get her into bed, she had no idea he was planning anything more than a one-night stand. Leaving her alone in bed while he showered had been a major tactical error, one he would remember.

The sexual chemistry between them was so hot it took his breath, and it was even more bewitching because he had known immediately she wasn't very experienced. Not ignorant, not virgin, but not . . . accustomed to making love. He suspected she controlled her sexuality as fiercely as she controlled her emotions. But last night, she had relaxed her control and turned into the sweetest, hottest woman he'd ever had in his bed. He hadn't known he could get a hard-on that often, but hell, he hadn't had any choice. She had been in dire need of loving, and he had risen to the occasion.

He *was* experienced, and their lovemaking had been more intense than anything he'd known before. The night must have seemed like nothing less than debauchery to her.

He reached for the phone to call her, then stopped. His temper had cooled, but he was still angry, and his own control was a little shaky after dealing with that little boy's murder. He needed to talk to her as soon as possible, so she wouldn't have time to buttress her resistance to him, but that need was balanced by caution. He wanted to yell at her, and yelling wasn't a good idea right now. She would withdraw even further and maybe refuse to talk to him again.

He forced himself to continue reading the notices from other police forces, flipping through the computer printouts. He paused when he saw the Mississippi state police had reported a body found just across the state line from Louisiana. The victim, a white male age fifty-seven, name of Rick Medina, had been shot twice with a .22; his money and credit cards had been stolen.

People were shot with .22s all the time; it was the most common of handguns. It was instinct alone that made him pull the report out of the stack. Maybe it was nothing, but this victim was approximately the same age as Karen's father, and Mississippi wasn't that far away.

He had his hands full with the little boy's case right now; he didn't have time to chase down such a tenuous, and probably nonexistent, connection. Still, he couldn't ignore it.

He found Shannon standing by the cold drink machine, flirting with one of the clerks. "Hey, Antonio."

Shannon straightened, his dark eyes alert. "See you later," he said to the woman, touching her arm as he left her. "What's up?" he asked, ranging himself beside Marc and tilting his head to read the sheet.

Marc handed it to him. "I've got to stay with the Gable case—"

"Oh, yeah, the little boy. His sonofabitch father killed the kid, didn't he?"

"Yeah, but I've got to do everything by the book, or

he'll walk. Do you have time to do some checking for me?"

"Sure." Shannon read the report. "You got something on this Rick Medina?"

"No, it's just a hunch. See if you can find any connection between Dexter Whitlaw and Rick Medina. They're about the same age; maybe they were in the military together. If they knew each other, it's coincidental as hell that they would both be killed with a .22 at about the same time."

"It's a long shot," Shannon said.

"Sure is," Marc agreed. "Just check to see if Medina was in the military, maybe served somewhere the same time Whitlaw did. Who knows what will turn up?"

Chapter 12

The patient in 11-A had survived an auto accident and extensive surgery to repair the damage, losing a kidney and his spleen in the process. His surgeon had deemed him well enough to be transferred out of SICU to the regular surgical floor, the patient being alert and stable, eating light but solid foods, his remaining kidney producing urine at a normal rate. His temperature was climbing, however, and he had declined to eat his evening meal.

The surgeon on duty had managed to hide himself where no one could find him, and he wasn't answering his page. Karen put in a call to Mr. Gibbons's surgeon and kept a close watch on the patient. If he had picked up a post-op infection, the sooner they caught it, the better. Concern over Mr. Gibbons kept her from brooding. It felt good to be back on the floor, in the familiar world of tile floors, medicinal smells, and beeping monitors. Her name tag was pinned to her short-sleeved tunic, the pockets of which were jammed with various bits of paraphernalia that might or might not come in handy. Her stethoscope was slung around her neck, and her rubber-soled shoes squeaked on the tile as she walked. Familiar. Good.

Despite her expectations, she had managed to grab several hours' sleep before coming to work. She didn't know whether to be glad of the sleep or sorry Marc hadn't called and disturbed her. Evidently, he had decided just to drop the matter, which, when she thought about it, was the most sensible thing to do. They had slept together, she had made a fool of herself, but it was over. He was in Louisiana. She was back home in Ohio, where she belonged. Maybe one day she would be in a reminiscent mood and tell Piper about the hot night she had spent with a New Orleans detective. Piper would be vastly relieved; in her opinion, Karen's love life was a contradiction in terms, because where there was life, there had to be activity.

Mr. Gibbons's surgeon finally called right before Karen went on break. As expected, he was grumpy. In the general opinion of nurses, all surgeons were assholes, but Dr. Pierini was a logical asshole. "Mr. Gibbons's temp is a hundred point eight," she said. "At midnight, it was ninety-nine point seven."

"Shit." He yawned. "Okay. I want a culture so we can see what's going on here. Tell the lab I want the results when I do morning rounds." He rattled off more instructions, then said, "Where the hell is Dailey?"

"Dr. Dailey isn't answering his page."

"Well, find him, god damn it, instead of calling me."

He slammed the phone down, but Karen shrugged as she hung up. She had gotten what she wanted, and whenever she woke someone up at three o'clock in the morning, she was inclined to cut him a little slack. She would be more than happy to find Dr. Dailey, if it were possible. No nurse on the surgical floor had ever performed that miracle, however.

She would be even happier if someone shoved a wire up Dr. Dailey's patootie, so she could hit a buzzer whenever she needed him and light up his life. He could then be found by following the yelps.

The nurses' break room was habitually strewn with newspapers and magazines, and the refrigerator harbored new life forms that no one wanted to investigate too closely. Four folding chairs sat around a small round table, and a lumpy sofa, covered in noxious orange vinyl, completed the furniture. A nineteen-inch television hung on the wall, but the video portion had been lost for several months, and the nurses had a lot of fun trying to figure out what was happening by listening to the dialogue and special effects.

Karen took a diet soda from the refrigerator and plopped down on Big Val, short for Valencia, as the orange sofa was not so affectionately known. Sighing with relief, she arched her feet and stretched her tired Achilles tendons and wished she had a basin of cold water in which to soak them. She would have liked to pull off her shoes but knew better; the feet would swell immediately, then she would have trouble getting her shoes back on, and they would be too tight for the rest of the shift.

Several days' worth of newspapers were scattered on the floor. Leaning over, Karen grabbed up several sections to see if anything exciting had happened while she had been gone. She doubted it, but maybe "Dilbert" hadn't been clipped out of the comic page. The cartoons had a way of winding up on bulletin boards in the hospital, with hospital employees' names penciled in. Administration didn't think it was funny.

She leafed through the papers, scanning headlines and photo captions. One photograph grabbed her attention because something about the burned shell of a house looked familiar. "A fire yesterday morning destroyed the residence of Nathan and Lindsey Hoerske—" Why, that was *her* house! Shocked, she stared at the blackened ruins in the photograph. It *had been* her house, rather. She had lived in that house for fifteen years. Oh, the poor Hoerskes, just married and so happy to have their own house. They had lost everything they owned, from the look of it. The newspaper said the fire started in the kitchen.

Almost as rattled as if she had lost an old friend, Karen laid the newspaper aside. House fires were never just about lost property, they were about memories and dreams. The fabrics of lives were woven together within the protective walls that provided sanctuary from the rest of the world. She had liked Nathan and Lindsey; though she had made up her mind to sell the house anyway, she was glad they were the ones who bought it. They had seemed so much in love, but settled, as if they had found their groove in life and nothing could jar them out of it. Karen had imagined them having a couple of kids, the rooms cluttered with toys and resounding with the happy, high-pitched shrieks of children at play. Now they would have to start over, find another place to think of as home.

Piper breezed onto the floor at six-thirty. She put her hands on her ample hips when she saw Karen. "Why didn't you call me?" she demanded, scowling.

"I didn't have time." Impulsively, Karen put down the chart she was notating and hugged Piper in apology. "The airline could only get me on a flight that was leaving in an hour. I just grabbed my clothes, called Judy, and ran."

"Well, I guess I'll excuse you," Piper grumbled, returning the hug. "I'm sorry, honey. It had to be rough, even though I know you weren't close to your father. What happened?"

"He was murdered. Shot."

Piper gasped, shocked, and the two other nurses at the station turned around with arrested expressions on their faces. Karen swallowed the lump in her throat. "It was a street shooting. There weren't any witnesses."

Piper blew out a breath. "Jeez, that's tough. Maybe you should have taken off another couple of days."

"No, working is easier." It always had been. If she could keep herself occupied, she could handle anything.

"Why don't you come stay with me for a few days—"

Karen rolled her eyes, then laughed. "You work days; I work nights. What would be the point?"

"Yeah, guess you're right." Piper pondered the situation. She was big-boned with a mop of short black curls and the most friendly face in creation. Just looking at her could make a patient feel better, not because she was a great beauty but because her good humor literally shone out of her. Her love life, unlike Karen's, was more active than Mauna Loa volcano. "Until you transfer back to days, you're on your own."

"Gee, thanks." Karen chuckled at the blithe callousness and hummed a familiar tune.

"I'll be there for youuuu," the two nurses behind her sang in unison.

Piper picked up a stapler and brandished it at them.

"You *can* be attached to those chairs for another shift, you know."

Judy Camliffe walked up, her stride brisk. "Hi, guys. Karen, you all right?"

Only a few days before, such concern, even from Piper, would have made Karen uncomfortable. Now, however, there didn't seem to be much point in trying to wall herself off; her defenses already had been breached. Despite all her caution and efforts, Marc had slipped through them like a hot knife through butter. And despite all the years she had spent building a wall of anger against her father, she had learned that she wouldn't have been so angry if she hadn't loved him.

She smiled at her friends. "I don't know if I'm all right, exactly, but working is better than not working." She paused. "Thanks for asking."

Judy nodded her dark head, then turned to the pile of charts. "Okay, what's cooking?"

Karen filled her in on Mr. Gibbons's worrisome fever, which was now up to a hundred one point three. Lab hadn't called with results of the blood tests, and Dr. Pierini was due to start his rounds in half an hour.

"I'll goose them a little," Judy said, reaching for the phone. "Oh, I found out what was wrong with Ashley."

"Diarrhea, you said."

"Yeah, but what caused it." She turned her attention to the phone. "Oh, hi, this is Judy on the surgical floor. Do you have anything yet on the Gibbons culture? Sure." On hold, she turned her attention back to them. "She thought it was food poisoning the first time it happened, and she raised hell in the cafeteria, but no one else had been sick, so they ignored her. This time, she narrowed it down. Jelly beans."

"Jelly beans?" Piper looked aghast. She loved pop-corn Jelly Bellies.

"She's on a diet, so she bought some sugar-free jelly beans for a snack when she went to a movie. Four hours later, the runs started." Judy snuggled the phone more comfortably between her neck and shoulder. "She went shopping yesterday, bought some more jelly beans, the same thing happened. This time, the jelly beans were all she had eaten. She said she bloated with gas and the cramps were awful."

"On the other hand," Piper said practically, "she probably did lose weight."

They all laughed. "Yeah," Judy said, "but she said it wasn't worth it." She turned her attention back to the phone. "Look, is there anything you can do to rush this along? The patient's temp is climbing. This may be staph. Okay. Thanks. I'll call back." She hung up and said to Karen, "They promised to have the results in another fifteen minutes."

"It usually takes them double the time they promise. They *might* have the results before Dr. Pierini starts his rounds, if he's running late." Karen glanced up the hallway as a doctor appeared, frowning as he studied a chart. It was the elusive Dr. Dailey, appearing for all the world as if he had been working hard all night. "What brand were those jelly beans?"

"Karen, honey, you don't want to go there," Judy warned.

"Oh, they're not for me. I was thinking of giving some to Dr. Dailey—for therapeutic reasons, of course."

"Of course," they all chorused, smiling, because the unanimous diagnosis among the nursing staff was that Dr. Dailey was full of shit.

* * *

Karen looked at her answering machine as soon as she entered the apartment. The little red light wasn't blinking. Well, it wouldn't be, she scolded herself. Marc knew she worked nights. If he hadn't called earlier, he certainly wouldn't have called in the middle of the night.

Sighing, she locked the door and headed for the shower. He had no reason to call, anyway, unless he wanted to swear at her some more. It was over. It had never even really started. There hadn't been any comments about seeing her again, only that relentless seduction. He had achieved his purpose, and now she had to let go of it, stop worrying the situation in her mind. It was over, she told herself emphatically.

But it didn't feel over. Marc had changed her view of herself. Standing in the shower, she was acutely aware of her body, in a way she hadn't been before. She felt . . . sensual. Female. Her nipples beaded under the pelting water, and she thought of Marc's mouth on them. She remembered the way his hard, callused hands had curved around her waist, her bottom, effortlessly lifting and turning her, positioning her for his pleasure, and hers. Her insides clenched on the swell of sexual arousal, and she could almost feel him there, thrusting into her.

Wow. She blew out a breath. Every woman should have a lover like him, just once in her life.

But she didn't want it to be just once. She wanted him again, every night for the rest of her life.

The question was, what should she do about it? It was hell, not knowing where she stood. She had doubts about his motives, about his feelings, about everything concerning that night except her own emotions, and in her experience emotions weren't a stable foundation on which to base important decisions.

Her experience—hah! Her experience in this man/woman stuff was nil. She had never loved a man before Marc.

The water had been getting progressively less warm, but all of a sudden there was nothing but cold water pouring from the showerhead. Stifling a shriek, Karen jumped out of the spray. She didn't know how long she had been standing there mooning over Marc, but it was long enough to exhaust the hot water supply. Hastily, she turned off the water, then wrapped a towel around her. She shivered as she dried off and hurried into a robe.

The inadvertent cold shower had dispelled her sleepiness, which was good; she handled night shift better if she waited several hours after getting home before she went to bed. She could watch the morning news, catch up on her mail, pay bills, do all the normal stuff. And just for fun, she might paint her toenails a daring scarlet, instead of the discreet pink she normally used.

Carl Clancy wasn't in any hurry. He had checked further than the phone book this time. Hell, how was he to have known the Whitlaw woman had sold the house but the new phone book wouldn't be issued until December with her corrected address in it? But he had found where she was living now, even discovered that she was a nurse at one of the local hospitals.

The question was, was she at home or not? Hospitals were twenty-four-hour operations, but he hadn't been able to find out what shift she worked, not without bringing a lot of attention to himself. People tended to remember someone asking specific questions about a particular person.

He looked at his watch. Eight-thirty. If she worked

first shift, she was now at the hospital. If she worked second, she should be getting up; third, going to bed.

He called the hospital, asked for her. He didn't have enough information about her, didn't know what floor she worked, but it didn't matter. The bitch who answered the phone replied in a frosty voice that nurses weren't allowed personal phone calls while on duty, except in case of an emergency. That was bullshit. Every floor had its own number, and the nurses made and received personal phone calls all the time. But rather than make a stink, he apologized and hung up. Dead end.

Next, he called her. After the screw-up in burning the wrong house, he had checked with the phone company and found that the number in the book was still the correct number; her new digs were within the same exchange area, so the number had simply been transferred with her. She might have the phone turned off so it wouldn't disturb her if she was trying to sleep, but that was a chance he had to take.

The rings sounded in his ear.

Karen's head came up when the phone rang. Her heart leaped, and she started to grab the phone, but then she remembered Marc knew she worked nights. He wouldn't be calling now, would he? Or maybe he would, thinking this was a good time to catch her at home, and it was still early enough that she might not have gone to bed yet.

She hesitated long enough that the answering machine picked up. Almost immediately, the caller hung up, and the message stopped. Not Marc, then. He would have left a message. Disappointment made her sick, but she shrugged it away. She wasn't going to spend her life waiting for him to call. If he hadn't called by tomorrow, she would call him. By running out the way she had, she had put herself in this quandary of not knowing if they'd had a simple one-night stand or if there could be something more between them. It was her fault, so she shouldn't balk at taking the first step.

Modern courtship was the pits, she decided, assuming this even *was* a courtship. Things had been much simpler when men declared their intentions, and the women then stepped out with them or not, signaling their own acceptance or rejection of the suit. She liked the orderliness of that, the emotional safety. Women's liberation had been great in terms of opening up jobs and beginning to equal out pay, but darned if the old social rituals didn't seem a lot better than the confused mess they had now.

Karen regarded her toes. Scarlet polish just did something for a woman's feet, she decided. A woman with red toenails wouldn't hesitate to call a man if they had an important, unresolved situation. Tonight, she decided. She didn't want to call him now and get all upset or excited, then not be able to sleep. If he didn't call today, she would call him tonight. And if he told her to take a long walk off a short pier—well, at least she would know and would be able to move on with her life.

Carl Clancy sighed. Okay, she hadn't answered the phone. She was either gone or asleep. If he had another day, he would be able to find out everything he needed to know, but Hayes was pushing him to get the apartment searched *now*.

He hoped she was at work. If she was at home, he would have to kill her.

Chapter 13

"You Antonio Shannon?"

Shannon looked up from his desk at the big, homely man who stood in front of him. "Yeah, I'm Shannon. What can I do for you?"

"My name's McPherson." He reached into his jacket and produced a leather ID folder, snapping it open with the practiced flip of the wrist that said Fed. Shannon took his time studying the ID. It looked official, but why would an FBI agent want to talk to him?

"First off," McPherson said quietly, "I'm not here in any official capacity. This is purely personal. A friend of mine got killed in Mississippi, and you put in a request for information about him. Rick Medina. Do you have any leads on who might have killed him?"

Shannon rubbed his jaw. Whatever response he might have expected to his request about information on the Mississippi murder victim, he sure hadn't expected an in-the-flesh visit from a Fed. That meant his little request had set off alarms somewhere. McPherson might or might not be acting in an official capacity, regardless of what he said. The victim in Mississippi might or might not have been this man's friend. It didn't matter. Rick Medina, whoever he had been, had some hot-shit connections.

"We don't know anything about that murder," he said slowly. "We were actually looking for something that would help us with one of our murder cases." He stood. "I think you need to talk to Detective Chastain."

Marc was on the phone with the ME. The child's autopsy was scheduled in an hour. His stomach tightened with anger at the thought of it, at the memory of the child's frail little body and matchstick bones. This was one of the times he wished he didn't have to adhere to the law; he would like nothing better than to kill the child's father with his bare hands, slowly, bone by bone and burn by burn, as he had tortured that child.

He had just hung up when Shannon entered with a tall, lanky, middle-aged man who nevertheless looked in remarkably good shape for his age. "This is Mr. McPherson with the FBI," Shannon said.

Marc shook hands, feeling the strength in the older man's grip. "I doubt it," he said mildly.

Shannon looked startled. McPherson gave a faint smile. "I have an ID that says so."

Marc shrugged. "I imagine you do. But if I call the local FBI office and have you checked out, what will they tell me?" If this man was an FBI agent, he was the first one Marc had ever seen who lacked that spit-and-polished look, an image the older agents clung to even more strongly than the younger ones. The differences were subtle: a haircut that wasn't quite short enough, a tie that was a little too individual and stylish. And his shoes were black Gucci loafers, which was a little out of the price range of most FBI agents. On the other hand, he was wearing a shoulder piece, though the cut of his jacket was good enough that it almost hid the bulge of the weapon.

The smile on that homely face grew to a grin. "I would tell you to go ahead and make that call, but hell, you'd probably do it. What gave me away? The shoes?"

"Among other things. The shoes were the clincher."

"It was worth a shot. Most people, even cops, aren't going to notice the shoes."

Shannon was looking in bewilderment at the shoes in question. "What's wrong with them?"

"They're Guccis," Marc explained.

Shannon still looked bewildered. "They're expensive," Marc enlarged. "Federal agents normally couldn't afford them." He looked back at his visitor. "So who are you, and why are you impersonating a federal agent?" He didn't add that doing so was against the law; this man already knew that quite well.

"My name really is McPherson."

"Then you won't mind if I check it out."

The older man sighed. "Son, have you always been such a bulldog? Do you mind if I sit down? I can see this is going to take longer than I planned."

"Please, have a seat," Marc invited, with a sardonic bite to his tone.

"Thanks, don't mind if I do." He folded his long length onto one of the chairs.

"You too, Antonio," Marc said. "But shut the door first."

Shannon shut the door and took the other seat, but

he positioned it so he was at an angle to McPherson. He was sharp; he might not know Guccis, but he had definitely spotted the weapon.

"Okay, I'm not with the FBI," McPherson said easily. Marc noted that he didn't seem worried—grimly amused, maybe, but not worried. "But I do work for the federal government, and the rest of what I told Detective Shannon is the truth. He requested information on the murder of Rick Medina in Mississippi, and that made me think he might know something about the case that the cops there weren't telling me. Rick was a friend of mine. I'm not here in any official capacity. It's personal. If you have any information concerning his murder, I'd appreciate it if you would tell me what it is."

Picking up a pen, Marc turned it end over end while he considered what the man had said. If he wasn't worried about impersonating a federal agent, which was a crime and he had just admitted doing so to a cop, then likely he did indeed work for the federal government in another capacity, one that he was certain would give him immunity from prosecution. National Security Agency, maybe, or CIA.

"Which agency?" he asked, still watching the pen.

The man smothered a curse and a sigh. "You know, this isn't something that generally comes out in conversation."

"No, I don't expect so. Satellites or pickles?"

"Are you speaking English?" Shannon wondered aloud.

McPherson answered. "What he means is, he thinks I must work for either National Security or the CIA. The National Security Agency deals mostly with satellites, that kind of stuff. The CIA is known, sometimes affectionately, as the pickle factory. He knows a lot, for a local cop."

Marc waited. He didn't have anything to tell McPherson about his friend's murder, and he did think McPherson was telling the truth about Medina being his friend. But something was niggling at him, an uneasiness or maybe even an awareness, as if he were about to put a piece of the puzzle in place if only he could turn it the right way.

"Was Medina one of you?" he asked.

"In a way. He did some jobs for us. He wasn't, however, working for us when he was killed."

"You would say that anyway." CIA, then, Marc figured. Otherwise, he wouldn't have bothered making a point about the victim not working for them at the time, since he had been murdered in the States.

"Of course I would. But it's true. We're in the dark on this, and Rick wasn't just a friend, he was a good friend." McPherson's eyes darkened. "It's damn hard to believe some punk wanting some quick cash for drugs could have gotten the drop on him like that and then not even take the car. It just doesn't feel right."

No, it didn't. Medina had evidently been very good at his job. Marc thought of what he had learned from Dexter Whitlaw's military records: Whitlaw had been a Marine sniper in Vietnam, and he had evidently been very good at his job, too.

"Did you," he said slowly, watching McPherson's face, "also know Dexter Whitlaw?"

McPherson stiffened, his eyes going flat and unreadable. "I know him. Are you saying you suspect him of killing Medina?"

"No. He was killed over on St. Ann the same day as Medina. Whitlaw was shot with a twenty-two. Did Medina and Whitlaw know each other?"

"Yeah. We all were in Vietnam at the same time." McPherson leaned back in the uncomfortable chair, pulling at his lower lip while he stared unseeingly at a spot on the floor. "So Dex is dead, too. Rick and Dex both. Same day, same caliber weapon."

"That's pushing coincidence a little too far," Marc said. "They know each other, they die the same day only a short distance apart, both killed with a twenty-two. Were they, say, maybe in the same line of work in Vietnam? And who would want both of them dead?"

"That's an interesting question." McPherson worried at his lip some more. "I'd like to know the answer to that myself. But, yeah, in a way they were in the same line of work. Both of 'em were damn good at it, too."

"Mr. Whitlaw was living on the streets, but he wasn't a bum; he was healthy, well fed, not on drugs or booze, so he had some means of income that I haven't been able to discover. Did Mr. Medina come down here to meet him, and if so, why?"

"No one knows what Rick was doing here. Personal business, he said."

"Then we still don't know anything. We can compare the slugs, see if they were killed with the same weapon, but unless you know something you aren't telling us, we're still at a dead end."

"I wish I did know something," McPherson said heavily. "Anything. Because this does smell real bad, but damn if I know why."

The noise was slight, little more than a rustle. Karen paused, her head tilting as she listened for a repeat of the small, odd sound. She was in the bedroom, plucking yellowed leaves off the potted ficus tree she had placed in front of the window.

There. A whisper, like fabric. And from a different location.

188

Someone was in the apartment.

Her scalp prickled, and a jolt of sheer terror made her heart almost freeze in her chest. She didn't move, couldn't move.

The bedroom door was open. She stood to the side, out of a direct line of vision, but if anyone came into the bedroom, he would see her immediately, and she was trapped against the wall. The only way out of the bedroom was that door. Her apartment was on the second floor, so she couldn't even climb out the window. It was a sheer drop to the ground, too far to jump.

He came to the bedroom door. She couldn't see him, just the faint shadow he threw across the floor. If she hadn't been looking, she never would have noticed. Karen's chest constricted, preventing her from doing more than draw in quick, shallow breaths. She couldn't move, couldn't even have screamed.

He didn't come in. After standing there for a moment, looking in, he walked on toward the kitchen, this time making much more noise, as if he thought there was no need now to be quiet.

Her ears rang, and her bedroom tilted oddly. Karen forced herself to take a deep breath, silently dragging in oxygen past the tightness in her lungs. Why had he gone on? Why was he making so much noise now?

She stared at her neatly made bed, and slowly it dawned on her: he thought the apartment was empty. The curtains were open, since she hadn't yet gone to bed, so the room was flooded with sunlight, and she had no need to turn on a lamp. There were, she realized, no lights on in the apartment at all for that very reason. The television wasn't on; she had watched it for a little while, but the morning shows hadn't been very interesting, so she had turned it off again after a few minutes. She hadn't been making any noise while she plucked the dying leaves from the ficus tree; to all intents and purposes, the apartment must seem empty to the invader.

She heard him systematically opening and closing drawers in the kitchen, prowling in the refrigerator—God, was he *hungry?* She should get out of the apartment, that's what all the experts said. Don't confront a burglar, just get out if you could, and call the cops once you were safe.

The eating area of the kitchen had a clear view of the living room. If he were there, he would be able to see her making for the door. What if he had a gun? He could shoot her where she stood.

All of a sudden, she felt calm—or at least much calmer. Whether or not he was armed, she had a better chance of getting through this unharmed if she got out of the apartment. She eased toward the bedroom door, her bare feet silent on the carpet.

Just as she came even with the door, she heard his footsteps approach the eating area. She froze one step short of stepping into view. Once again, her breath hung in her chest, caught on the icy shards of terror. If he came on into the living room—

But furniture scraped across tile, and she knew he was still in the eating area. Her brow furrowed. It sounded as if he were turning all the chairs upside down.

Surely that wasn't normal behavior for a burglar. Look for valuables, take the television and small stereo, and get out. But he hadn't even come into the bedroom to look for jewelry, which was where most women kept their valuable bits and pieces.

She slid that one step more, framed in the doorway but staying far enough back that she could see only a small portion of the eating area. She saw the legs of a chair sticking out. He *was* turning them all upside down.

He was looking for something . . . something in particular.

Get out and then call, the advice went. She looked at the phone by the bed. The apartment was too quiet; the only sounds were that of the refrigerator running and the noises he was making. If she called 911, she would have to whisper, and he might be able to hear even that. If she didn't say anything, would they send someone out anyway? Could 911 pinpoint individual apartments?

It didn't matter if they could or not, she realized, so long as they came with sirens blasting.

Damn him, he was *searching* her apartment. Abruptly, the terror left her, and other emotions flooded through her. She felt outraged, violated. He was looking through her things, disturbing the tentative feelings of home she was beginning to form. This was the only home she had now; the house she had always considered home, still thought of as home, was nothing but a burned-out shell. She wasn't going to abandon her home to this bastard.

Karen took a step back, away from the doorway. Gently, so gently, moving slow and easy the way her father had taught her to walk in the woods, she eased toward the telephone. Not turning her back on the doorway, she carefully lifted the receiver out of the cradle and shoved it under her pillow to muffle the noise of the dial tone. Then she punched 911, wincing at the faint click of the buttons.

A weapon. She needed a weapon. But she didn't own a handgun, and the knives were all in the kitchen. When he finished the rest of the apartment and came into the bedroom, he would see the phone under the pillow and know someone was there, hiding. She would lose the element of surprise, which was the only advantage she had, so she had to find something before then.

There was nothing in the bedroom she could use, unless she wanted to hit him with her purse, which was sitting beside the chair in the corner—another dead giveaway of her presence, if he happened to see it.

Quickly, she did a mental inventory of the bathroom. The disposable shavers she used wouldn't send him screaming in fright, unless he had a phobia about being shaved. The worst damage one of those shavers could do was a shallow slice. She had perfume, hairspray . . . hairspray. That was it. He would have to get close, but a gun was the only weapon that afforded distance. She wouldn't have had that luxury even with a knife.

The bathroom door was open only halfway. Karen sidled toward it, taking care not to brush against anything. Her heart was pounding so hard she could feel her pulse throbbing in her fingertips, but she felt calmer now, more purposeful.

The door hinges creaked at the least movement, she remembered. She couldn't touch the door.

The carpet seemed to drag at her feet. The distance was only a few steps, but it felt like yards. She was in full view of the open bedroom door if the man came far enough into the living room to look through it. How much longer would he be occupied in the kitchen? How many places in a kitchen were there to search? He had already looked in the cabinets and drawers, the refrigerator, under the chairs and table. The only place now to occupy him before he came back into the living room was a small closet to the right of the doorway before you went into the kitchen. If he was methodical, that would be the next place he would search.

Please, let him be methodical, she prayed.

The bathroom door wasn't open as much as she had hoped. She eyed the narrow opening. It looked *too* narrow, large enough to let a child slip through, but she wasn't a child. Still, she had lost weight. Maybe she could do it—maybe.

Have a plan, just in case.

In the kitchen, he began putting the chairs upright again, sliding them into place. He was a neat burglar, as if he didn't want her to know he had been inside her home. His neatness gave her a few seconds of warning.

She took several quick, silent breaths, visualizing what she was going to do. The hairspray was sitting on the left side of the vanity. The towel hung on a bar on the right. Grab the towel with her right hand, pick up the hairspray can with her left, use the towel to muffle the sound of the cap coming off. She wished *she* were less neat and had tossed the cap as soon as she bought the spray. She never threw away any cap, though, until the container was empty.

She exhaled to collapse her chest and sucked in her stomach. Pressing her back hard against the doorway, so hard the edge scraped her skin, she sidled through.

Her breast just brushed the door; the hinges gave a single, small squeal.

She didn't stop. Freezing now could be disastrous, if he had heard that betraying squeak. She slipped into the small, dark bathroom, grabbing the towel with her right hand and the hairspray can with her left. She didn't bang against anything, just moved smoothly and quietly. After wrapping the towel around the cap, she twisted it off. That, too, made a slight sound, less carrying than the creak of the hinges.

Turning around, she faced the bathroom door, standing just where she wouldn't be visible through either the opening or the crack. Quickly, she checked behind her, to make certain the mirror couldn't be seen, but from the angle of the open door, all that was visible was the tub and shower enclosure.

Holding the can in her left hand with the nozzle pointed outward, she waited. She didn't like being caught in this tiny space, but after the squeak of the hinges, she didn't dare step out into the bedroom again. She already knew he could move quietly, because she hadn't heard him enter the apartment. He could be standing on the other side of the door, playing cat and mouse, silently waiting for her to come out.

Her scalp prickled again. She could almost feel him there, a patient, malevolent presence.

But she could be patient, too. The one who moves first is the one who loses, her father had said. How could she remember all this? She had been only a child, and he was a scary stranger, though she knew he was her father. But he had talked, showing her how to be a successful sniper, and she had listened. She didn't have a gun in her hand, only a can of hairspray, but that knowledge had been her father's legacy to her, and perhaps now it would save her life.

She didn't hear any sounds coming from the living room. If he hadn't heard the hinges, he would be searching as he had before, moving about normally, making noise. The apartment was silent; he had heard her.

She gauged the distance to the door. If he shoved it

open, it would hit her, knocking her off balance and ruining her aim. Silently, she stepped back against the vanity, hoping that would be enough clearance. She raised the can and waited.

She had a slight advantage in that she *knew* he was there. He suspected her presence, but he didn't know—unless he had noticed her purse. Or the telephone under the pillow. *Oh, God.*

Picture what you're going to do, Dexter had said. Be prepared to do it without warning. Don't hesitate, or your ass is dead.

Karen didn't want her ass to be dead. She wanted to live a long, long time—

The door crashed violently inward. Instantly, she extended her arm and sprayed at the head of the menacing shape silhouetted in the doorway. "Aghh!" He staggered back, his hands going to his eyes. One of those hands held a gun.

Karen hit him in a rush, shoving him with all her strength and sending him sprawling backward across the bed. He grabbed at her, catching her gown and pulling her with him. She screamed, hoping the sound would go through the pillow and that the 911 operator was still on the line. He rolled, pinning her down; she saw his contorted face, his red and streaming eyes, and she hit him with another blast of the hairspray. She missed his eyes, and the spray went up his nose. He choked, gagging. She sprayed him again, kicking violently, squirming, hitting him in the face with her right fist. Her foot hit the lamp and knocked it off with a crash, the ceramic base shattering.

"You . . . bitch!" he howled. Blinded, he struck out with his fist and caught her on the cheekbone. The impact bounced her head on the mattress, blurred her vision. She wasn't aware of pain, only of the stunning force of the blow. She hit him across the nose with the can, splitting the skin and sending blood spraying across her and the bed. She managed to get her legs up and kicked out with both of them as hard as she could, one foot hitting him in the stomach and the other lower, almost in the groin. He staggered back, his breath exploding out of him. Karen rolled off the bed, scrambling on her hands and knees for the door. He pulled the trigger then, enraged, cursing, but he couldn't see, and the bullet punched a hole in the wall above her head, sending plaster flying.

The carpet burned her knees as she lunged through the door. Panting, her vision still blurred, she staggered to her feet and lurched for the front door. Another shot exploded through the wall.

She wrenched the door open as he stumbled out of the bedroom. Wiping his sleeve across his streaming eyes, he raised his arm. Karen dove out the door, sprawling in the hallway and rolling as she hit. The shot splintered the door. She surged to her feet, stumbled for the stairs, and ran into two policemen who were coming up the steps with their weapons drawn, faces white.

Dizzily, she sank to the floor. Down the hall, she saw a blurred face in the doorway of one of the other three apartments on this floor. "Get down!" she gasped.

Hearing her voice, the burglar staggered through the door, arms extended, pistol in a two-handed grip. Both policemen reacted instantly, firing so close together that the two shots sounded like one. The impact of the bullets slammed the burglar back against the wall, and for an instant a look of mild surprise crossed his face. He looked down at the red stain spreading across his chest, blinking his streaming eyes as he tried to focus them.

"Drop the gun! Drop it!" both policemen yelled.

The burglar laughed. The sound gurgled in his throat, but it was a laugh. "Fuck you," he said, and lifted his pistol, pointing it in Karen's direction. He pulled the trigger just as both policemen fired again.

Chapter 14

McPherson punched in a number on his secure cell phone. "This thing is getting curiouser and curiouser," he said when the call was answered. "Dexter Whitlaw was killed the same day in New Orleans, which isn't all that far from where Rick's body was found, same caliber weapon. The detective working the case is a sharp son of a bitch; he made me the minute I walked in his office. He put in the request for info on Rick on a hunch. I'd say he's got a hell of an instinct."

"Who's Dexter Whitlaw?" said the voice on the other end. "I don't know him."

"He was a Marine sniper in Vietnam, damn good one. Sneaky son of a bitch. Patient. He could outwait the second coming of Christ. Anyway, we got acquainted with Dex in Saigon, and he and Rick were . . . well, I don't know that I'd go so far as to say friends, but they respected each other, you know?"

"So he and Dad met up in New Orleans."

"Seems like it. Don't know why, though. But it made someone nervous, someone who didn't want the two of them together."

"That means it was someone who knew both of them." The voice was cool, unemotional.

"I'd even say it was someone who knew them from Nam. As far as I know, Dex dropped out of sight after he got back from Nam. Couldn't handle it; went native. The detective said he'd been living on the streets but evidently had a source of income because he was healthy and well fed."

"His family probably sent money to him. I'll check out his next of kin. Has Vinay found his leak yet?"

"No, and he's damn pissed."

"I'll stay outside channels when I talk to him. About this detective. He made you. Does this need taking care of?"

"Only if you're thinking of recruiting him—which wouldn't be a bad idea, by the way. He looked at my shoes and pegged me for NSA or the Company. He's that sharp, that quick. He doesn't need two twos to come up with four."

A sigh came over the line. "Those damn Guccis."

"I couldn't see buying wingtips for the occasion."

"So you think we should use him as an asset?"

"Unless you recruit him outright."

"He might be more valuable where he is."

"Agreed." The Gulf Coast cities were prime gun-running ports. Knowing when and where the weapons were going could give their analysts valuable insight on where the next brush-fire war was going to pop up. Sometimes the fire needed to be lit, sometimes it didn't. Sometimes the shipments would be inter-cepted, sometimes they wouldn't.

"The funeral is at two tomorrow. Will you be here?"

"Unless you need me to do something else." With John, you never knew. He was like a spider, pulling on six invisible threads at the same time.

"It will be interesting to see who's around."

Meaning who would be surveilling the funeral to ID John. Just getting a photograph of him would be worth a lot of money to a lot of people and quite a few governments. There was always the possibility that Rick had been killed for no other reason than to draw John into a public situation. Not that any photograph of him tomorrow would be worth a shit. McPherson had known John most of his life, and he probably wouldn't recognize him tomorrow even if he was standing right next to him. "Will Vinay have a net on the area?"

"I'd like an extra set of eyes. Someone closer in."

And *that* meant John hadn't ruled out an inside job. At this point, he hadn't ruled out anything, though the information about Dex Whitlaw meant the possibility that Rick had simply been the victim of a robbery/murder was just about down the tubes. As Detective Chastain had said, that was straining coincidence a little too far.

But John was a cool, subtle thinker, which was what made him so dangerous and so valuable. He weighed probabilities, percentages, possibilities, saw shadows and details others missed. Jess McPherson didn't completely trust many people, but John Medina was one of them. Frank Vinay was another. And Rick Medina had been on that list as well. Losing him hurt.

"I'll be there," he said gruffly, and disconnected.

* * *

Marc checked his watch: nine forty-five. The small, pitiful body on the autopsy table was telling a tale of horror, of a short life spent in pain and terror. He had checked the area hospitals and come up with a list of visits to the emergency departments that made him cringe. Little James Blake Gable had already had ten "accidents" this year, accidents serious enough to warrant medical attention. The Gables had avoided attention by using a different hospital each time. One of the doctors should have picked up on the signs of systematic abuse, but no one had.

What about the families? Hadn't either Mr. or Mrs. Gable's family noticed something was wrong? Hadn't they noticed their grandson was slowly being murdered or that Mrs. Gable had become reclusive? Sure they had. What Marc couldn't understand was how they had just let it go, ignored it, probably hoping things would get better. Well, things never got better unless someone *did* step in. Now it was too late for the little boy, and Marc had a sinking feeling that time was running out for Mrs. Gable, too.

He checked his watch again. Even with everything he had going on right now, he needed to call Karen. The urge to do so tightened his stomach, knotted his nerves. It wasn't just that he wanted to get things settled between them; he felt uneasy, restless.

He hadn't talked to her in twenty-four hours, and suddenly, he thought it was twenty-four hours too long. He wanted to know she was all right, tell her how he felt, get her back to New Orleans, somehow. Maybe it was because the CIA, in the form of Mr. McPherson, had come sniffing around after he had Shannon put out the feeler on Medina. All the details about Dexter Whitlaw's murder that had struck him as unusual—the neatness of the hit, the lack of noise that indicated silencers, the expensive pistol in Whit-law's possession—took on a lot more importance when teamed with the information that he had known the other murder victim, who just happened to have worked for the CIA. A simple street murder had become complicated.

No, it wasn't that. He struggled to pay attention to the autopsy, but the tension in his gut wouldn't go away. As soon as this was over, he would call her. He should already have done it. Never mind needing to calm down; what he needed was to talk to her. This was two mistakes he'd made, he thought grimly. The first was leaving her alone yesterday morning, the second was not calling until he finally got her instead of the answering machine.

His radio crackled to life. Dr. Pargannas looked up and scowled at the interruption. Marc listened to the code for a suspected murder in the Garden District. The address was very familiar to him. "Ah, shit! The son of a bitch has killed his wife!" He spat the words out as he ran from the autopsy room.

Defeat was a bitter taste in his mouth. He'd been afraid of this. He had been caught between the need to have everything right so the bastard couldn't get off on a technicality and the need to hurry, to do something *now*. In another two hours, he would have had an arrest warrant, and Mr. Gable would be safely locked away. For Mrs. Gable, two hours was now a lifetime too long.

When he got to the house, the wide, tree-lined street was choked with patrol cars. The heat and humidity wrapped around him like a blanket as he walked up the sidewalk and into the cool, high-ceilinged ele-gance of the house. He was sick with fury and helplessness, but he shoved his feelings aside so he could do his job—for all the good that would do Mrs. Gable now.

"Where?" he asked one of the patrol officers.

"Upstairs." The woman looked rattled.

He climbed the wide, curving stairs and followed the commotion to a bedroom. The room was huge, probably thirty by thirty, and decorated like Hollywood's idea of European royalty. The big bed was draped with white net that hung from the ceiling. Ornate mirrors and original oil paintings decorated the walls, and furniture was arranged into two formal conversation areas. Tall alabaster vases held arrangements of irises coordinated with the color scheme of the room, which was white and gold with accents of peach and blue. A new color had recently been added to the room: red.

A lot of red. Red that sprayed, red that pooled, red that was turning rust-colored as it dried.

Mrs. Gable sat on one of the sofas. The back of her head was gone. She hadn't fallen over, simply slumped back against the cushions as if now she could relax. Her eyes were open, empty with death. Death wasn't peaceful; it was just nothing. Everything gone. No more sunrises, no more hopes, no more fears. Nothing.

She wore a white silk gown and negligee, low-cut, sheer. Sexy. Marc crouched in front of her, his gaze cataloging the mottled bruise on her neck he had glimpsed yesterday, as well as all the other marks. There was a small purplish mark on the upper curve of her breast, the sort of mark lovers left on each other. He suspected that the autopsy would find Mrs. Gable had had sex not long before her death. The bastard had probably thought making love to her, treating her tenderly for a change, would keep her quiet about how their little boy had died.

Maybe that was what had pushed her over, the fact that he had killed her son and then come to her for sex. Maybe she had planned it anyway.

Marc turned his head and looked at Mr. Gable's body, or what was left of it, sprawled in the bathroom doorway. She must have waited until he was about to step into the shower, then walked into the ornate bathroom and emptied a pistol into him. From the looks of it, she had then reloaded and kept shooting until the gun was empty again. The remnants of body parts were splattered around him. She had been very particular in what parts she shot off. Then she had reloaded once more, walked to the sofa, sat down, put the gun barrel in her mouth, and pulled the trigger.

The letter of the law was not always the same thing as justice. Mrs. Gable had sought justice for her son and achieved it by her own ends. Perhaps she had then killed herself because she couldn't face prosecution, or because she couldn't face life without her child—or in atonement for acting too late to save him.

Marc stood, his expression grim and set. All that was left for him to do was the paperwork.

Karen sat curled on a bed in one of the emergency department cubicles. She didn't know why she was here, but she was too numb to protest, even to care. She couldn't go to the apartment; the police had it roped off until they finished their investigation. She didn't *want* to go to the apartment. She wouldn't ever be able to sleep there again, even after that man's blood and gray matter were cleaned from the door . . . the carpet . . .

The medics had been insistent that she have medical attention, though she told them she was a nurse and was capable of assessing her own injuries, none of which required hospitalization or even emergency care. Her face was bruised, she had carpet burns on her knees and a small cut, too minor to require stitches, on her foot, and her ribs were sore, probably from the struggle. None of the shots had hit her, though the last one had been close enough that bits of Sheetrock had gotten in her eye, but eyewash had taken care of that problem.

All in all, she was in good shape, considering that man had been trying his damnedest to kill her.

She had no doubt about his intention. Once he had known she was in the apartment, he hadn't fled, which was what the run-of-the-mill burglar would have done. Instead, he had come after her, pistol in hand.

But why? That was what the policemen had asked, and she had asked it herself. Violent home intrusions happened. She was a woman living alone, a prime target. She hadn't lived in the apartment long; perhaps the man had thought someone else lived there. But he hadn't ransacked her apartment looking for valuables. He had carefully searched it and neatly returned everything to its place. And then he had tried to kill her.

Bad things happened in groups of three, the old saying went. Dexter had been shot. Her old house had burned. And now this. If the old saw was accurate, her life should be peachy keen now.

But she hugged a blanket around her shoulders to fight off the chill she couldn't shake and tried to control a sense of impending doom. What else was going to happen?

"Ms. Whitlaw?"

It was one of the detectives, standing outside the

drawn curtain of her cubicle. Her apartment had been swarming with detectives, uniformed policemen, medics, and people from IA, since any shooting by a police officer was automatically investigated. Outside the building, reporters and spectators had gathered. Every local television station had been represented.

"Yes, come in," she said.

He parted the curtain and stepped inside. He was middle-aged, his face shiny with sweat. How could he be sweating? It was so cold in here, the air conditioning must be turned on maximum. He sat down in the single chair in the cubicle, and Karen pulled the blanket tighter around her, shivering.

He watched her with that cool, assessing cop look, as if he didn't believe anything anyone told him. Marc had that look, too, she thought, and she wanted him here so much she ached inside. She had never felt safer than when she had been with Marc, and just now she needed that security.

"Detective Suter," he said by way of introduction. "Do you feel like answering some questions?"

They had taken a brief statement from her at the apartment, but since there was no question about the manner of the man's death, her importance to them was as a witness, not a suspect. The medics had wanted to transport her to be checked out, so they had let her go and taken care of more pressing matters.

"Yes, I'm fine," she said automatically.

He gave her an assessing look but didn't argue. He flipped open a small notebook. "Okay, in your previous statement, you said you were in the bedroom when you heard the suspect enter the apartment—"

"No, he was already inside. I didn't hear him enter. I heard him stop outside my bedroom door and look in." She knew what she had said, and it wasn't that she had heard him enter.

206

He looked back at the notebook and didn't comment. Maybe he had been testing her, to see if the details still matched.

"But he didn't see you?"

"No. He didn't come into the bedroom. I was standing off to the right, next to the window. The bedroom door opens to the right, so I was hidden from view unless he came all the way into the room."

"What did he do then?"

"After that, he wasn't as quiet. Since he didn't see me, he must have thought no one was at home. He went into the kitchen and began . . . searching."

"Searching?" He seized on the word.

"That's what it seemed like. He looked in the cabinets, because I could hear the drawers and doors opening and closing. He even looked in the refrigerator."

"What for?"

She raised her hands in a helpless gesture. "I don't know."

"Okay, what did he do then?"

"He turned the kitchen chairs upside down and looked under them." Her voice mirrored her bewilderment.

He wrote in his little notebook. "What did you do?"

"I—I didn't think I could get out of the apartment; from where he was, he had a clear view of the door. I tiptoed to the phone by the bed and put the receiver under a pillow to muffle the noise, then dialed nine-one-one."

"Good thing you did," he said. "The responding officers were less than a block away. They didn't know what apartment, but the street address was enough to get them there."

"They figured out what apartment," she said, staring blindly at the floor. "It was the one where shots were being fired."

He cleared his throat. "Uh—yeah. What happened then?"

"I tried to sneak into the bathroom, because that's where I keep my hairspray."

He gave a brief smile, and for a moment he was a man instead of a cop. "Smart. That stuff gets in your eyes, it burns like hell."

"I know. It was all I had." She swallowed, trying not to remember the terror of facing an armed burglar with nothing more than a can of hairspray. "The bathroom door squeaked a little. He heard it. I—" She took a deep breath. "I thought he must have, because the noise from the kitchen stopped. I just stood there in the bathroom with the can in my hand, watching the door to see if it moved. He shoved it open, and I sprayed him in the face. He had the gun in his hand," she finished, and fell silent.

"Did you know him?"

She shook her head.

"Maybe seen him around?"

"No."

"So what happened then?"

"I shoved him, but he caught my gown, and we both fell on the bed. I sprayed him again, and he hit me." Unconsciously, she touched her cheekbone. "I hit him on the nose, with the can of hairspray. I remember kicking him with both feet . . . then I rolled off the bed and crawled to the door, and he started shooting." She fell silent, remembering the blur of details, the terror, the rage.

Detective Suter didn't ask any more questions, didn't prompt her, but she could feel him waiting for the rest of the story, for what happened after the police officers arrived. She rubbed her forehead, trying to get the details straight. "I made it out the door of the apartment . . . the officers were just coming up the stairs. I almost ran into them. The man came out of the apartment and aimed his gun at me, and they shot him. He didn't fall. He . . . he *laughed* and shot at me again, and they shot him again."

"Did anyone say anything?"

"Both officers yelled at him to drop the gun. That's when he laughed and said . . . ah—" She looked at the detective and cleared her throat. Funny, she normally wasn't such a prude, but she simply couldn't say the word in front of this man who was old enough to be her father. "To paraphrase, he said, 'Screw you.' Then he shot at me the last time."

He looked down at his notes and nodded, as if she had corroborated something he already knew. He closed the notebook and slipped it inside his jacket. "That's all for now. Where can I get in touch with you, if I need to talk to you again?"

She stared at him. "I don't know," she said blankly. "You won't let me back into my apartment."

"Do you have family here?"

"No." Her throat closed. "No family."

"Friends?"

"Yes, but I don't—" Piper had offered her house, her company. "Maybe Piper Lloyd. She's a nurse here at the hospital, too." She gave him Piper's number. "Even if I'm not staying there, Piper will know where I am. Or you can reach me here at the hospital. I work nights."

He gave her a shrewd look. "I bet you won't work tonight."

"Of course I will," she said, automatically rejecting the notion that she wasn't fit. Why did everyone keep acting as if she had suffered more than some minor bruising and a small cut?

He sighed and rubbed the back of his head. "Ms. Whitlaw, it's none of my business, but I think you should cut yourself some slack. You handled the situation just about as well as possible, under the circumstances. You kept your head, didn't panic, alerted nine-one-one, and defended yourself with the means you had at hand. But you haven't had any sleep, you've been in a fight—and believe me, you're going to start feeling all sorts of bruises and aches. Look at you. You're shivering and huddling under that blanket, but it isn't cold in here. You're a nurse. What does that tell you?"

Shock. Her mind immediately supplied the diagnosis. Her blood pressure had dropped after the surge of adrenaline that allowed her to fight off the burglar. Karen was annoyed. She should have recognized the symptoms and been lying down. This was twice she had been oblivious to what her own body was telling her, she who was one of the best on the surgical floor at looking at patients and quickly summing up their overall condition.

"All right, so maybe I won't work tonight," she admitted. "I need a uniform, anyway. How do I get my things from the apartment?"

"Make a list of what you need, and I'll have a policewoman pack a bag for you."

"How long will it be before I can get back in?"

"A couple of days. I'll try to hurry things along."

"I can't live there again."

He sighed and reached out as if he would pat her knee, then paused without making the gesture of comfort. She diagnosed his hesitation as fear of lawsuits. "No," he said, "I don't guess you can."

The sound of running feet caught her attention, and a moment later Piper burst into the cubicle. She was red-faced and panting. "Karen! My God, are you all right? One of the emergency nurses called upstairs and told us you were here. You were *mugged?*"

"Not exactly."

Detective Suter got to his feet. It looked like an effort. "I'll be in touch, Ms. Whitlaw. And I'll get your things to you."

"Thank you," she barely had time to say, before Piper shifted from concerned friend mode to nurse mode and pushed her down on the bed.

He hadn't heard from Clancy, who was always prompt about reporting. Hayes waited, growing more annoyed and worried by the minute. Finally, he called his source in Columbus.

"Anything interesting happened today?"

"Ah, yeah. The good guys killed a burglar in a lady's apartment. She was at home, surprised him, put up a good fight and got away. The word is he was a pro; the piece he was carrying had the serial number filed off."

"No shit. Did he have anything else on him?"

"Nothing on him, but a rental vehicle was located in the parking lot, and a wallet with his license and credit cards was found in the glovebox."

Hayes hung up and sat drumming his fingers on the desk. Clancy was dead. How in hell had that happened? He'd been one of the best.

Moreover, nothing had been found on him, so that meant he hadn't found the book. Hayes spared a moment for regret that the book hadn't been on him; it would now be in police possession, but he would know where it was, and getting it *out* of police possession was child's play.

Karen Whitlaw was beginning to worry him. This was twice things had gone wrong. The first time was a logical mistake, but now he wondered *why* she had moved. To make herself harder to find? How much had her father told her?

Hayes's preference was to find the book, not kill the woman. But, logically, she was the only one who would know where the damn thing was hidden. If he couldn't find the book, then obviously he had to get rid of her.

Chapter 15

"You see what a problem it is, Raymond," Senator Lake said. The big, gray-haired man nodded in acknowledgment. They sat in the parlor of the senator's Washington townhouse, lingering over their morning coffee. Raymond had gotten a late flight out of Minneapolis the day before and arrived in Washington well after midnight, so the senator had left word for him to get a good night's sleep, and they would talk in the morning.

The senator had gotten, for him, a late start; he had slept until eight, and now it was ten-thirty, the morning sun bright and hot. "I had my doubts about the way Hayes handled the matter of Medina," he said slowly, "and now it looks as if he lied in order to get me to do things his way. I can't imagine any reason why Frank Vinay would deny knowing about Medina's death, if he already knew, or any reason for him to say Medina had no family if in fact he did. I wasn't asking for classified data, and I *am* chairman of the Senate Intelligence Committee."

"Hayes must have his own agenda," Raymond said, his thick brows furrowed as he thought. He looked like a boxer who had gone one round too many, but there was an agile brain behind the battered appearance.

"That's what I thought, too. I wonder if perhaps he is gathering ammunition with which to blackmail me. Whitlaw could have given him the idea." The one good thing about that scenario, the senator thought, was that it proved Hayes's minions hadn't discovered the notebook and he had kept it himself. If Hayes had the notebook, he wouldn't need any other means of blackmail.

"You know what I think about loose ends." Raymond shook his head. "They're dangerous. You don't use people you can't trust. You said Hayes used people you didn't know to take care of Medina?"

"Yes. He swore they knew nothing about me, that they thought he was the head, but if he's lied in one thing, then nothing he says is trustworthy."

"Get their names from him," Raymond said. "I'll take care of it."

Raymond had always taken care of things. Senator Lake could remember, as a child, hearing the burly man quietly say to his father, "I'll take care of it," and his father had always smiled and nodded, and it was done. It was reassuring now to hear him say the words, to know his affairs were being handled by someone he could trust with his life.

"Do you have Hayes's address?"

"Yes, of course." The senator had made it a point to find out. He had not, however, written it down in his address book or had his secretary add it to his computer files. No, anything to do with Hayes was stored only in his head. In his position, he knew too much about the capabilities of current technology to believe anything in his computer was private, and though he took the security precautions any sane man would take, he didn't assume his system was inviolate. If it wasn't written down, then it wasn't accessible; that was the most secure any information could be. He rattled off the street number to Raymond, whose lips moved slightly as he memorized it.

"I'll get right on it," Raymond said, and the senator knew everything was going to be all right.

"Are you sure you're all right?" Piper asked for the tenth time as she and Karen walked across the hospital parking lot to Piper's car. There was a parking deck, but it was reserved for the doctors and administrative staff, so they wouldn't get wet or have to walk very far. The nurses and other peons, who were evidently all in good shape and not allergic to water, had to use a parking lot that was half a block away from the hospital.

Karen squinted into the hot afternoon sun and wished she had her sunglasses. "I'm fine," she said, for more than the tenth time. Piper had insisted on taking Karen home with her. Several of her friends and colleagues had stopped by the emergency department to check on her. Ice had been applied to her various bruises, the cut on her foot had been anointed with antiseptic and covered with a bandage, and she had been made to lie down for several unnecessary hours while they plied her with food and fruit juices. She didn't feel shocky any longer, she just felt tired and harassed.

Piper carried her suitcase, having refused to let Karen lift it because of her sore ribs. Detective Suter had been prompt about having her things collected, earning Karen's undying gratitude. Her options until then had been wearing either her own blood-splattered gown or a hospital gown. The hospital gown had won the contest, but just barely. Now she was dressed comfortably and securely in the all-American uniform of jeans, T-shirt, and sneakers.

"It's too hot to cook," Piper said. "Let's get some take-out on the way home. What are we in the mood for? Mexican or Mexican?"

"I don't know. I think I'd rather have Mexican."

"Say, that's a good idea. Do you want Taco Pete's or—"

A car pulled out of a parking slot and headed down the aisle straight toward them. Karen stopped listening to Piper rattling on and watched the car. A man, probably one of the maintenance workers, was driving. There wasn't anything unusual about the car; it was a beige Pontiac, several years old. But it was going too fast, and she edged Piper more to the side to give the car plenty of room to pass.

If she hadn't been attacked that day in her own home, she probably wouldn't have paid the car more than cursory attention, but she was on edge, something deep inside her still frightened and outraged that the sanctuary of her home had been violated. She didn't feel safe. And so she watched the car, watched it gaining speed as it came down the aisle of the parking lot.

The driver was wearing sunglasses. She saw him clearly through the windshield as the car bore down on them, and she had the impression he was looking at her.

Piper broke off her running list of Mexican restaurants and said, "He's going too fast."

The fine hairs on Karen's arms stood up. She stopped, staring at the driver. Closer, closer. He gunned the engine, and the car rocketed toward them. Karen turned and drove her shoulder into Piper, knocking her sideways into the space between two parked cars. There was a loud crash, and metal screamed as it tore and bent. They both hit the pavement hard, sprawling on the grit, Piper under her and the suitcase tangled between them. The car beside them rocked wildly on its suspension as it was hit, the rear end skidding around toward them. The front end of the car crashed into the car on the other side of it and bounced back, coming to rest with the rear tire only an inch from Piper's head.

Tires squealed in the parking lot. Someone shouted, and they heard running feet. Then tires squealed again, and there was the sound of a car engine roaring as it turned its maximum rpms, rapidly growing fainter with distance.

Gingerly, Karen sat up. She was already sore, and this latest insult to skin and muscle only aggravated the previous injuries. Now her hands were bleeding as well, from sliding on the pavement, and her right knee throbbed.

Piper sat up also, a hand on her head. She leaned against a tire and looked at Karen.

"Are you all right?" they both said together.

They stared at each other another second. "Yeah," Karen finally said. "How about you?"

"Oh, your standard contusions and abrasions. That car almost hit us!"

"Are you two all right?" Another nurse practically vaulted over the fender to reach them. "He didn't even stop!" She knelt down beside them, dragging things from the pockets of her tunic. Her name tag announced her name was Angela, and the tiny koala clinging to her stethoscope with Velcro paws announced she worked in pediatrics.

Most of the nurses on first shift had already left; Piper was running late because she had swung by emergency to collect Karen. But there were still a few people around, and they all came over. "Go get some gurneys from emergency," Angela said to an orderly, her voice crisp and calm.

"We're all right," Karen and Piper said in unison.

"Don't be silly. You both need to be checked out. You know, sometimes people can't tell if they're injured until several hours later, because of the shock." Angela would have made a good general; maybe it came from dealing with kids all day long.

"Here," another nurse said, tearing open a disposable package containing an antiseptic wipe and handing the package to Angela.

"Do you have any more of these?" Angela asked, taking Karen's hands and wiping her raw, bleeding palms.

"No, just that one. Let's see." The second nurse dug in her pocket again. "Here's a gauze pad, but that's it." She climbed over the bumper, since the car was now sitting at such an angle that its front end was almost touching the bumper of the car beside it. Karen and Piper were sitting in the slight V-shaped space between the two cars, with Piper in the wider part of the V. The nurse crouched beside Piper and pressed the pad to a cut on her forehead, which was sullenly oozing blood. "Someone needs to call the police," she said positively. "That creep not only almost hit you, he left the scene. The owners of these two cars will need an accident report for their insurance companies."

"I've got a cell phone," someone else said. "I'll go call."

Within minutes, the parking lot was swarming with emergency personnel, both the medics who happened to have been in the department at the time and one of the emergency department doctors as well as two of the nurses. Two gurneys were brought, despite Karen's and Piper's groaning objections. Piper tried to stand and sank back to the pavement with a startled exclamation. "I think I must have sprained my ankle," she said sheepishly. "I guess I'll need that gurney after all, unless someone wants to lend me a pair of crutches."

A patrol car pulled into the parking lot then, and they all got to tell their stories to the policemen. The orderly said, "Man, he didn't even have license plates on the car. I got a good look when he was leaving the parking lot, because by then it was obvious he wasn't going to stop."

No one recognized him, but it was a big hospital; it was impossible for everyone to know everyone else. And since there was no security at the parking lot, anyone who wanted to could park there regardless of whether or not they worked at the hospital. All the cars were supposed to have employee decals on them, but no one ever checked, so the decals were useless.

Angela said, "I was standing just over there. It looked to me as if he *tried* to hit them." She didn't speculate about what sort of chemicals might be zipping around the driver's bloodstream, but several others did.

Karen knew better. When she could, she said quietly to one of the police officers, "I'd appreciate it if you would notify Detective Suter about this."

He gave her a "Get real" look, and she added, "This

is the second time today someone has tried to kill me. I'm sure you heard about what happened this morning, when two officers shot and killed the burglar. That was my apartment."

He got serious fast. "You think this was deliberate?"

"I know it was. He aimed for us." She managed to keep her voice even, but she was trembling inside with rage. The driver hadn't cared that Piper would have been seriously injured, possibly killed, too. Anyone with Karen was apparently as expendable as she was.

She couldn't say just when she had arrived at the conclusion that someone was trying to kill her—maybe while she had been airborne between the two cars, hearing the impact behind her. But she wasn't stupid, and she wasn't paranoid. As improbable as it seemed, someone really was trying to kill her.

Detective Suter thoughtfully tapped his notebook against his knee. Karen sat quietly, having finished what she had to say. She had outlined her father's murder and the burning of her old house. Added to both of that day's incidents, it was enough to make anyone thoughtful.

Piper's ankle had been X-rayed, revealing a hairline fracture. No cast was necessary, but the ankle was securely wrapped, and she was under orders to stay off it for a week. Karen's scrapes had been cleaned and bandaged, but she was free to go. The question was, where?

"Ms. Whitlaw," Detective Suter said slowly, choosing his words so as not to give offense, "you've had a very rough day. Anyone who has endured what you have could be forgiven for thinking there's a conspiracy against her. I'm sorry about your father, too, but from what you tell me, he was living on the streets, and those types of crimes are all too common. As for the house fire—" He looked helpless. "How can you tie that in with anything else that's happened?"

"I looked in the phone book," she said. "The new ones don't come out until December. My address is still listed as the house that burned."

"Still—"

Karen leaned forward. "Someone knew I was still at the hospital this afternoon, that I would be going home with Piper. Why else would he have been waiting in the parking lot? I work third shift; I wouldn't normally be there this time of day. *You* knew I was going with Piper, because you were here when she asked me. Who else knew?"

The detective's face went hard and blank. He said slowly, "I see what you mean. I guess I'm glad you're not accusing me of anything."

She didn't entirely trust him, either, but she didn't tell him that. She thought he was a straight, honest cop, which was why she had asked for him, but at this point she wasn't taking anything for granted.

"Your whereabouts weren't a secret," he said slowly. "Several people asked your condition, and I told them you were okay and would be going home with one of the other nurses when her shift ended. For that matter, maybe someone called the hospital and checked."

"Only a condition report would be given, not my plans for the evening."

He looked distinctly unhappy. "Ms. Whitlaw, looking at things in that light, I agree that something unusual is going on here. But why would someone be trying to kill you? Do you owe a lot of money to someone? Did you witness something you shouldn't have? Do you know a terrible secret?"

Karen shook her head to all those questions. "No,

none of that. I don't *know* why anyone would want to kill me, but all the indications are that someone is trying to. And that man who tried to run me down in his car wasn't concerned that he might hit Piper, too. My friends are in danger, Detective. I can't stay with anyone without worrying they might die in a house fire or get shot if they step in front of me at the wrong time. What am I supposed to do?"

"I don't know." He turned the notebook around and around. "I can't help. I can't even justify investigating, because there's nothing to go on. The only dead person is the guy who broke into your apartment. If we run across a beige Pontiac with no license plate, a damaged right fender, and paint scrapes, we can get the owner for leaving the scene of an accident, but that's all. Not attempted murder. I don't know what to tell you, except that you should take a leave of absence and go somewhere safe. Don't tell anyone where you're going, either."

A leave of absence? She sighed. At the hospital, there was no such thing as a leave of absence unless you had a medical reason. Administration would grant her request for a leave, but whether or not there would be an opening for her when she came back was the sixty-four-thousand-dollar question. It would also have to be an *unpaid* leave of absence, which would eat up her savings. Because of the life insurance policy on her mother and the proceeds from the sale of the house, she had more money in the bank than she had ever thought she would have, but by no means could she simply quit work.

"Just think about it," Detective Suter said.

This time, Karen walked alone to the parking lot, to retrieve Piper's car and then pick Piper up at the emergency department. Night had almost fallen; twilight was still hanging in there, but the street lights had come on. She would have asked an orderly or another nurse to walk with her, but after the hit-and-run, she didn't want to take chances with anyone else's life.

The entire situation felt like a *Twilight Zone* episode, with danger lurking all around her, and she didn't know what form it would take or why she had been targeted.

Leave. That's what Detective Suter wanted her to do. Hide. But if she didn't know what she was hiding from, how would she know when it was safe to come *out* of hiding?

It all tied together somehow. All of it. From her father's murder to the two attacks today, they were all for the same reason.

She was so tired, too tired to think clearly. Surely, when she was rested, she would be able to see a picture that eluded her now. But she'd had very little sleep in two days, and today had been a shock to her nervous system from start to finish.

She could think clearly enough, however, to know she couldn't go home with Piper. Her conscience hurt her, because Piper was on crutches and *she* needed someone. But Karen's presence brought danger, and she was too tired tonight to stay awake and alert.

On the other hand, Piper couldn't go home, either, because *he* had known Karen planned to go home with her. Having missed once, the logical thing would be for him to try to get to her at Piper's house. He might already be there, inside, waiting for them.

Chill bumps roughened her skin at the thought of walking into a dark house, to be met by a stranger with a gun.

A motel, that was the ticket. Just for tonight, for both of them. Piper wasn't dumb; she would see that the only logical thing to do was not take the chance of going home. Tomorrow—well, tomorrow she would think of something else. Piper had a sister with whom she could stay.

And Karen knew where she was going. If she had to hide out, then she intended to hide out in the one place she really wanted to be. She was going to New Orleans. To Marc. All she had to do was stay alive until then.

Marc replaced the phone, frowning. Karen still wasn't at home. He had called twice, even though he was still royally pissed, because after the blood bath in the Garden District, talking to her had suddenly seemed more important than cooling down. Even if he was angry, she needed to know that he cared enough to get in touch. In trying not to spook her, he thought, he had made the mistake of not letting her know she meant more to him than just a hot time between the sheets. He usually wasn't that clumsy in love affairs, but hell—

He ran his hand over his face. The operative word before had been *affair*. Now the emphasis was on the other word.

Love. He'd never been in love before. He had greatly cared for some of his lovers but never before felt this fascination, this obsession, with a woman. He loved her, and it scared the shit out of him. What if he did the wrong thing? He seemed to be walking a delicate tightrope between not coming on so strong that he scared her off, and holding back so much that she thought he didn't care at all.

To hell with it, he thought. From now on, he was going to go with his instinct, which was to move as fast as possible and make damn sure she and everyone else knew his intentions. The primitive urge to stake his claim went beyond the physical; making love to her was wonderful, but he wanted all the legal ties, he wanted his ring on her finger for all to see.

But where in hell was she?

If he knew Karen, she had worked last night, never mind having gotten very little sleep the night before, never mind the hassle of navigating airports and wrestling luggage. He hadn't called earlier because he figured she would be asleep, but it was late enough now that she should be awake. Night had fallen, and the Quarter was alive with tourists looking for good food, hot music, cheesy strip joints, all of which were readily available.

It occurred to him that she didn't know his home phone number, and she couldn't get it by calling information because it was unlisted. He dialed her number again and left a third message, giving her the number and ending with, "Call me, sweetie. No matter what time you get home, call me."

She did have his voice-mail number, though. Just on the off chance she had called it, he punched in some more numbers and listened to his messages. There were only two, one from a gutter punk trying to make points by feeding him some info he'd already had for two days, but the second message was from Karen. His heart thumped against his ribs when he heard her voice.

"This is Karen. Someone is trying to kill me. I'll be on flight sixteen twenty-one, American, arriving at ten-thirty in the morning."

Every hair on his body stood up. Swearing, sweating, Marc waited to see if there was an addition to the message telling him where to reach her now, but the line clicked off, and nothing but silence followed.

God *damn* it! He stood and slowly paced around the living room, thinking. This had to be tied to her father, just like the Medina murder. But how? Why? A comparison of the slugs taken from Rick Medina hadn't matched the one that had killed Dexter Whitlaw, but just because they hadn't been killed with the same weapon, that didn't mean the murders were unconnected. Neither was this. Every cop instinct he had developed after years on the job told him Karen was in danger for the exact same reason her father had been killed. The problem was, he didn't know why, he didn't have a clue who was behind it, and Karen was evidently in hiding somewhere and he didn't know how to get in touch with her.

"Son of a bitch," he muttered, and picked up the phone one more time. He had some instructions for Shannon.

The only seat available on the flight was a window seat, in the very last row. Karen stared down at the blue bowl of Lake Pontchartrain and the brown coil of the Mississippi River, with New Orleans sandwiched between them. It had all started here, with Dexter. Even if Marc wasn't interested in her personally, he would still help her, because he was a good cop, and Dexter had been murdered in his territory.

She still hadn't talked to him. When she called from a pay phone last night, she had gotten his voice mail again. The message she left was to the point: "This is Karen. Someone is trying to kill me." Then she gave him her flight number and arrival time and was too tired to think of anything else to say, so she hung up.

Maybe going to Marc wasn't such a bright idea, but he was the only person she could think of who might help, and she would certainly be safer in New Orleans than she had been in Columbus. She had had to use her real name to get the airline ticket, since passengers were now required to show a photo ID when checking in for the flight. Assuming her pursuer had the expertise, contacts, and funds, he would be able to trace her movements to New Orleans, but once she was there, she planned to check into a motel under a false name and pay cash, so there wouldn't be a paper or electronic trail for him to follow. New Orleans was a big city, a tourist city, with thousands of tourists every week and a lot of hotels and motels to accommodate those tourists. She could easily hide.

It occurred to her now, after she had gotten some sleep and could think again, that she could just as easily have remained in a Columbus motel under the same conditions. Columbus was more dangerous, though, because people knew her, could, if anyone asked, say, "Oh, yeah, I saw her a couple of days ago. She was in the supermarket on Such-and-such Street." A lot of people passed through the hospital, and a lot of them remembered her. Strangers were constantly speaking to her, telling her of their stay in the hospital, and she always smiled and nodded, but she seldom remembered anything about them.

She didn't want to be in Columbus. She wanted to be in New Orleans, with its heavy, sticky heat and air of casual, cheerful wickedness. And so she was here, though she had no idea if Marc would be at the airport or what sort of welcome he would give her even if he *was* there. If he wasn't, she would take a cab to the city. He had a job, a busy one. Just because he had made time for her before didn't mean he could, or would, do so again.

The plane landed with a slight bounce, and they taxied to the terminal. As soon as the plane lurched to a stop at the jetway, passengers ignored the instructions to remain seated until the captain turned off the seat-belt sign and crowded into the narrow aisle, taking down bags from the overhead bins, dragging them out from under seats. Karen remained seated; the rear of the plane was always the last to empty, and she was in the very last row. Except for stretching her legs, standing up would serve no purpose because she certainly wasn't going anywhere for a while.

But eventually, the line began to snake forward, and the plane emptied in fits and starts. Karen crawled out of the cramped seat, wincing at her sore ribs, her sore knee, her sore hands. She ached all over. This morning, she and Piper had solemnly bandaged each other, then hugged good-bye and laughed and cried at the same time. Piper had argued at first against the entire preposterous idea that someone was trying to kill Karen, but the more she thought about it, the more worried she became, and finally she had agreed the safest thing to do was get out of Dodge.

Piper had been right about something, too. With her hands bandaged, people rushed to handle her one suitcase for her.

Though her wardrobe was limited to what the policewoman had packed, when Karen finally stepped off the plane into the heat and humidity of the jetway, she realized she was better dressed for New Orleans weather now than she had been before. Other than a couple of uniforms, her wardrobe currently consisted of two pairs of jeans, a lightweight flowered skirt that fell to mid-calf, three cotton tops, some socks and underwear, sneakers, and a pair of sandals. She wore the skirt and sandals and felt much cooler than she had before.

Marc nabbed her as soon as she set foot in the terminal. That was the only word for it. A hard hand closed over her nape, dragging her to a halt, and he said with suppressed violence, "What the *hell* is going on?"

Chapter 16

He was still angry, Karen thought. No, *angry* wasn't
an adequate word; he was furious, his eyes glittering,
his lips a thin grim line, pale around the eyes and
nose. She was so glad to see him that she closed her
eyes as a sigh of relief soughed out of her lungs. "Hi,"
she said, another inadequate word.

Then she was in his arms. He eased her there, as if
afraid of hurting her. She felt his heart hammering
under her cheek, his breath soft on her hair, the hard
bulge of his gun in the holster at his waist, and it felt
so wonderful to be where she was that the cessation of
solitude was almost painful. She had never felt this
connection with anyone else, this rightness as her
body touched his, this pure, delicious sense of home-
coming.

"You look like hell," he said, the blunt statement so
far from his usual courtesy that she thought he must

be rattled. She did look rather battered: limping, both hands bandaged, a bruise on her cheek, and that overall pinched, pale look that came from too little sleep and too much stress.

"Yesterday was an eventful day."

"Are there any injuries I can't see?" The words were tight.

"Ribs. Sore, but not cracked."

He muttered another curse under his breath. "Let's get out of here. Any bags?"

"One."

"Do you need a wheelchair?"

She leaned her head back and gave him an appalled look. "No! That would make me more conspicuous. My knee is stiff, but I can walk perfectly well. Let's just get my suitcase and get out of here."

The line of his mouth didn't relax, and the hard glitter in his eyes didn't soften, but he slowed his long stride to match her much more leisurely gait, his arm around her waist as if he felt she needed steadying. The more she walked, the more her knee loosened, and if she went slowly, she didn't limp.

She said, "If someone had the means, how long would it take him to find out I took a flight here?"

"If someone had the means, he could have someone here waiting for you or be here himself." He looked as if he wanted to do something violent.

She stopped, her heart jumping with panic. "Get away from me," she said fiercely. "If you're with me, then you're in danger, too."

He turned to face her. "You're going with me," he said between clenched teeth, "if I have to pick you up and carry you. *Then* you'll be conspicuous." He took her arm and steered her toward the escalator. "After your message, I took precautions. I'm not here alone."

She decided not to push him any further. From

what she could tell, his temper hadn't subsided at all during the past two days. He looked dangerous, his gaze hard and restless as he surveyed the people around them, and she suspected he would welcome the chance to unleash that temper on someone.

Getting off the plane had taken so long that the luggage was already being unloaded. After a few minutes, the carousel chugged her suitcase around; she pointed it out, and Marc snagged it.

He was parked at the curb. Another car had pulled up close behind him, and a lean, good-looking young black man stood on the sidewalk beside them, his eyes shielded by sunglasses. "See anything?" Marc asked as he stowed the suitcase in the trunk. He had put on sunglasses, too, making him look hard and expressionless.

"Nothing out of place. Everything's calm as a convent."

"Good. Karen, this is Antonio Shannon. Antonio, Karen Whitlaw."

"Pleased to meet you," Karen said. "Are you a detective, too?"

"Yes, Ma'am." Shannon smiled at her. Like Marc, he wore a jacket despite the heat.

Marc opened the passenger door and ushered her into the car, his hand warm on the small of her back. The touch was so familiar, so possessive, that she shivered.

"I'll watch your six and make sure you aren't followed," Shannon said quietly to Marc.

"Thanks. I've put in a call to McPherson, but I'm routing everything through you so there won't be any direct connection to my house or my home phone."

Shannon nodded. "Got it. Go on, get her stashed. I'll handle things."

Marc clapped Shannon on the shoulder in appreciation and slid behind the wheel. As he pulled away from the curb, he watched in the rearview mirror as Shannon did the same, falling back far enough that he could see if anyone tried to follow Marc. Shannon had good instincts, maybe a result of his military training, maybe because he was naturally sharp.

Karen cleared her throat. "Is Detective Shannon your partner?"

"Detectives in New Orleans aren't teamed. But he worked with me on your father's case, and we get along. I trust him."

"Who's McPherson?"

"Someone who might be able to give us some information. Now—" His tone was measured, but she still heard that suppressed violence beneath the control. "Tell me what happened yesterday."

She did, as calmly and concisely as possible. She also told him about her previous home burning to the ground. He digested everything in silence for a minute. "Do you know the name of the bastard who entered your apartment?"

"Carl Clancy." Detective Suter had told her his name, to see if she recognized it.

He indicated the bruise on her face. "He did that?"

"Yes, but the hands and the knee are courtesy of the other bastard, the hit-and-run one. Actually, my hands are just scraped. Piper put these impressive bandages on them so people would help me with my suitcase. With my sore ribs, it was difficult for me to handle it."

He said something under his breath again, something vile and inventive. Karen stared straight ahead. If Marc was swearing like that, he was a volcano waiting to blow.

"I know it sounds far-fetched," she blurted. "Maybe I panicked. But twice in one day seemed a little too

232

much for coincidence, and when I added it to my father being murdered and my old home burning, I—what's the legal term? A preponderance of evidence? That's what it felt like. Or am I being paranoid?"

"No, I don't think you're paranoid. Something else turned up on your father's case that makes me real uneasy." He checked his rearview again.

"What?" She turned around and checked behind them herself. "Is anyone following us?"

"Just Antonio."

"Tell me what turned up."

"Another body, in Mississippi. The other man and your father knew each other, and they were probably killed at the same time. The other man was in a car in the hot sun, so the coroner can't pin his time of death down as accurately as we could with your father, but it's close enough."

"What was the other man's name?"

"Rick Medina. Your father knew him in Vietnam. Did you ever hear of him?"

She shook her head.

"He worked for the CIA."

Startled, she said, "Dad wasn't CIA."

"I know, but they knew each other anyway. At first, when I found out about Medina, I thought maybe he had been the primary target and your father got in the way. But now . . ."

Now, with the attacks on her, it seemed likely the situation was reversed.

She rubbed her forehead. "Why come after me? I don't know anything about what he did."

"Someone evidently thinks otherwise."

"Do you think this has anything to do with the CIA?"

He shook his head. "They seem to be as much in the dark as we are. Medina did occasional work for

233

them, but he wasn't in their employ at the time. No one knows why he was here."

"Another dead end."

"Or a lead. Whoever dumped Medina's body did it across the state line, probably thinking we wouldn't link the two murders. Medina's murder looked like a robbery, except they left the car, which was worth a lot of money if that was what they were after. It was as if they wanted him to be identified without any trouble."

"Why would they want him identified?"

"Because they wanted someone to know he was dead. Who and why?"

"We keep saying *they*."

"I don't think one person could have managed both murders so cleanly, with no witnesses."

So what were they dealing with? she wondered. An army of assassins? People she wouldn't recognize, who could walk up to her door at any time, perhaps wearing a police officer's uniform, and kill her when she opened the door? Would she ever feel free to cross a street again without wondering if one of the cars waiting at the traffic light was going to make an early start and run her down?

Now she *was* being paranoid, but where did it end?

She stirred, realizing they had been silent for some time and were almost in New Orleans. "If you don't mind, take me to a nice, quiet motel that's within walking distance of a supermarket. I'm paying for everything with cash, so if I check in under an assumed name, I should be safe enough."

His jaw tightened. "I'm taking you to my house," he said evenly.

His house. Her stomach clenched in a rush of mingled desire and terror. "I can't stay with you. If they find me, you'll be in danger, too."

"And if they find you, you'll be a hell of a lot safer with me than you would alone in some motel room."

It was blind instinct that had sent her back to New Orleans, a panicked need to be near Marc, but now that she was here, she knew she couldn't live with herself if anything happened to him because of her. "I can't take that chance. Once they trace me to New Orleans, wouldn't your house be the first place they would look?"

"Why would they? Contrary to what you seem to think, no one except the two of us knows we spent the last night you were here screwing all night long like a couple of minks."

He said it so smoothly, the rich, dark tones of his voice shaping the words almost into a caress. If he meant to shock her, he succeeded. If he meant to forcibly remind her of the intimacy they had shared, he succeeded in that, too. She felt her face get hot as a blush spread from her breasts upward.

She tried to ignore both her blush and his comment, doggedly sticking to her guns. "You're the one who investigated Dad's murder. Of course, they would watch you—"

"I would almost welcome them," he said, very gently. "I'm armed, and I'm pissed."

Yes, he was—royally pissed. Again. Or still. She stared blindly out the window.

He exited off I-10 and worked his way over to Canal Street, then down Chartres, then left on St. Louis. He hit the garage door opening, and Karen managed not to duck as he drove under the yawning door with inches to spare.

"How long are you going to pretend it didn't happen?" he asked, getting out and opening her door, then collecting her suitcase from the trunk.

She bit her lip as she preceded him up the stairs.

She felt herded, as if she had no choice but to go in the direction he had chosen. "I'm not pretending. I know very well what I did. You have a right to be angry, and I apologize. I acted like a fool, running away the way I did. I'm not used to—well, anyway, I'm sorry."

"You're not used to sleeping with a man," he finished, unlocking the door and stepping aside for her to enter. He followed, locking the door behind him and setting her suitcase down with a thud. "Now, tell me *why* you ran."

Uneasily, she moved away from him, embarrassed all over again. "The main reason was lack of nerve. I didn't know—I couldn't figure out why you'd done it."

For once, he looked totally flabbergasted. "What?" he asked blankly.

To give herself something to do, she began unwrapping the enormous bandages covering her hands, concentrating on making a neat roll of the gauze as she unwound it. "The least upsetting reason I could come up with was that you were just horny, and I was handy."

"You were right about the horny part." He reached for her hands and took over the job. "But I didn't use you as a substitute for my fist. I wanted *you*. If that was the least upsetting reason, I'm not sure I want to hear the other one."

"Other two."

"God. All right, what was the next one?"

"That you felt sorry for me."

His hands stilled at their task. Slowly, his head came up, disbelief written on his face. "You thought I kept a hard-on all night because I felt *sorry* for you?"

"You had been so kind," she tried to explain, feeling helplessly inadequate for the task. "I couldn't have managed without your help. But then I broke down at the funeral, and I thought you felt you couldn't leave me alone at the hotel—"

"Karen." He shook his head a little, as if trying to clear it. "That's carrying sympathy a little far, don't you think? My bed isn't a charity ward."

She bit her lip again and fell silent. He bared one of her hands, turning up her raw palm so he could inspect it. He got that grim look on his face again but took her other hand without comment and began the unwrapping process on it. "Okay, what's the third reason you thought of?"

This one was the tough one, but she owed him a full explanation. It was an effort to keep her voice even. "That first day—I knew you didn't like me. I wasn't imagining that, was I?" Despite her best try, she couldn't keep the pain from showing.

He kept his black head bent over her hand. "No," he finally said. "You didn't imagine it."

Karen swallowed, feeling her insides shred. "I didn't think so," she whispered, then said in a stronger voice, "So, anyway, the most likely reason I could think of was that you'd done it for . . . oh, not revenge, but as a sort of put-down."

"Use you, then kick you out?" He still wasn't looking at her, but she saw the muscle in the side of his jaw clench.

"Something like that. Because you didn't like me." She said it again, trying to impress it on herself, trying to face it head-on so she wouldn't crumple under the hurt of it.

"Not at first, no." He paused, and his big hands tenderly cradled her sore one. "Or rather, I was angry, but it didn't take me long to figure out you weren't what I'd first thought. Within an hour, actually. I began to get the idea when you almost passed out on me, but then when you watched that video and tried to act so calm, so untouched . . . you were falling apart, and I knew it."

"How?" she demanded, feeling a little truculent. She had tried hard to remain in control, a technique she had perfected over the years. She didn't like thinking she had been so transparent.

"You were clenching your fists so tight they were almost bloodless. You're a marshmallow, sweetie. Instead of not feeling enough, you feel too much. You try to take care of everything and everyone, and then beat yourself up when you can't do it." He slanted a glittering look at her from under his lashes. "By the way, did you get any of my messages?"

"Of course I did. 'God damn it, Karen,'" she quoted, and watched his olive skin darken as blood ran into his cheeks. She was almost glad he was embarrassed, because it balanced her own sense of vulnerability. He saw too much; she felt stripped naked, even more so than when he had actually removed her clothes. She was accustomed to shielding herself emotionally, and it knocked her off balance to realize how transparent she was to him.

"I'm sorry," he said gruffly. "I was so mad I— anyway, I left three messages yesterday."

"Oh. With everything that was happening, I didn't think to call the machine and check messages. What did you say?"

"To call me. Please. Then I got *your* message, and I was scared shitless until you got off that plane." He took a deep breath and shuddered as he let it out. "We need to talk."

"We're talking," she pointed out.

"Not like this." Abruptly, he leaned down and lifted her in his arms.

Startled, she grabbed his neck for balance. "What

are you doing?" she half shrieked as he carried her into the bedroom and set her on the bed.

"Checking you out," he replied, going down on one knee beside her and taking her hand again to finish the unveiling. He inspected that hand, too, then folded her skirt back to look at her knees. Both were skinned and bruised, but he could see for himself none of her injuries was serious. Lifting each foot, he slipped off her sandals. "So, on the basis of a first impression, you ignored three days of intensive court-ing?" He flashed her another of those glittering looks. "Well, as intensive as I could make it, under the circumstances."

"When I thought about it, everything seemed so . . . orchestrated. Planned." She gave him an angry look of her own. "You were already wearing a condom while we were dancing!"

"And kept it on the whole time we were dancing, too, by God, which should tell you something about how turned on I was." He stood and removed his jacket, tossing it aside. Then he started unbuttoning his shirt, his movements jerky, his nostrils flaring with anger. "I was *trying* to be *considerate*. I didn't think you'd appreciate having to worry about a pregnancy or disease at the beginning of our relation-ship."

Karen watched him, her eyes big, her mouth dry. She didn't say, "What are you doing?" which would be stupid because it was obvious what he was doing. She didn't say, "What relationship?" because she didn't want to inquire too closely in case she had heard wrong. She wanted to say she *did* appreciate his consideration in wearing a condom, but she didn't say that, either.

She just watched him, her heart pounding, her

nipples tightening. Greedily, she took in his sleek, strongly muscled shoulders and nice, broad, hairy chest. Clothed, he looked broad-shouldered and trim; naked, he was more muscular, with a flat, ridged stomach and a line of downy hair running down the center of it straight to his groin. She thought of following that line with her tongue and taking him in her mouth; his entire body would go rigid, and he would give that wonderful, deep, gut-wrenching groan. She wanted him. Oh, God, she wanted him now and forever.

He dropped his shirt to the floor and kicked out of his shoes, then peeled off his socks. "I can't believe you were mad about the rubber," he muttered, glancing up at her, and for a moment his gaze was so blazing hot she felt scorched.

She reached out and touched his stomach, feeling his hot, smooth skin and the hard pad of muscle underneath. "It wasn't the condom, it was that everything felt so *deliberate,* as if you were following a plan."

"I was," he said bluntly. "I'd been working for three days to get you in bed, and I was afraid stopping to put on a condom would give you a chance to think twice about what we were doing and back out. So I put the condom on first."

"And kept it on, too, by God," she teased him, smiling. Her fingers trailed down his belly to the waistband of his pants, following the line of silky hair.

His eyes were brilliant as he looked down at her. "Take off your clothes." The words were low and rough, almost a whisper.

Her heart pounded harder. She stood and began removing her clothes, her breath rushing in and out in excitement. She felt the clenching of desire deep inside, the twin yielding and demand of utter need. She dropped her blouse to the floor, then unfastened her skirt and stepped out of it. His gaze was locked on her breasts as she unclipped the front clasp of her bra and let it fall, and she noticed his breath was coming faster, too.

Critically, he eyed her ribcage as he dropped his pants, trousers and underwear going down in one smooth movement. Her ribs were marked with bluish splotches, and his hands clenched into fists before he deliberately relaxed them, reaching out to touch the bruises. "Are you too sore for this?"

"No," she said softly, eyeing his thick erection and appreciating his concern even more because it was obvious he was urgently aroused. But then, so was she. She removed her panties and sat down on the bed.

Instantly he was there, a strong arm wrapped around her, supporting her as he eased her down and in the same fluid motion mounted her. Lying between her legs, he carefully propped his weight on one elbow and fondled her breasts with his free hand, lightly rubbing her nipples until they were throbbing. Her own hands were on his chest, stroking, delivering pleasure. His erection nudged between her folds, but he didn't enter her.

"I'm not wearing a condom now," he said, kissing her.

"I know." Karen wrapped her arms around his neck as ancient instincts surged to the fore. Their gazes locked, his fierce and bright, hers soft and darkly mysterious, yielding. She didn't make this decision lightly; she knew full well what she was doing. "I don't want you to," she murmured, arching her hips a little. She wanted all of him, now. She wanted his seed, the possibility of his child. She felt unbearably aroused, though he had scarcely touched her.

"We're taking a risk." His voice was thick. His mouth moved down her neck.

"Yes. Please." She arched again, desperate, hungry, aching.

He pushed into her, hard and urgent, as if he couldn't hold back a moment longer. The head of his penis was already slick and eased his penetration. She cried out as satisfaction replaced desperation, pleasure replaced pain.

He groaned, and sweat beaded on his forehead, dampened his close-cropped black hair. "Have mercy," he whispered. "I haven't done this since I was a teenager."

She clung to his shoulders, her hips rising eagerly to meet his restrained thrusts, enveloping every inch and trying to hold him. "Making love? I know better." Speaking was an effort when everything in her was concentrating on the tightening spiral of desire. She was almost there, trembling on the edge, hanging on a point of pleasure so sharp it was exquisite, wonderful pain.

"Not wearing a rubber." He shuddered at the tight internal clasp of her. Suddenly, he gripped her shoulders and began thrusting hard, fast, deeper with every stroke. "I can't wait," he said tightly.

He didn't need to. Her nails dug into his shoulders, and she arched, crying out in the intense grip of orgasm. He made a rough, helpless sound and began coming, spurting into her, milked dry by the rhythmic pulse of her climax.

He hung over her for a few moments, his head down, his arms trembling as he supported himself rather than letting his weight down onto her. Karen managed to stroke his shoulder with one hand, but even that small effort exhausted her, and her arm fell to the bed. Finally, he eased out of her and collapsed on the bed beside her, breathing hard, his eyes closed.

Drowsily, she turned on her side and nestled against him, sighing at the pleasure that was quite apart from the sharp need of sex. Tears prickled her closed eyelids as she tried to contain a happiness so acute she ached with it.

He groaned. The sound was that of an unconscious man struggling toward awareness, and it startled her into laughing.

A smile tugged at his lips, and he rolled onto his side to face her, sliding his arm under her neck and draping his other arm over her hips to anchor her close. "You need to laugh more often." He kissed the tip of her nose. "Every time I see your solemn brown eyes, it's like being kicked in the gut."

"I laugh," she protested sleepily.

"Not enough. And before your fertile imagination comes up with any more off-base scenarios about what just happened here, we are deeply involved in a serious relationship. Is that clear?"

"Clear," she whispered, barely able to get the word out over the pressure in her chest. She felt shaky inside, as if she might crumble. She loved him so much it actually hurt, but it felt good at the same time.

"If you get pregnant, we get married. I refuse to let a child of mine grow up illegitimate. I don't care how many actresses do it or whether or not a woman really needs a man around now to help her raise their children."

"You're damn right we'll get married," she said with sharp force. "The odds are I didn't get pregnant this time, but if you don't plan to stay around, we'd

243

better decide on a method of birth control and stick to it. I don't want a broken marriage." Knowing what being abandoned by her father had been like for both her mother and herself, she was determined her own children would never know that pain if she could possibly help it.

He caught her hand and carried it to his lips, being careful not to hurt her raw palms. She snuggled against him, unable to decide which she wanted to do most: turn cartwheels or sleep. She didn't do either, because she'd never been a head-in-the-sand type of person, and reality at present was a bit dicey.

"It all comes back to here," she murmured, unable to hold the thoughts at bay any longer. "To Dad. His murder is at the center of it, because otherwise why would I be targeted? But I don't know anything about what he was doing. I hadn't seen or talked to him in years."

"What about your mother? Did she have any contact with him?" Marc brushed her hair back from her face, kissed her forehead, and held her closer as if he couldn't get her quite close enough.

"More often than I did. After I grew up, I refused to see him when he blew in for a couple of days, usually when he was out of money, but I know he called her sometimes, though not very often. She didn't tell me much about his calls because she knew how angry I was at him."

"Had there been any calls from him since she died?"

"If he called, he didn't leave a message, but then he wouldn't." A memory surfaced, pulled out by his questions. Marc thought like a cop, looking at angles she hadn't considered. "Wait. She died at the end of January. A few weeks after that, I got a package he'd mailed to her. I was still in shock and hurting a lot, and getting that package made me so angry because she loved him all of her life and he didn't stay in close enough touch that he would know she was dead. I almost threw the package away."

A subtle tension had invaded the muscled arm under her neck. "Did you open it?"

"I opened it, but I didn't go through it. I remember the box had some papers in it. I closed it up and put it in with the rest of her things I had boxed up for storage."

"Where is it stored? Your apartment?"

"No, I don't have room there. I rented a storage unit. That's it, isn't it? The reason why he was murdered is in that box."

"Maybe. It's a lead, and God knows we've been short of those. I want to hear from McPherson first—"

"Who's McPherson?" she asked, as she had before. His earlier answer hadn't been very informative.

"CIA."

"Are you going to tell him about the package?"

He didn't hesitate. "Hell no."

"So you don't trust him, either?"

"I don't know him. He may be who and what he says he is. I'll give him a little information, see what he gives me in return, but I sure as hell won't tell him you're here with me or anything about the package until I've checked it out."

"So what do we do in the meantime?"

"What do you think?"

Chapter 17

"Your people are incompetent fools," Senator Lake said coldly, hiding the fear that twisted his stomach. "The woman has disappeared, and you still haven't found the book. She could use that information at any time, thanks to your bungling!"

Hayes lowered his eyelids. He didn't protest or make excuses. The hard truth was that he hadn't performed his task; though the people he used were normally reliable, things had gone wrong. Clancy had gone into an occupied apartment, and the Whitlaw woman had somehow managed both to call the cops and to escape, and now Clancy was dead. Yamatani had missed completely in his attempt to run her down. Not only had he failed, but the Whitlaw woman would have to be a fool not to have figured out something was going on, whether or not she knew where the book was. She had gone into hiding, and he hadn't been able to find a trace of her yet. He could, but not without setting off alarms at the sources he would have to use, and Hayes wasn't willing to stick his neck out that far for the senator. The last thing he needed in this operation was to draw the attention of certain people.

"What do you plan to do now? I would like to remind you that the more people brought into this, the more likelihood there is of a leak."

"They're professionals. They don't talk."

"But they haven't proven themselves completely reliable, have they? I'd like their names, please. I seem to be in an undesirable position, with these people knowing about me while I know nothing about them."

"They don't know about you," Hayes reassured him, his tone weary. "Senator, I've kept you completely out of this. So far as anyone knows, the trail ends with me."

"So you say, but then you haven't been completely reliable, either, Mr. Hayes. Even your information about Rick Medina was in error."

Hayes kept his eyes hooded, but his interest sharpened. "In what way?"

"About his son. Medina didn't have any children."

"Who said so?"

"Franklin Vinay, the DDO. I'm sure he would know."

Hayes felt a chill run from his head all the way to his toes. Even his blood felt cold. "You asked Vinay about Medina?"

"It was a way of finding out what they knew. In my position, it's perfectly normal for me to hear about such things and ask about them."

Except that it wasn't perfectly normal for him to ask about Medina's *son,* whose existence and activities were so closely guarded that his name wouldn't turn up on any data file of employees. For the senator to ask about him would elicit any number of reactions from Vinay. First and foremost, he would deny that Medina had any children. Then, assuredly, he would try to uncover the senator's source. He would look first in his own office, but when that failed, he would begin looking at the other end of the equation and asking himself how the senator could have gotten any information about Rick Medina in the first place. A cop would say that knowledge indicated involvement; the senator had laid a trail right to his own door.

Discovery was just a matter of time. Not only had the senator involved Franklin Vinay, he had brought the son's attention down on them, and Hayes had heard enough about that shadowy figure to know the game was up. The best thing he could do now was cover his ass, his tracks, and disappear.

"I'll take care of the notebook personally," he said, feeling no compunction about lying. A man who would do something as stupid as arousing the suspicions of the deputy director of operations at the CIA wasn't a man for whom it was safe to work.

"Do that," Senator Lake said.

After Hayes left the office, the senator sat where he was for some time, thinking. He drummed his fingers on the desk. He didn't like these personal meetings with Hayes, but at the same time, he didn't trust the telephones. He could have *his* office swept for bugs, but who was to say Hayes didn't have one of those tiny tape recorders in his pocket, recording everything they said?

Something about Hayes had been . . . different, there at the end. He knew Hayes underestimated him; a lot of people had made that mistake. In fact, he sometimes deliberately encouraged such errors in judgment, giving himself an advantage.

He didn't consider himself an evil man, though it was true that in his lifetime he had been forced to make some difficult decisions. He didn't like the idea of harming the Whitlaw woman, but the book contained information he could not allow to be made public. The good of the few must not outweigh the good of the many. If she stood in the way, she would simply have to be removed.

And as for Hayes . . . the senator narrowed his eyes as he thought. Dexter Whitlaw had taught him an important lesson about tying up loose ends, a lesson Raymond had reiterated. Hayes would have to be dealt with. Perhaps, if he could make it look as if Hayes were in the employ of a nation hostile to the United States, and arrange things so it seemed as if Rick Medina had been involved . . . or maybe it would play better if Medina had been trying to *stop* Hayes. After all, Frank Vinay said Medina had been a patriot. Yes, that sounded better, more in character.

Of course, it wouldn't do for Hayes to be picked up and questioned. No, unfortunately, Mr. Hayes would have to die. All the loose ends had to be tidied. Of course, he would allow Mr. Hayes to take care of Miss Whitlaw first, and find the notebook; then he could take action.

He had depended on Hayes to arrange such matters, but now he would have to use other means. Thank God he had Raymond. This time, he would make certain there weren't any loose ends.

There was nothing about Frank Vinay's house that would call attention to itself. It was neither more ostentatious nor plainer than most of the other houses in the upper-middle-class neighborhood. He didn't drive a fancy car, preferring a slightly used domestic model. His neighbors assumed he was one of the thousands of faceless bureaucrats who battled D.C. traffic every morning for forty-five thousand dollars a year and a nice pension.

The house, however, did have certain modifications that made it different from the others. There was a very good security system, for one thing, backed up by a black and tan German Shepherd named Kaiser and a .9mm named H&K. Every morning and every night, the phones were checked for taps and the house swept for bugs. A parabolic mike aimed at the house would pick up only an annoying buzz instead of any sensitive conversations, because of the sophisticated electronic system designed to thwart such eavesdropping.

Jess McPherson felt safe in Frank Vinay's house, more because of Kaiser and the .9mm than the electronic stuff. Satellites and computers were great shit, but he was at heart an old-fashioned guy. When he retired, he planned to get him a dog. When he walked into Frank's den, he glanced at Kaiser, lying contentedly on the rug at Frank's feet. Kaiser returned the regard and gave a wag of his tail, as if saying, "Relax, everything's okay."

"I haven't been able to find a leak in the office yet," Vinay was telling John. "Damn, this has me worried. Have a seat, Jess, and add your brain to ours."

McPherson chose a comfortable armchair, folding into it and stretching out his long legs. "I can add something better than that. I got a call from that New Orleans detective. I returned it and didn't get to talk to him, but I did talk to the younger guy, Shannon, who put in the first request for info on Rick. Seems the detective got a call from Dex Whitlaw's daughter, in Ohio. She knows him because she flew down to ID Dex's body. Anyway, two attempts have been made on her life since she got back to Ohio, and, not being an idiot, she figures this has to tie in with her father's murder and wants to know if the detective has found out anything."

"Hmm. That means Whitlaw was the main target, then, not Rick." Vinay frowned. "What information do we have on Whitlaw since he got out of the Marines?"

"Not much," Jess said. "He bummed around the country, did some short time in Maryland for some penny-ante stuff about ten years ago, nothing since."

"Any indication he contacted Rick during that time, or vice versa? Were they ever in the same part of the country at the same time after Vietnam?"

"We'll have to do some deep digging to find out."

"While you're at it," John said from the corner, "see what acquaintances they had in common."

Vinay looked thoughtful. Exploring common acquaintances that far back would require major searches that went far beyond tracing the movements of both men. On the other hand, John's instincts were uncanny. "I'll put someone on it immediately."

"I don't believe," John continued, "that Whitlaw's daughter has any idea what's going on, or she wouldn't be calling the detective to ask him about it. On the other hand, someone else definitely thinks she *does* know. It might be interesting to put a tail on her, see who turns up."

"And step in if anyone tries to dispose of her?" McPherson asked.

"Yes, of course." John said it casually but without hesitation. He was like his father, McPherson thought. John spent his life in the shadows, constantly putting his life on the line in a world where people were assets and nothing was ever what it really seemed. Everything was fluid, shaded with gray. And yet John, like Rick, had kept a few absolutes. He was, first and foremost, a patriot. He loved his country.

251

Beyond that, he would back his people to the death. And underlying all that was his belief that for an employee of his country as he was, the ordinary citizen was his real benefactor. His job, boiled down to its essence, was to protect them.

"We'll shift our focus," Vinay said, "to Whitlaw's daughter. With Whitlaw dead, she's now the center of whatever's going on. John, how long are you stateside?"

"I cleared myself a week, max. I may have to leave at any time."

"But you're officially on leave. Jess, as of right now, you're officially on leave, too. This isn't a Company operation, and I don't want to fuzz the legal lines."

"Do I pass anything along to Detective Chastain?"

"Is there any need?" Vinay asked. That was what it always boiled down to: need to know. "If we agree Ms. Whitlaw is the center of it, and she's in Ohio, then any benefit a New Orleans detective would be to us is negligible."

"But she called him," John said. "She evidently trusts him. If she's hiding, he might be our only link to her."

"I've been up front with him so far," McPherson put in.

"Have you run a check on him?"

"A-one citizen," Vinay answered. "Excellent military record, did time in the Marines. He's from an old New Orleans family, the kind with a mile-long pedigree but no money. He got his college degree on the GI Bill, majored in criminology, started work on the NOPD as a patrol officer, worked his way up to detective. He'll make lieutenant easy, if politics don't get in his way. Or he might switch over to the state police."

"My take on him is he's tough but honest, the kind of cop a cop should be." McPherson spread his hands. "So is it quid pro quo or not?"

"I vote yes," John said.

Vinay considered the situation. "Okay, keep him briefed on what we know and what we're doing, so long as what you tell him doesn't touch Company business. If this veers into some old operation Rick was running in Vietnam, then that information stays in-house."

"At first, that's what I thought it would be." Hands in his pockets, John strolled over to the bookshelves and studied Vinay's reading material. "But now we know the focus was on Whitlaw from the beginning, so that theory doesn't hold. Our best bet is to find Ms. Whitlaw, and for that we may need Detective Chastain."

Marc watched Karen sleep, curled up in his bed, her shiny dark hair tousled around her head and her face delicately flushed with contentment. When she had stepped off the plane that morning, her face was white with tension. He knew he was part of that tension, but he hadn't been able to control his reaction at seeing her frightened and bruised. Pure, savage rage had seized him; in that moment, if he could have gotten his hands on whoever did that to her, he would have killed him without hesitation or remorse.

His woman was in danger. Every protective, primitive instinct in him was working overtime, fueled by fear and anger. If he hadn't had to deal with the sheer tragedy of little James Gable's murder, he likely would have flown to Columbus to settle things between them once and for all, and he would have been there to protect her. He wished he *had* been there when that son of a bitch broke into her apartment and tried to kill her. If she hadn't kept her head, he would have succeeded.

She had defeated the would-be killer, using nothing more than a can of hairspray. The thought made him cold all over, thinking of her facing a gun with such a puny weapon. When she had told him about it, she seemed almost apologetic for not having something more serious at hand for self-defense. Her sheer guts awed him, and the too-detailed knowledge of a cop told him how close he had come to losing her.

On a remote level, Marc was amused at himself. He had lightly loved before; he had argued with women, been angry at them. What he had never before done was lose control, but he had lost it with Karen. There was nothing light about the way he felt. It was dark and powerful and startlingly primitive. He, who had never before treated a woman with anything but the utmost courtesy, had been torn between the simultaneous and uncivilized urges either to spank her bare ass for leaving him, and therefore putting herself in danger, or to throw her on the bed and make love to her until she knew deep down in her bones she belonged to him and would never leave again.

He couldn't do the first because he couldn't lift a hand to her, and he knew it. His primary instinct had always been to protect, not abuse. The only way he would ever be able to strike any woman would be to protect Karen herself, or a child, from attack. His second urge had been abated by Karen's physical condition; she wasn't in any shape to be thrown on the bed. But having to restrain the force of his lovemaking had made it, in a way, even sweeter.

Until she went into his arms, he had been afraid. Afraid he hadn't read her correctly, afraid she didn't feel the way he did. He didn't know how she would take the suggestion, the question, the demand, but one way or another, he was going to marry this woman.

He hadn't worn a condom. Sweat beaded on his forehead as a wave of pure lust seized him. He had been in relationships where the lady was on birth control pills and it hadn't been necessary for him to wear a condom, and the sex was good; but today was the first time he had ever made love knowing there were no barriers, chemical, latex, or hormonal, against pregnancy. It had been incredibly arousing. He wanted to make her pregnant, wanted to come inside her, time and again, until his child began growing within her.

The bedroom was warm and darkened, the blinds closed. She had pulled the sheet over her before going to sleep, but she was beginning to perspire. Gently, Marc folded the sheet down. This was better anyway, he thought. This way, he could see all of her. He supposed he knew, rationally, that she wasn't the prettiest woman in the world, but if his eyes saw any imperfections, his heart didn't care. The things that made her different made her Karen. He loved the way she looked. She turned him on—God, did she turn him on. She was neatly formed, trim, toned. Her breasts were high and round, and he had satisfied his curiosity about how firm they were. They were very firm, with scarcely any jiggle even when she wasn't wearing a bra. Her flat stomach flowed into curvy hips, curvy hips into smooth, nicely muscled legs. Nothing about her was flashy, but Lord have mercy, she was sexy. He'd never known a woman more responsive, and her pleasure increased his.

She was lying on her side, one breast plumped by her arm. Gently, Marc rubbed a knuckle over the velvety, slightly swollen texture of her nipple and watched, fascinated, as it immediately tightened and elongated, the pinkish beige color darkening almost to red.

Her heavy eyelids fluttered open, and a sleepy smile curved her lips. "I'm sorry," he murmured. "I didn't mean to wake you."

She reached out and wrapped her fingers around his swollen penis. "Oh, I think you did." Her voice was drowsy, sensual. Lazily, she stroked him up and down, bringing him to full erection.

He laughed and moved her hand away from him before she aroused him to the point where all he cared about was orgasm. She shifted closer until they were lying pressed together and lifted her mouth to his. "How long before you expect to hear from that McPherson man?"

"I'll give him until tomorrow afternoon."

She looked wide-eyed and solemn. "Are we going to spend the entire time in bed?"

"Probably."

"Don't you have to work?" She traced his lips with one fingertip, then trailed it down his chest to circle his flat nipples.

"I took some personal time off. A case I was working cleared yesterday, and I didn't have anything else urgent." He didn't let himself think about *how* the case had cleared.

"So we can stay right here?" She hadn't lost the solemn look. Marc inhaled deeply as that slender finger worked its way down his torso, bypassing his erection to reach beyond and stroke his testicles.

"Right here." He did a little of his own stroking, down her spine to the crease of her buttocks, back up, down again. Each time his fingers stroked farther down. She gasped and arched against him, her buttocks tightening. Her nipples were pebble hard.

"What do we do if he doesn't call?"

"Proceed on our own." He squeezed her bottom, then eased one finger into her. She felt like warm, wet satin inside, tight on his finger, shivering delicately with arousal. He thought it was Henry Miller who had said entering life by way of the vagina was as good a way as any, and he heartily agreed. He could happily spend the rest of his life with some part of his body inserted into Karen, feeling her excitement, watching her little squirms.

She didn't have much patience. Her brown eyes were almost black as she suddenly put both hands on his chest and shoved him onto his back. He laughed as she straddled him, using both hands to position his penis and sliding down onto him so completely that his laugh changed to a groan. Oh, yes, he was definitely going to marry this woman.

His beeper sounded.

"You said you're off duty," she accused, frowning.

"I am. That would be Antonio." He stretched to reach his beeper and checked the number. "Bingo."

"He can wait five minutes," Karen said firmly.

"And you can't?" He was teasing. He didn't think he could, either.

"No," she said, and proved it.

"You sound as if you've been running," Shannon observed when Marc called him, ten minutes later.

"I was downstairs," Marc replied. It wasn't a lie. He *had* been downstairs—about two hours ago.

"McPherson just called back. They're looking into any acquaintances Whitlaw and Medina had in common, but right now they don't have anything. Ah, he did say they were going to put a tail on Karen, to see if they can spot anyone else following her and also to step in if she's in danger. I didn't tell him she's here."

"Good. Hold off on telling him for a while. I might change my mind later, but for now I don't want anyone but the two of us to know."

Marc wanted to think more about the situation before he gave away Karen's location. Involvement by the CIA, even peripherally, made him uneasy. He didn't assume, as a lot of people did, that they were either bad guys or assholes, but by nature of the Agency they dealt with a lot of bad guys.

On the other hand, it could be handy to have McPherson's shadow following them when he and Karen went to Columbus, to that storage unit. Tomorrow should be interesting.

Chapter 18

He couldn't just walk away. Hayes came to that
realization during the night, in the middle of his plans
to do just that. He had kept careful records of each
meeting, what was required, and the results. The
records incriminated him, but they also incriminated
the senator, who had much more to lose. It followed
that if *he* had kept records, so had the senator, the
mistrustful son of a bitch.

Hayes had no doubt Vinay would come snooping
around. There were two ways to play it. The smart
way, he decided, would be if he could arrange for it to
seem as if he were on the senator's staff in, say, a
security position. Everything above board. Vinay
might have some snooping done by his own guys,
though if he went by the book, he would involve the
FBI in the investigation. CIA or FBI, that didn't
matter, so long as his name popped up easily before
they really began digging. Any half-assed check would

turn up the information that he had done some work for the Company himself, a couple of decades ago. His name would shoot to the top of Vinay's list. When questioned, he would say, yeah, he told Senator Lake about Rick Medina's death and also mentioned that the word was he had a son who was also a Company man. That was logical, because he had been in a position to know those things. Bingo, mystery solved, no further investigation needed.

That was the smart way. The problem was, the senator would balk at having himself linked to Hayes. Maybe he could convince the senator otherwise. He decided to give it a shot, though he didn't have much faith in the outcome.

The second way, the dumb way, the risky way, was to find the senator's records and destroy them.

That would be a job. Hayes hoped to hell the senator didn't have the records in his congressional office; that was the most dangerous place to keep them, where they were most likely to be turned up by accident.

In his Georgetown townhouse? Possible. His estate in Minnesota was more likely; it was larger, more hiding places, plus the senator had grown up there. He knew the house, the grounds, intimately. Then there was the summer house in Cape Cod, but the senator hadn't been there this summer, so Hayes thought he could dismiss that possibility.

If he had stashed the records in a safe deposit box somewhere, which was what Hayes had done, then they were beyond reach. He would have to find out which bank and what name the box was rented under, get the key, and learn how to copy the senator's signature. Hayes had a lot of talents, but forgery wasn't among them. Then there was the possibility that rather than deposit the papers himself and take the chance of being recognized, the senator had had his wife do it under her name. Mrs. Lake was a sweet, cheerful, uninquisitive person, and she adored her husband. She would do whatever he told her.

The possibilities were endless. The one place the records wouldn't be was in a computer. The senator was computer-illiterate; hell, he had never even learned to type. From birth, he had been surrounded by wealth, and if he wanted to send a letter, he simply dictated it to a secretary or scrawled it by hand if he wanted it to be personal. From the beginning, Hayes had been relieved to know that; his personal opinion was that if you wanted sensitive information to get out, you put it in a computer. They were notoriously unconfidential. He wondered how many people would use accounting programs in their on-line computers if they knew the information could be accessed. Using the bank account number, a thief could then wipe out the account.

Bank accounts. Something about bank accounts niggled at him. Something he should have thought about days ago.

Suddenly, he knew what it was, and he wanted to kick his own ass. He had overlooked something so obvious that he shook his head in disgust.

He had been thinking only about covering his ass when Vinay came looking, so the DDO wouldn't link him to Rick Medina's death. Instead, now he was pretty sure he had figured out how to find the book.

He had wondered about the damn book, wondered exactly what was in it that the senator wanted kept quiet. Wouldn't it be a bitch for the senator if the man he sent after it kept it and used it against him the way Whitlaw had done?

Hayes almost laughed aloud. He didn't like Senator

Lake, and he sure as hell didn't trust the lying, sanctimonious, murderous bastard. On the other hand, he definitely liked the idea of a neat little double-cross. Why, it made him glad all over.

If Whitlaw had hidden the book somewhere that only he knew, then the book was gone. Hell, maybe he had buried it somewhere. At any rate, under those circumstances, the senator was reasonably safe, because what were the odds it would turn up during his lifetime?

On the other hand, if Whitlaw had sent the book to his wife or daughter . . .

The wife had died in January. She and the daughter had lived together; the daughter would have her mother's effects. Then, only a couple of months later, the daughter had moved, from a house into an apartment. She would have been pushed for space. Where would the excess stuff go?

Into storage.

Columbus was a city of about six hundred thousand people. A city that size would have hundreds of storage companies, but there was a simple way to narrow the search: canceled checks.

She would pay the monthly storage fee with a check. She might even write the unit number on the check, but if she didn't, that wasn't a big obstacle. All he would have to do would be to break into the company's office and locate her name in their files, then break into the unit. Most people just put small padlocks on the things anyway; bolt cutters would clip them right off.

She was in hiding; no one would be at her apartment. The police would have it sealed off with crime-scene tape anyway, until they finished their internal investigation into Clancy's death. Any IA investigation could take days, even one as cut-and-dried as this one.

All he had to do was find her bank statement and go through the canceled checks. Even if she only got photocopies from the bank, he would have the information he needed.

Hayes chuckled, feeling very pleased with himself. In the morning, he would make a phone call to the senator to tell him he had a lead on the book, to calm him down, and then he was going on a little trip to Ohio.

Jess McPherson was tired. It was four-thirty in the morning. His eyes burned, and every time he blinked, a pound of sand scratched across his eyeballs. The lines of data on the computer screen kept blurring, and he kept blinking. He had personally drunk two pots of coffee, and his stomach was burning worse than his eyes. He needed to take a piss, and he needed to sleep, in that order.

He wondered how John held up the way he did. The stamina, the absolute concentration, amazed McPherson, and he wasn't a man who was easily impressed. But the younger man had been sitting in front of a computer screen even longer than McPherson had, so totally focused he scarcely blinked. He had flown thousands of miles, crossed about eight time zones, and dealt with his father's funeral. He had to be both jet-lagged and stressed out, but none of that showed in his face. Looking at him, no one would suspect what he was.

His brown hair was neatly cut and combed, his white oxford shirt neatly pressed, his slacks unwrinkled. He wore a pair of wire-frame glasses to ease eye strain from working at the computer for so many hours. He had a manicure, for God's sake. He could be any Ivy Leaguer, any lawyer or banker, or an investment broker, the guy next door.

But he wasn't. His long fingers danced over the keyboard, agile testimony to his complete familiarity with computers and their workings. McPherson was competent, but John was a master at ferreting out information.

He was also the most dangerous man McPherson had ever known.

He loved John like a son, but he knew no one *knew* him completely. It was anyone's guess what went on behind those calm eyes, the thoughtful manner. No, it wasn't just a manner; John really was thoughtful. Most people saw only the surface; John saw multiple layers and intuitively knew how to manipulate those layers so people reacted the way he wanted, causing certain events to unfold.

He also knew how to kill in more ways than most people knew even existed. He had trained with the Navy SEALs, going through the rigorous physical conditioning as well as the classroom stuff. He had learned about computers from some legendary techno-wizard. He could fly a plane, sail a ship, set a bone, and probably sew a dress.

The CIA gathered information on roughly a hundred and fifty countries. John Medina had been in all of them.

He had been married once, in his early twenties. The young woman had died. Rumor had it she was a double agent and John had killed her himself rather than let her compromise a highly placed mole in the Kremlin. McPherson never met the young woman, and he didn't necessarily believe the rumor, because there were other ways to prevent her from passing along information, and John didn't kill unnecessarily;

nevertheless, he admitted John was capable of the action.

The computer screen blurred again, and McPherson leaned back in his chair, stretching his legs out and yawning. "Damn, whoever would have thought they would know so many of the same people?"

"They were in Vietnam," John murmured, his fingers skimming the keys. "Hundreds of thousands of troops were over there at any one time. Dad was in and out of the country several times, multiplying the possibilities. Whitlaw did multiple tours of duty. They met a lot of people, not necessarily at the same time."

"Jesus, some of these people have been dead over twenty years. Can't you weed out the dead guys, shorten the list a little?"

"Sure." John tapped some keys, then paused with his finger poised over the mouse. He typed in another command. A hard copy began spitting out of the laser printer beside McPherson.

"What's this?" McPherson reached over and picked up the first sheet lying in the tray.

"A list of the dead guys."

Squinting at the names, McPherson said, "Why?"

"Because the answer may be in someone who's already dead. Maybe Dad and Whitlaw were just next on someone's list." John shrugged to show the endless possibilities. "The wider the search area, the more likely I am to see a pattern."

"So you're looking for people who have recently died."

"I'm looking for anything. If I see anything interesting, then I'll run a match to see if any of the people on the deceased list also knew any of the people on the present list. There has to be a link."

The printer stopped printing. McPherson gathered

up the sheets and handed them to John, who tilted back in his chair and began scanning the list of names and the dates of their deaths. Ten minutes later, he paused, his gaze returning to one name, and he stared at it thoughtfully for a moment. Then he leaned forward, pulled up another file on the screen, and typed in a name.

"Hmm."

"Did you find something?"

"Maybe. It's . . . interesting. I'll check further."

McPherson rolled his chair over beside John's and read the information on the computer screen. "Huh."

"Did you know him?"

"No, but we sure as hell know his brother, don't we?"

"Wake up, honey." Marc smoothed his hand over Karen's shoulder, cupping his palm over the smooth, cool ball of the joint. "Here's a cup of coffee."

She blinked sleepily. "What time is it?" she mumbled.

"Not late. Seven-thirty."

"Then why are you up? You said you don't have to go to work." She pushed herself up in bed, yawning as she reached for the cup of steaming, fragrant coffee. The sheet slid to her waist, and Marc's hand almost automatically went to her bare breasts, stroking, rubbing her nipples. Karen leaned against him and nestled her head on his shoulder as she sipped the coffee, enjoying his fondling.

"I don't, but we do have to go to Columbus. I called the airline and got two seats on the ten-thirty flight."

She was silent, a little frightened at the thought of returning to the city she had fled in fear only the day before. It had to be done, though. Marc could go alone, but she didn't want to be separated from him, and he seemed to feel the same way.

He tilted her head up and kissed her, long and slow. She was amazed at how relaxed she felt with him, how comfortable and secure. It didn't bother her that she was naked and he was clothed. They had just spent roughly eighteen hours in bed together, making love, dozing, making love. He had let her get up only to go to the bathroom. When she got hungry, he brought food to her.

The pampering had worked. She felt much better than she had the day before, not nearly as sore. She was well rested, and she was happy. She felt guilty for being so happy, because her father had been murdered a week before and her own situation was serious, but the giddy, light hearted sensation that filled her chest was undoubtedly happiness.

After all her anxious, uncertain over-analyzing before, she felt calm now, and confident. They had committed to each other, and she trusted him. She had no doubt they would soon be getting married; otherwise, he would never have made love to her without using birth control, no matter how good the lack of barrier felt or how tempted he was. Marc was infinitely responsible and reliable. He had shown her that in a hundred small, different ways from the moment she first met him. For the rest of his life, he would be there.

The strong coffee hit her system with a jolt of caffeine, stirring her brain to activity. She needed to shower and wash her hair; she wanted to put down the coffee cup and pull Marc down on the bed with her again, but she wasn't certain they had enough time. She slid her hand up his thigh to check out the situation.

"You're wasting your time," he said ruefully. "After last night, I couldn't get a hard-on now if my life depended on it."

"Are you certain?" She found what she was looking for and began stroking him.

"Not one hundred percent certain, but fairly confident." He grinned. "Trust me, the two nights we've spent together are aberrations."

Tilting her head back against his shoulder, Karen smiled at him. "So what is your usual—ah—level of performance?"

He laughed. "Twice a day is plenty. Once is normal."

"Every day?"

"If I say yes, are you going to hold me to that?"

"Rain or shine."

"In that case, yes. But if I'm tired, you'll have to do the work."

"Oh, all right, if I have to." She stopped teasing him and took her hand away. "I'd better get ready. Want to shower with me?"

"I have breakfast ready. Eat first, then we'll shower."

After breakfast, he called Shannon to let him know where they were going. "I'm going to let McPherson know, too," he said.

"Are you on to something?"

"Karen remembers getting a box in the mail from her father. We're going to see what's in it."

"When will you be back?"

"Tonight, if we can get a flight. I didn't book a return ticket because I don't know how long this will take. Tomorrow for sure."

"Okay. I'll keep an eye on your house while you're gone, in case any suspicious characters start nosing around." He paused. "Watch your ass."

"I will. I'll let you know when we get back."

Then he called the number McPherson had given him, having decided to go with his instincts and trust the man. McPherson picked up on the second ring. "Yeah."

"This is Chastain. Miss Whitlaw is with me, and we're going to Columbus this morning to look at some papers of her father's that are in storage. I've notified Shannon, and he knows I'm calling you."

McPherson snorted. "Cautious soul, aren't you?"

"Cautious enough."

"It's a smart thing to be. I'll get someone there to tag along behind you."

"Tell me what he looks like, so I won't get nervous."

McPherson paused. Marc had the impression he covered the mouthpiece. Then he said, "Ah, okay. Tall, early to mid-thirties, dark brown hair, glasses."

"Got it."

"He—um, he'll be wearing a Cincinnati baseball cap. Red. And, um, change the glasses to sunglasses."

Either the man who would be following them was standing right there in front of McPherson telling him what he was going to wear, or McPherson was making a list of instructions. Marc suspected the former, otherwise why cover the mouthpiece of the phone?

"Can he get there ahead of us?"

"No problem."

"How will he spot us?"

"We have ID photographs of both of you."

"That was quick."

"As a fox," McPherson said.

"Have you turned up anything yet?"

"An interesting possibility, but no way to verify it. I hope you find something in that box that will help."

269

Chapter 19

Columbus, Ohio

Hayes studied the setup of the apartment building. It was an older building, in a good neighborhood, only four stories, probably two to four apartments on each floor. It was the kind of building where the residents knew one another and kept track of what was going on. That wasn't good. On the other hand, there wasn't much in the way of security: lights on each corner, and the glass double doors to the small foyer were certainly locked at night, but if they were supposed to be locked during the day, then someone wasn't following the rules, because people came and went without hindrance. Not many people, true, but enough that he was cautious.

Her apartment was on the second floor, 2A. That should mean it was the closest to the stairs.

He paused before he entered the building, taking a casual look around to make certain no one was watching him. A car turned into the small parking lot, and Hayes calmly opened the door and went inside, for to stand outside the door watching the car would get him noticed.

A small elevator in the rear of the foyer serviced the upper floors; the mailboxes were on the right wall, the stairs on the left. Hayes took the stairs.

As he had surmised, apartment 2A was at the top of the stairs, the door just to the right of the steps. Yellow crime-scene tape was attached to the hand rail and stretched across the hall to the wall, creating a small alcove. Tape also had been placed across the door.

Looking down, he saw the large rusty stains in the beige carpet. The door had holes in it, jagged, messy holes. The smell of death, of blood and urine and feces, still lingered, and would until the carpet was cleaned.

Hayes took a pair of latex gloves from his pocket and pulled them on. Ducking under the crime-scene tape, he tried the door. As expected, it was locked. Otherwise, the scene would have been an irresistible lure to teenagers and the morbid; they might even have gotten up the nerve to ignore the warning on the tape and go inside. People were incredibly nosy.

The locked door was a minor barrier. He had it open within fifteen seconds. If anyone came out of the other apartments and saw him, they would think he was a police detective. After all, he wore a suit and latex gloves. The suit was a definite sacrifice in ninety-degree weather; obviously, no one would be wearing one unless his job required it. That made him official; he doubted he would even have to show a badge, though he had one with him just in case. It wasn't a bad fake, either, considering how fast he had gotten it.

The inside of the door was covered with the same rusty stain, streaks smeared across the white surface, on the door jamb, part of the wall. Other than that, the apartment was neat. Clancy always had been particular about how he did a job. He was neat. No one would ever know their place had been searched; everything was back in its previous location, nothing taken, nothing sliced up. Clancy had claimed he could tell if anything had been hidden inside a cushion without taking it apart, by carefully studying the seams.

Yeah, Clancy had been an artist. Hayes had watched him toss a room before. He had tapped walls, gotten down on his hands and knees and studied the floor, inspected books and lamps and bric-a-brac. *Nothing* in that room had escaped his notice. And he had found the file for which he had been searching, hidden in the bottom of an upholstered chair. The particle-board bottom had been unscrewed from the frame and the file placed inside, then the bottom screwed back on. Clancy had noticed the small scratch marks on the particle-board where the screws had been removed and then replaced.

Not many people had that kind of patience or eye for detail. Hayes would miss having his services.

Hayes closed the door behind him, then stood for a minute looking around, getting oriented. He didn't want to disturb anything unnecessarily, either, because the cops undoubtedly had photographs of the scene, and some sharp cookie might notice if anything was moved.

He was in the living room. There was a nice twenty-seven-inch television set in the entertainment center, and a small stereo system. Against the wall just as you came in the door was a small desk where an answering machine blinked and a cordless phone sat in its cradle. Hayes resisted the urge to listen to her messages, because if a detective was here later and noticed the messages had been played, he would wonder who had been in the apartment.

He opened the center drawer of the desk. There were pens in there, notepads, rubber bands, stubs of movie tickets, but no bank statements. A couple of magazines had been tossed onto the desk. He picked them up; there was nothing under them. Carefully, he put them down in the same location.

Okay, nothing there. Some people did all their paperwork at the kitchen table. Hayes walked in there, checked the drawers, but came up empty. Ditto the small closet on the right just before entering the kitchen.

Okay, that left the bedroom. Again, he was struck by how *neat* everything was. The bed was made, there hadn't been any dishes in the sink, no clothes lying tossed around. Hell, no wonder Clancy had thought no one was home.

There were three taped and sealed cardboard boxes stacked in the corner near the window. So she hadn't yet got everything unpacked after moving in; that made Hayes like her a little better, made her seem more human. It also gave him an excellent place to look, because if he were lucky, the book would be in one of those boxes, and he wouldn't have to dig around in a metal storage unit in this heat.

"Winter clothes" had been written on the sealing tape on the top box. Hayes took the box down and opened it. Sure enough, it was full of clothes. He took each item out, taking care not to disturb the folds, and felt to make certain nothing had been inserted between them. Nothing. Not a single stray item was in that box, nothing that wasn't an article of winter clothing.

The second box had "Insurance papers, books, photographs" written on the tape. That looked promising. The box had been carefully packed with the heaviest items, the books, on the bottom, then the photographs, then the insurance papers. The insurance papers were in a manila file folder, but when he flipped through them, he found nothing but . . . insurance papers. The photographs were framed and few. Hayes inspected the books. Fiction, nonfiction, medical books, books about nursing. Nothing was hidden inside any of them.

The tape on the third box said "Christmas decorations, wrapping paper, bows." Hayes groaned. Damn, he didn't want to look through a box of fucking Christmas decorations, but he didn't dare leave it unexplored just because the other boxes had contained exactly what the labeling said.

There were Christmas decorations. And wrapping paper. And bows.

A woman that organized needed killing.

He opened the dresser drawers. Underwear, neatly separated and folded. Pajamas. Nightgowns. Socks. Nothing.

In the closet, a few dresses hung on one side, pants and jeans and tops on the other, with crisply starched uniforms hanging in the middle. A name tag had already been clipped to a uniform, the one she had chosen to wear next, and a stethoscope was secured around the crook of the clothes hanger. Below it were thick-soled white walking shoes.

There were some boxes on the top shelf of the closet. Hayes took down the closest one. Written on top were the words "Bank statements."

Bless her neat little heart.

Laughing to himself, Hayes took out the top envelope. An adding machine tape had been stapled to the statement, to show that her figures matched the bank's. He unfolded the sheets of photocopied checks and ran his finger down each column until he found one that read "Buckeye Stockit and Lockit." The notation on the check read: "Unit 152, July." Just what he wanted to know.

He put the statement back into the envelope, the envelope back into the box, and the box back on the shelf. All he needed now was an address. He found the telephone book and looked up Buckeye Stockit and Lockit, writing down both the address and the phone number. The storage company would be fairly close by, he was certain, because Ms. Whitlaw was too organized to have it otherwise.

Raymond Hilley waited in a parked car across the street from the apartment building Hayes had entered. He had cut the engine off and slumped down in the seat; even though he had managed to park the car in partial shade, the heat was intense. He rolled down the window but didn't start the engine; people would notice a seemingly empty car left with its motor running. He had waited a lot longer, and in a lot tougher conditions, during the years he had worked for Mr. Walter.

Mr. Stephen wasn't half the man his father had been, or even the man William had promised to be, but Raymond loved him, would do anything for him. Mr. Stephen *tried*. No matter what, he never shirked his duty, and Raymond respected that. Just look at the way Mr. Stephen took care of his father, spending time with him every day, making certain Mr. Walter was as comfortable as possible. It broke Raymond's heart to see Mr. Walter in such shape, a living vegetable instead of the forceful, dynamic man he had once been; at least Mr. Stephen honored his father instead of dumping him somewhere and forgetting about him, just waiting for him to die.

But Mr. Stephen had always adored his father and tried so hard to please him. Mr. Walter had known that and had been patient with Mr. Stephen's shortcomings; in the end, he had also been proud of him. Mr. Stephen hadn't set the world on fire, but he had accomplished a lot in his cautious, methodical way.

Following Hayes to Columbus had been pathetically easy; he had always taken care, the few times Hayes had been to the Minnesota estate, to stay out of sight. Raymond knew exactly what his role was in the Lake household: he was a weapon, an enforcer. A weapon was most effective when it was unexpected.

He had simply gotten a seat on the same flight with Hayes—two rows behind, as a matter of fact. Senator Lake had taken the next flight, using a fake driver's license Raymond had procured for him. He had even given the senator a disguise, and the photo on the license had shown a man with a full gray mustache and completely gray hair. Raymond had achieved the effect with an authentic-looking fake mustache and a can of gray hairspray such as makeup people in Hollywood used to give actors an interesting touch of gray at the temples when it was needed. The stuff washed off with shampoo, adding to its convenience. The name on the license was one he had taken out of the D.C. phone book. He had even established a debit card in that name, so the senator could rent a car and get a hotel room without a hassle. He had done everything he could to smooth the way for the senator, though he still had no idea why Mr. Stephen had insisted on coming along. It wasn't as if Raymond was a novice at this.

Raymond had a pistol shoved into his belt. Mr. Stephen had wanted a weapon, too, "and one of those big silencers," so, against his better judgment, Raymond had provided him with a .22 pistol. Mr. Stephen had protested, wanting something more macho, until Raymond had pointed out that only a subsonic round could be effectively silenced, and the larger calibers had too much power.

He had been cautious about the weapon he had procured for Mr. Stephen. A .22 pistol was cheap, readily available anywhere, regardless of what laws were on the books, because people who sold firearms illegally didn't give a shit about the law. The pistol he had given Mr. Stephen would be impossible to trace. Mr. Stephen had been a little shocked at how easy it was to get a weapon, because he honestly thought all his efforts to make the streets safer for American citizens had had some effect. Mr. Stephen said he intended to write and begin pushing legislation that would go after the manufacturers of Saturday night specials. If no more were made, they would certainly become more difficult to obtain.

Such innocence made Raymond feel both sad and protective.

One of the glass doors opened, and Hayes came out of the apartment building. Raymond slid farther down in the seat, so that even if Hayes noticed the car, it would look empty.

He heard a car start and sneaked a quick look over the dashboard. Quickly, he started his own car, sighing with relief as cool air washed from the vents, and watched as Hayes drove out of the parking lot. Raymond waited a few seconds, let another vehicle get between them, then pulled out behind Hayes's rental car.

* * *

Ahead of Raymond, Hayes checked his mirrors. There were two cars behind him. One was the car that had been approaching when he pulled out into the street, the other was one he hadn't seen before. That didn't necessarily mean anything. The car could have pulled out of a side street while he wasn't watching, but safe was better than sorry.

He speeded up and kept careful watch behind him. The second car made no attempt to pass the first car and catch up with him. Naw, there was nothing to it, just old habits and jumpy nerves. Still, it wouldn't hurt anything to take a leisurely drive before going to Buckeye Stockit and Lockit, just to make certain he didn't have a tail.

Raymond flipped open his secure cell phone and dialed the senator's cellular. "He searched the apartment, and I'm following him now."

"Where are you?"

Patiently, Raymond gave the street and direction. "Just one street over from you, but don't fall in behind me. Don't let him see your car. He may take some evasive action whether or not he thinks he has a tail, just as a matter of course. I'll hang back, keep him from getting a good look at me, let him do some ducking and weaving. He hasn't spotted me yet, and I followed him all day yesterday."

"For all the good it did," Senator Lake said fretfully.

Raymond didn't reply. Mr. Stephen had been very disappointed when Raymond's search of Hayes's home hadn't turned up anything interesting. In Raymond's estimation, Hayes was a careful man. He wouldn't keep any incriminating papers in his home.

Up ahead, Hayes took an abrupt right turn. Raymond fell out to pass the car ahead of him, putting that vehicle between him and Hayes's line of sight as they drove past the bisecting street. If Hayes followed his previous pattern, the right turn would be followed by two lefts, then a right back into this street.

Child's play, Raymond thought.

"Did you see anyone?" Karen asked as she and Marc climbed into their rental car.

"I spotted a red cap. I suspect he let me see him, because I haven't been able to pick him up since." He shrugged out of his lightweight jacket, which he had worn only to cover the pistol clipped to his belt, and tossed it into the backseat. Otherwise, he was dressed in jeans and a T-shirt, and so was Karen. She didn't remember exactly which box she had placed the papers in; they were going to have to dig around in the storage unit in the hot sun, and it had seemed wise to dress as comfortably as possible.

"While we're here, I want to call Detective Suter. Maybe I can pick up some more of my clothes. I need to check on Piper, too, and let my supervisor know—how long will I be gone, by the way?"

Marc reached for her hand. "We'll talk about this after we find that box, okay?"

He didn't think even that much contact would be safe, until this was over. She squeezed his hand. She had been trying to hide how nervous she was, but she didn't know how good a job she was doing. Logically, she knew she probably hadn't even been traced to New Orleans yet, much less back to Columbus. She had the key to the storage unit on her keychain, so she didn't have to retrieve it from her apartment—or, rather, Marc didn't have to retrieve it. If the police hadn't completed their investigation, the apartment would still be secured. He probably wouldn't ask the CPD for permission, but neither would he have let her be the one to go in.

They were safe. She tried to tell herself that. They could slip in and out of the city without anyone knowing she was there, except for Mr. McPherson and the man he had following them.

"You're worrying," Marc said. "Stop it."

"I shouldn't have dragged you into this. I've put you in danger—"

He gave a bark of laughter. "Darlin'," he drawled, "if you hadn't turned up in New Orleans yesterday, I would already be at your apartment this morning. Not only would I be very upset, but if anyone was watching your apartment, he would have made me for sure. Get the tag number, call the rental company, and he would not only have my name but my address."

Despite her worry, Karen caught her breath at the way "Nooawlins" sounded when said in that black magic voice of his. If Piper ever heard him, she might bump Karen off herself just to clear out the competition.

The traffic was heavy, the pace slow. The summer sun glared at them from a milky sky. She watched Marc drive, marveling at how physically fascinating she found him. She felt almost sick with apprehension, and yet that somehow intensified her fascination. She studied his hands, strong and well shaped, the way he gripped the steering wheel. His wrists were twice as thick as hers, and small, almost colorless hairs glinted in the sun. What if something happened to him? What if this were the last time she would be able to watch his hands move, study his profile, reach out and touch him?

She couldn't let herself think such things. He was a

cop, though, thank God, he wasn't in narcotics or on the SWAT team, where his life would be at risk on a daily basis. But as a cop, a homicide detective, he obviously dealt with people who were capable of killing other people. Murder was what he saw every day, and at any time a suspect could turn on him. She couldn't hamper him emotionally by letting herself get paralyzed with fear every time he went out the door.

"On the other hand," he said, "maybe we should talk about it now."

"What?" She blinked at him, not quite following.

"The entire situation. Your job. Let's get this out in the open. I don't want you living in Columbus while I live in New Orleans, not even for a little while." He slanted a quick look at her, gray eyes brilliant. "And maybe I should wait until I can get down on one knee, but I think now is the time. Karen, will you marry me?"

Her heart leaped into her throat. "Yes," she said. Then, "Take this exit."

He obeyed, glancing over his shoulder to check the traffic before easing into the right lane and then taking the exit ramp. "I know I'm rushing you, not giving you time to get used to me, to the idea of a steady relationship. But I don't want room for any misunderstanding, either. We can have a long engagement, if you want—but I don't want you to live here. I want you in New Orleans. Specifically, my house."

"Okay." She could barely speak. Funny. She had expected they would get married eventually, perhaps even soon, but hearing him actually say it out loud was a shocker.

"Okay?" he echoed, giving her another of those fast glances. "Is that all you have to say?"

"Well, I could say I love you."

He muttered a curse under his breath, then very evenly said, "Yes, why don't you?"

"I love you."

Another curse, one that turned into a laugh. He looked at her. She was grinning. "I love you, too."

She touched his arm, wanting to throw herself at him. He was the most considerate man she'd ever met, and the hell of it was he was so damn *alpha*. She hadn't known the two qualities could blend together so wonderfully. There he was, brimming over with testosterone, a gun-toting macho cop, who danced with her on a balcony and prepared breakfast for her.

"Do you mind moving to New Orleans?" he asked.

"No," she gently reassured him. "I'll miss my friends, but I don't have any family here, or a house. I can be a nurse just as well in Louisiana as in Ohio. You have roots and that marvelous old house in New Orleans. Of course, I'll move there. Besides, I would hate for you to lose your accent. Turn left at the next traffic light."

"I don't have an accent, honey. You do."

"If you say so. But if you by chance meet Piper, don't open your mouth, or your chances of getting out of Ohio go down drastically."

He smiled and winked at her. "You'll protect me."

The words reminded them both of why they were here, and the smile faded from his face. Karen blew out a deep breath. "What if we don't find anything here? What if the papers are just . . . papers, with nothing important in them?"

"Then I'll keep working on the case, and so will McPherson. Between the two of us, we'll figure this out. In the meantime, however, *you* will be in a safe place. Not my house, not for much longer. I'm not in the phone book, but hell, there are a hundred different ways of getting someone's address if you really want it, and most of them aren't that difficult."

"How reassuring. Turn right two blocks down, at the McDonald's. The storage company is about five miles down that road, on the right. Buckeye Stockit and Lockit. There's a sign. Turn just past the sign, into the center alley." She paused. "Is that guy following us?"

"I haven't seen him." Their shadow would have removed his baseball cap, because red was so noticeable, but Marc hadn't been able to pick up a particular car behind them, either—and he had been watching. He hadn't been driving fast, hadn't made any sudden turns, so he should have been able to spot him. Either he was remarkably good, or Marc had inadvertently lost him.

They didn't speak again until Marc turned at the Buckeye Stockit and Lockit sign. The gravel alley separated twelve sections of storage units, six sections on each side. Chain-link fencing surrounded each section, accessible by a numbered gate secured by a combination lock. "Gate number three," Karen said, pointing. She opened her wallet and looked at the combination, which was changed each month and which she always wrote down and stuck in her wallet. "Six-four-three-eight."

"I'll get it," Marc said, stopping in front of gate three and getting out of the car.

He unlocked the padlock and swung the gate open, then slowly drove down the row of storage units. "Number one fifty-two." Karen pointed at it and took out the padlock key.

They both got out of the car, and Marc took the key from her. After opening the lock, he slid back the lever that kept the door from being raised, then bent and caught the handle and lifted the overhead door with a rattle of metal.

The smell was musty but not, she was thankful, mildewed. Her throat caught as she looked at the boxes, the pieces of furniture. Her mother's bedroom suite, all her clothing, the other things Karen hadn't had room for when she moved.

Marc lifted one of the boxes down. Taking out his pocket knife, he neatly sliced through the sealing tape.

Hayes checked his rearview mirror, then, at the next intersection, made a hard left turn, barely missing the oncoming traffic. Behind him, nothing happened.

He grunted in satisfaction. If there had been a tail, he'd lost it for certain. There was no way he could have been followed after that turn, not without a lot of tires squealing, horns blowing, and maybe some metal contact.

Time to find this storage place.

Chapter 20

All the packing boxes were neatly labeled, but Karen couldn't remember in which one she had placed the smaller box. The first box Marc opened held Jeanette's clothing. She carefully took out each garment, trying not to think of her mother, blinking fast when her vision blurred, and then folding and replacing all the clothing when the search came up empty.

"I think—I think I already had the boxes packed, and all I did was set the other box on top of the stuff already there."

"Then we won't have to dig through the entire box. All we have to do is open each one and see if the small box is there."

"Theoretically. I was still pretty much in shock at the time. I'm not certain what I did."

He was patient, and the heat wasn't as dreadful as she had feared. In fact, the shade inside the storage unit made their work more bearable than if they had been in the broiling sun. Occasionally, a small breeze managed to work its way among the row of units, further cooling them. Still, Marc's T-shirt began to show damp patches and cling. Clinging was good. She eyed him appreciatively.

He sliced open the fifth box and grunted. "Here we go, I think." He lifted out a small cardboard box, not much bigger than a shoe box. Karen saw her mother's name printed on top.

"That's it."

She took the box and opened it. Inside were some papers and a small black-bound notebook, the type available in every discount store in the country, secured with a rubber band. She slipped off the rubber band and flipped through the papers. Seeing some letters in her mother's handwriting, she took a deep breath and handed the papers to Marc, keeping the notebook for herself.

"You look through those," she said, taking a seat on an end table.

He gave her a searching look, then glanced at the papers and nodded in understanding. He scanned the letter Dexter had sent with the box. "He says the papers might be worth some money someday." He propped himself against the dresser and crossed his feet at the ankles.

"I thought he was being sarcastic." Karen flipped open the book and stared at her father's handwriting, unusually neat for a man. He had used a small, square style, almost like printing, very legible.

"January 3, 1968," was listed on the first page. Bewildered, she read a description of the terrain, the weather conditions including wind velocity and direction, distance to target, spotter's name—Rodney Grotting—and other information such as the make and model of rifle he used, technical details about the ammunition, and the final notation: "Head shot. Kill made at 6:43 A.M. Viet Cong colonel." Below, Rodney Grotting had scribbled a verification and signed it.

Blinking, Karen turned the page. Another date, another description of conditions, ending with the casual, chilling outcome.

More pages. Most of the time, he took a heart shot, but sometimes he went for the head. Once it was the throat. She had seen such a wound once: the high-caliber slug had torn out half the throat, and the victim had bled to death. For such a terrible wound, with the jugular destroyed, there was nothing that could have been done even if medical personnel had been there when it happened.

She couldn't read any more. Her face white, she closed the book and handed it to Marc. "Take a look at this."

He eyed her sharply, consideringly, then turned his attention to the book. Watching him, Karen didn't see any expressions of shock or distaste at such a sick record.

"It's his kill book," he said.

"Good God, do you mean *everyone* kept them?"

"The snipers did. I was a Marine, too, you know. The snipers in the Vietnam war were legendary. The best ones could take out a target at a thousand yards. Their kills had to be verified, so they kept track in their kill books."

The idea still made her feel ill. "But wouldn't the Marine Corps have kept the books?"

"I don't know. I wasn't a sniper, so I never asked. Maybe they did. Maybe he kept two books, one for his own records. It was a bad war, honey. It messed up a lot of good men."

He continued flipping through the pages, scanning each one. When he reached the last one, he said,

"Sixty-one kills. He was good at his job." He started to close the notebook, and the pages fluttered; there was some writing on the last page, though about forty pages had been skipped and left clean. Frowning, Marc opened the small notebook to the last page.

"Holy shit," he said slowly.

Karen had been watching him, had seen the way his pupils flared, the quick compression of his lips. "What is it?"

"Another kill," he answered, then lifted his gaze to hers. "An American soldier. He was paid twenty thousand dollars to do it."

Karen's stomach twisted. Dear God. Her father was a murderer, a paid assassin. Killing the enemy in war was one thing, but killing a fellow soldier was hideous.

"I'll take that, thank you," a strange voice said, and a man stepped in front of the open unit. He was burly, middle-aged, but hard looking; the pistol in his hand was aimed straight at Marc's head. He was in his sock feet, which explained why they hadn't heard him approach. "I've been wondering what was in that little book that was so damn interesting. I suppose I should thank you for saving me the trouble of looking for it. Just put it down on the box, there." His tone was easy, his manner anything but. "You, cowboy, ease that piece out of the holster and toss it on the ground. Gently, now. Two fingers."

Karen sat frozen. Marc's face was expressionless, but a slight shake of his head told her he didn't want her to move a muscle. Carefully, he did as the burly man said, using his thumb and finger to ease his pistol from the holster. He tossed it to the ground at the man's feet.

"Good boy." The man didn't even glance at the

pistol, didn't take his eyes off Marc. "Who the hell are you? Boyfriend? Cop?"

"Cop," Marc answered, leaving it at that. If he admitted to a personal relationship with Karen, the man would know he could force him to do anything by threatening her.

"I was afraid of that." The man sighed. "Okay, toss over your backup piece."

Silently, Marc removed a small pistol from his ankle holster and tossed it to the ground beside the other.

"Shit," the man said. "I really don't like killing a cop. It causes all sorts of trouble."

"Then rethink your position," Marc said. He started to straighten, and the man shook his head warningly.

"Just stay where you are. Sorry about this, Cowboy, Ma'am." Oddly, his regret seemed genuine. It didn't matter. He was going to kill them anyway. Karen watched his finger tighten on the trigger, horror slowing her perception so that the tiny movement seemed to take forever. Without thinking, she cried, "No!" as she reached out as if she could catch the bullet in her hand and prevent it from striking Marc.

The man jerked, just a little, his attention fragmented by her sudden cry. Marc uncoiled like a snake striking, shoving Karen to the ground with his left hand while his right one whipped down and out. There was a blur of something shiny, then the man made one of the worst noises she had ever heard, a mixture of a cry and a gurgle, and with his free hand he clawed at the knife sticking in his throat, the knife Marc had been using to open the boxes.

He was a professional. He pulled the trigger anyway.

There was only a coughing sort of noise. Marc staggered back, caught his balance, launched himself forward. He hit the man in the chest and drove him backward to the ground. There was another coughing sound, and the mirror in the dresser shattered.

Scrambling up, Karen dived for Marc's pistol. The two men sprawled, struggling, in the rough gravel. Marc's left hand was locked around the other man's right wrist, forcing the weapon upward. With his right hand, he jerked the knife blade sideways.

The man choked, gagging. Blood spurted from the gaping wound in his neck. His face took on a bluish tinge. Rolling so he straddled him, Marc slammed the man's gun hand hard against the ground, twice, three times. Finally, the thick fingers loosened, and the pistol dropped from his grasp. He coughed, a rattling sound, and his legs quivered. He clawed at his throat.

Marc slumped forward, breathing hard, his head down.

"Oh, God," Karen whispered as she skidded to the ground beside him, ignoring the pain in her already abused knees. She forgot about the pistol in her right hand as she put both arms around him, easing him upright so she could assess the wound and his condition.

The front of his T-shirt was already soaked bright red. There was no exit wound in his back.

She spared only a glance for the man on the ground. He wasn't dead yet, but he would be shortly. His chest heaved as he tried and failed to suck in oxygen; his face was turning darker and darker, it was almost purple now.

Marc pressed his hand hard over the wound. The bullet had hit him high in the left chest, so high it had missed his heart but hit his lung. Karen heard the terrifying whistle from his chest as air escaped from his lung. The blood seeping through his fingers had bubbles in it, and a pink froth lined his lips.

"It's okay, sweetheart, you're going to be okay," she heard herself murmuring as her mind raced. Plastic. She needed some thin plastic, like Saran Wrap, to seal the wound and keep the lung from collapsing.

Sucking chest wounds were critical, and God only knew what kind of collateral damage the bullet had done tumbling around inside his body. He would die if she didn't seal the wound and get him to a hospital, quick.

The man he was sitting on began to spasm. Marc's teeth clenched as the movements jarred him, but the "Unnnhh" of pain escaped anyway.

"Don't bother," another voice said behind her. "I regret the necessity of this, but I really can't let either of you live."

Chapter 21

Marc sagged in Karen's arms, and she struggled to hold his weight. His head turned toward two newcomers, a trim, good-looking man, in his fifties perhaps, with a gray mustache and gray hair, and an older, heavier man who looked as battered as some old fighter. Both were standing slightly behind them, each holding a silenced pistol in his right hand. The pistols were aimed at them.

They couldn't see the gun she held, Karen realized, staring at the weapon in her right hand. And where in *hell* was the man McPherson had sent to follow them? Unless—horrible thought—he was the man who had just tried to kill them.

"Hello, Senator Lake," Marc said in a strained voice, and coughed.

The younger man looked startled and aggravated. "How did you recognize me?" he snapped.

"I was . . . kind of . . . expecting you. I . . . read the book."

"Don't talk," Karen begged him. Painfully, he dragged his left arm up so he could touch the pistol. She knew he was telling her to let him have it. But he was too weak, she thought, in too much pain; he would never be able to handle the heavy weapon. She tightened her grip on the gun, her jaw locking as she stared at this new threat.

Marc closed his hand around the pistol, groping. His shaking finger found the safety, clicked it off. The sound was a tiny snick. Karen barely heard it, but she knew what he had done.

Senator Lake's gaze went to the small, stained notebook lying on top of the box. "Keep them covered," he said to the bigger man, and quickly stepped into the storage unit to retrieve it. He flipped through the pages, then tucked the book into his shirt. "Yes, this is it," he said, and smiled at Karen. "How gratifying that someone has *finally* found it." He sneered at the dead man on the ground. "Hayes certainly couldn't manage to do the job, though he finally figured out where to look and led us here. He thought he was so sharp, with all his evasive maneuvers, but once again he underestimated my, ah, capabilities."

Senator Lake was very pleased with himself and the way the day had turned out. Not only was Hayes out of the way, but the notebook had been found. This whole aggravating nightmare was almost over with. He was especially pleased with the weapon in his hand; the pistol itself wasn't much, but the best silencer made anywhere in the world was screwed onto the barrel. Nothing more than a slight cough would be heard when he fired it. Hayes had told him once about walking up to a target on a busy street, shooting him with a silenced .22, and no one around them paid any attention until the target keeled over on the sidewalk. By then, Hayes was already several steps beyond the target, blending with the crowd. He should have known then that Hayes couldn't be trusted, because what sort of man would brag about something like that?

He was amazed sometimes at how well things worked out. How convenient of Hayes to leave town at just the right time. Disposing of him in D.C. would have been a problem, even for Raymond. For one thing, reporters were always snooping around. For another, Hayes would have been missed. That was where he lived; he had associates, neighbors, people who would have been able to identify him. Here . . . well. This was all working out very nicely. There would be three bodies here, and nothing to tie any of them to him.

All in all, he was rather proud of himself. He seemed to have a knack for this type of thing. All one had to do was plan carefully, but really, he had found most people too stupid for such meticulous thinking.

"Shoot them," he said to Raymond.

Karen tensed, her gaze locked on the big man's pistol. She started to lift her right hand, knowing even as she did so that she wouldn't be fast enough, not with the big man already aiming at her. She felt Marc gather himself.

"How much . . . are you paying . . . for our murders?" Marc gasped between phrases, his chest moving in jerks as he tried to breathe. The froth at his mouth dripped down his chin. "As much as . . . you paid Whitlaw . . . to kill . . . your brother?"

The big man froze. "What?"

The revelation rocked through Karen. Horrified, she stared at the man she had seen so many times on television, a man known for his integrity. So that was what Marc had read, what he hadn't had time to tell her. That was why her father had been killed.

"You had your own brother killed," she said slowly. "You hired my father to do it. He was blackmailing you, wasn't he?"

"Don't be ridiculous," the senator said, his tone uneasy as he glanced at the big man beside him.

"Mr. Stephen." The big man was white, haggard. "Mr. Stephen, let me see that book."

"Don't be ridiculous," the senator said again. "Don't tell me you believe this . . . this pack of lies!"

"It was in Vietnam," Karen said.

"Shut up!" The senator rounded on her, pointed his pistol at her.

"My father was a Marine sniper," she continued, though she was shaking in every limb. "You paid him twenty thousand dollars to kill your brother."

"Kill her, Raymond," the senator said, infuriated.

The older man, Raymond, still looked stunned, but he was recovering. He said, sadly, "Mr. Stephen," as he turned his weapon on the senator.

Senator Lake calmly turned and fired. Raymond staggered back, a look of astonishment and sorrow on his face. Senator Lake fired again, with no sound except that ominous little cough Karen knew would haunt her dreams, and Raymond fell.

"Damn you," the senator said furiously, wheeling on Karen. "Why couldn't you keep your stupid mouth shut?"

Marc lifted his bloodstained hand, pulling the senator's attention to him. "What about . . . Medina?"

Marc's entire body was trembling with effort. Karen gripped him tighter with her left arm, thinking fast. If she tugged him to the ground, it would get him out of the line of fire, but the sudden motion might cause the bullet to shift, causing even more damage. She couldn't see that she had any other choice.

"Whitlaw thought he could blackmail me with the book. No one else could track him down, so I called in Medina for the job. I told him Whitlaw had killed another contract agent in Vietnam, one of Medina's friends. It was a lie, of course, but Medina had some troublesome morals. I needed him, and that was the only way I could get him. He knew Whitlaw, so he had an advantage the others lacked."

Karen felt her breathing slow, get deeper. Her vision narrowed as she stared at the stylishly dressed man, until she could see only him. This man was the one who was the cause of everything. He had paid to have his own brother killed, then had her father hunted down and executed.

"Medina?" Marc gasped again. He sagged to the left, away from her. Desperately, she locked her fingers in his shirt, holding him upright. The muscles in her left arm strained and shook.

"Oh, well, obviously I had to have him taken care of, too. He wouldn't have liked finding out I lied to him. Those pesky morals of his again."

"Tell me . . . something."

The eyebrows rose. "As a sort of last request? Of course."

"What kind of . . . shithead . . . brags about . . . murder?"

The senator jerked a little, outrage flaring in his eyes as if he couldn't believe Marc had called him a shithead. His hand came up. Something erupted in Karen's chest, an inhuman sound that was very close to a growl. She felt as if she were moving in slow motion, but so was he. Using her grip on Marc's shirt, she dragged him down and at the same time lifted his pistol.

She had fired a pistol before, and a rifle. Her father had taught her those things, too, during those walks in the woods, crouching behind her and helping her hold the heavy weapons steady. She had been only a child, six or seven years old, but the memory was suddenly clear and bright, every image sharp. When Jeanette found out, she was frightened and angry, and they quarreled.

Odd how quiet everything was, how still. She centered the sights on his chest and pulled the trigger. The boom was muffled. The recoil jarred her arm.

The slug hit him in the chest, right where she had aimed it. She saw the bloom of red on his white shirt, between the open lapels of the linen jacket he wore. Why, then, did his head kind of explode? Blood and brain matter sprayed out of a large hole on the left side of his head. His eyes bulged a little, and he dropped in a boneless heap.

Abruptly, everything kicked back to normal time. She could hear again, though her ears were ringing. She could see everything in color, with a full field of vision. The harsh smell of cordite burned her nose. And Marc was collapsed on his side in the dirt and gravel.

She dropped the gun and seized him with both hands, hauling him over onto his back. She pressed her fingers into the base of his neck; his pulse was fast, thready. His eyes were half open, watching her, but she knew he was slipping out of consciousness. "I'll . . . make it," he promised, his voice barely audible.

"You're damn right you will," she said fiercely,

tearing his T-shirt open. The edges of the dark hole were blue tinged, and bright red blood continued to bubble and froth as it left his body.

She had to get the wound sealed, now. As she turned toward the burly man's body to search it for something usable, a flash of red caught her eye. She whirled back, grabbing up the pistol, crouching over Marc.

"Easy, there," a tall, lean man said, stepping fully into view. He wore a red baseball cap and sunglasses, and he held a pistol in the expert, two-handed grip of cops and other warriors. He surveyed the remains of the senator, then stepped over the body and approached Karen, tucking the pistol into his waistband at the small of his back as he did so.

McPherson's man. "Where have you been, damn it?" she said furiously, dropping the pistol again and scrambling to the other body. She patted all his pockets, searching for a pack of cigarettes. The cellophane wrapper around the pack would make a good seal. Her frantic fingers found only a wallet. "Damn it, damn it, *damn it!* Doesn't anyone smoke anymore?"

"Do you need a cigarette?" the baseball cap man asked politely but with mild puzzlement.

She whirled on him with a snarl. "I need a thin piece of plastic to seal that wound."

His eyebrows arched over the rims of the sunglasses. Silently, he reached into his front jeans pocket and pulled out a pair of thin latex gloves. "Will these do?"

She snatched them from him. Some gloves were too thick, the latex not pliable enough to do the job, but these were almost paper thin, like the ones put in boxes of hair coloring. "Perfect." Hastily, she slapped a glove down on Marc's chest, covering the hole and holding it tightly in place. He gasped but immediately began to breathe better as air stopped leaking from his damaged lung. "I need something to wrap around him, to hold this tight," she said. "There are some clothes in a box in there." She jerked her head toward the storage unit behind her. "Cut something up."

"Yes, Ma'am." Baseball Cap looked around for a second, spied the knife in the burly man's throat. "Jesus Christ, Hoss, you play rough," he said to Marc, a certain amount of admiration in his tone, and stepped over him to lean down and pull the knife free.

Karen looked at the bloody blade and thought of AIDS. She thought of means of sterilization, none of which she had with her. Looking back at Marc, she decided he was in far greater danger of dying from that wound than he was from catching AIDS from a strip of cloth cut with a bloody knife.

Baseball Cap was almost frighteningly efficient, plucking a shirt from the box and slitting the seam, then tearing off strips of fabric. The first two he folded before he handed them to Karen, and she pressed them over the wound. He pulled out a dress and repeated the steps, first slitting, then tearing. The resulting strips of cloth were sufficiently long for Karen to wrap around Marc's chest. Baseball Cap helped her do that, holding him upright while she worked. She pulled the fabric as tight as possible, and tied it off with the knot right on top of the wound to apply even more pressure.

"Phone," she said harshly, switching her attention to the next priority.

"I'll take care of it." Baseball Cap jogged down the row of storage units and disappeared out the gate. His progress was silent; he didn't seem to make any noise when he moved.

Karen checked Marc's pulse again, watching the

second hand of her watch. One thirty-two, way too fast. He was going into shock, his body fighting both blood loss and lack of oxygen, as well as the trauma it had suffered. She dragged his legs up, propping them on the burly man's chest, then positioned herself so her body blocked the sun from Marc's eyes.

"Are you still with me?" she asked, forcing her voice to calmness.

He slowly blinked and managed a faint smile. "Yes, *Ma'am*," he murmured, duplicating Baseball Cap's sardonic tone. "Status report?"

"The bullet hit your left lung. You've lost a lot of blood, and you're shocky, pulse rapid and thready—"

He took a quick, painful breath. "Serious . . . but survivable."

"Yes." She admitted her fear of the one, her hope for the other. "Stop talking. Baseball Cap has gone to call nine-one-one."

"I need . . . to talk to him."

"He'll be back." At least, she thought so. He might clear out while the clearing was good.

But he returned within a couple of minutes, approaching as silently as he had left, going down on one knee beside Marc. The cap was pulled low, and his sunglasses were very dark, effectively hiding his eyes. His hair was dark brown, Karen noticed that much. She knew, however, that if she walked past him within the next five minutes, minus the cap and sunglasses, she wouldn't recognize him.

"Here." He pulled the pistol from his waistband and reversed it, handed it to Karen. "You'll need this, to match the ballistics. We don't want the cops to come up with any strange bullets, do we? Let's see, what would be a logical sequence of events to account for three dead guys, one wounded, and *six* weapons, not counting the knife?" He paused. "This is going to get complicated."

"I'll handle it," Marc rasped.

Baseball Cap smiled grimly, little more than a quirk of his lips. Standing, he walked over to the senator's body and stood looking down at it for a moment. "You son of a bitch," he said to the dead man.

"Did you . . . hear?" Marc asked, gasping again.

"I heard."

Something in the grimness of the tone caught her. Karen looked at the senator's body, then at Baseball Cap. "We both shot him," she said. "At the same time."

The bill of the cap dipped once. "Both shots were kills," he said briefly.

"He had my father hunted down and killed." She was surprised at the fierceness of her tone.

"I know." He started to say something else but changed his mind, pressing his lips together.

Marc gathered himself. "Can . . . this man . . . be linked to you?" He tapped the burly man's body with his heel. Karen understood what he was asking. McPherson had stuck his neck out offering his aid; Marc didn't want anything brought out that would bring the CIA into the situation.

"No. We're clear."

"The . . . kill book."

"Make it public." Baseball Cap's mouth twisted. "Let everyone know what a bastard Stephen Lake was. It's proof of his motive." His head shifted a little, and Karen knew he was looking at her. "Is he going to be all right?"

"I think so. Yes." She touched Marc's face, and he turned his head against her palm. "But he's not going to be very happy with things for a while."

"You'll keep him in line." In the distance, sirens began to wail. "Jess was right," he murmured. "You're a natural, Chastain. If you ever get bored with local work, give m—give McPherson a call."

"I'll do . . . that," Marc said, and waved his hand. "Leave, before they . . . get here. I'll . . . handle things."

Baseball Cap pulled a card out of his pocket. It was a plain white card with a number scribbled on it in pencil. He gave it to Karen. "Call this number, and let us know how he is."

"All right." She slipped it into her jeans pocket.

He raised two fingers to the bill of the cap in brief salute, then walked away, his stride fluid but unhurried, eerily silent.

Karen knelt in the dirt, the bright sun glaring down on her head, and held Marc. He clasped his long fingers around her wrist, and they waited together, listening to the sirens draw closer and closer.

Ten hours later, Karen slipped out of Marc's SICU cubicle and went to the pay phone. The surgery had gone well, actually better than she had expected, and feared. The bullet hadn't done as much damage as it could have, because, after piercing Marc's lung, it had lodged in a rib, preventing it from tumbling around. He had required two units of blood, but he was now stable, actually awake, and as unhappy as she had predicted.

She took the white card out of her pocket and punched in the phone number, then her own calling card number. The call was answered on the first ring.

"Yes?" was all he said, but she knew it was Baseball Cap.

"The surgery went well," she reported. "He's stable, will probably be in SICU for another day, and home in a week to ten days."

"Good. Thanks for calling."

Sensing he was about to hang up, she said, "Wait!" He paused.

Fury bubbled up in her. "What *did* take you so long to get there, damn it?" she said fiercely, spitting the words out between her teeth.

He sighed, and in the long moment of silence that followed, she thought he wasn't going to answer her. Then he said, "I wanted to know why. I didn't know about the kill book, so . . . I listened."

"What difference did the why of it make?" she demanded, so angry she was shaking. Marc could have been killed while this man *listened*.

There was another long pause, then he said, very quietly, "Yours wasn't the only father killed, Miss Whitlaw."

He hung up so gently she barely heard the click on the line, then the dial tone buzzed in her ear. Slowly, she returned the receiver to the cradle and made her way back to SICU.

Marc was still awake, his face as white as the pillow beneath his head. He lay very still, not wanting to disturb any of the tubes running into his body in various locations, especially not the ones for which special holes had been made. But his mouth curved into a smile, and he cautiously moved his hand to reach for hers.

She cupped both of her hands around his. "Medina was his father," she blurted. "Baseball Cap, that is."

Marc considered it, his eyelids drooping sleepily as the morphine drip worked on him. "Then I'm glad they were both kill shots," he said simply.

Yes. Karen caught her breath. If it was possible for

anyone to be killed twice, she and Rick Medina's son had both avenged their fathers.

"I love you," Marc murmured. "Have I told you how damn wonderful you were, snarling 'Doesn't anyone smoke anymore?' You'll make a great trauma nurse."

Somehow, despite everything, he was actually smiling. Karen bent her head and pressed her lips to his hand. "Don't get smart with me," she warned tenderly. "Don't forget, this is my hospital, and I can get the nurses to do all sorts of nasty stuff to you."

He winced and kept on smiling. "They've already done some of it. I think I've lost my virginity."

"I'm sure of it," she replied. "Go to sleep now, sweetheart. I love you, and I'll be here when you wake up."

"I know," he said. "You won't ever leave." Then his eyes drifted shut, and he slept while Karen held his hand, and watched over him, and stayed. As she had promised, and as he expected, she was there when he woke.

John Medina sat with his steepled fingertips pressed to his lips, staring thoughtfully into space. It was good that Detective Chastain was going to be all right; Jess had been right in his assessment of the man. A man who could take a bullet in the chest and still cut his assailant's throat was a man to be respected.

He had to leave shortly, return to his assignment, but John allowed himself a few minutes of reflection. He had kept it all inside, because only then could he function at his peak, but his father's murder had hit him hard, harder than anything since Venetia's death. Now that it was over, now that justice—and vengeance—had been served, he could let loose the grief, the rage.

The press was in an uproar, of course. Dexter Whitlaw's kill book was in police custody, and the section of it pertaining to William Lake's death had been released. The news reports were rampant with speculation about Stephen Lake's motive for having his brother killed, but John was fairly certain the late, unlamented senator had regarded it as nothing more than a career move. He had killed the heir apparent and then smoothly stepped in to take his place.

John checked his watch. Time was getting away from him. He stood, tossing the red baseball cap into the garbage and running his hand through his dark hair. A plane was waiting for him, and he had to be on it.

He'd have Jess send Miss Whitlaw and her detective a very nice wedding gift.

Kill and Tell

Proof-of-Purchase

1511